SEXTET

MARK L. FOWLER

Copyright © 2018 Mark L Fowler

The right of Mark L Fowler to be identified as the Author of this work has been asserted in accordance with the Copyright, Designs and Patents Act 1988.

First published in 2018

All Rights reserved. No part of this publication may be reproduced, copied, stored in a retrieval system, or transmitted, in any form or by any means, without the prior written consent of the copyright holder, nor be otherwise circulated in any form of binding or cover other than that in which it is published and without a similar condition being imposed on the subsequent purchaser.

All the characters in this publication are fictitious, and any resemblance to real persons, living or dead, is purely coincidental.

For my wife Fiona with all my love

PROLOGUE

Penny and Susan Henderson lived in the town of Valemore, North Staffordshire, sharing a rivalry that Cain and Abel would have been proud of. For most of their seventeen years they both had long hair, black as crows, and few could tell the twins apart. More recently, Penny had cut her hair off and dyed what remained the colour of straw ...

Hearing her mum and dad leaving the house early, Penny dozed, fitfully. Her waking mind was circling over recent events, while her dreams ranged back to six years old, their stupid parents still telling anyone who'd listen that they'd brought two angels into the world.

Fallen angels more like. Cast out of heaven for acts of rebellion.

Penny would have loved to see how a truth like that went down at Sunday worship. It was a gift having parents who didn't know the first thing about you. Or about the games you played right under their noses.

Games like *Good Susan, Bad Penny.*

That was the best one.

The game would begin with Susan playing a funeral march on the piano. Then Penny taking a prisoner, and inflicting a little suffering. Spiders were a favourite, wasps and bees, too. They kept their captives in marked matchboxes, with a cage hidden in the woodshed big enough for mice and birds. Susan handled the healing and insisted that if the creature survived they would release it. That was only fair. Susan would write music "capturing the tormented creature's soul."

Susan could be full of shit sometimes.

They tried frogs, rabbits, hamsters, cats, and dogs before extending their techniques to children in the neighbourhood. Babysitting was a godsend. Penny made voodoo dolls, and Mum's sewing box was always full of needles. When the voodoo failed, they tried injecting simple poisons into chocolates and sweets, Susan as always supplying the music.

The results were patchy. Penny wanted to have a go at being the healer, but Susan wouldn't hear of it. Then Susan became ill and Penny wrote a melody to help.

It failed miserably. Susan said that was because *she* was the healer, Penny the tormentor. It was just how things were. Like Susan was always the more popular. Boys loved her. They were identical twins, and still the boys went for Susan every time.

Then one day Penny met Carl.

Now, Carl was a real sweetie, and Penny liked him a lot. Until the time she walked through the park and saw Carl running after Susan, shouting and waving his arms like he was chasing after the most beautiful girl in the world. Later, realising his mistake, he apologised to Penny. Carl and Susan both saw the funny side; after all, it hadn't been the first time someone had mistaken the girls.

Penny didn't see the funny side, though. She punched Carl in the face and told him to crawl away and die. Susan said that if Penny didn't want him, she didn't see what was stopping her from going out with Carl herself.

Penny said they could go to hell together for all she cared.

And so Susan and Carl started seeing each other, and Penny began knocking around with Daz Johnson. Daz was leader of the Gonzo Gang, and he could get things done. Penny told him that her sister needed teaching a lesson. Daz said that could be arranged.

Penny was the kind of girl Daz liked; a girl who could be very accommodating when the mood suited. He didn't want money. There were lots of people giving him money. When he asked Penny how much of a lesson Susan needed, she told him to make it one that her sister would never forget. That kind of lesson didn't come cheap, Daz told her, and Penny agreed to give him everything he wanted.

One evening, as Susan was heading out of Valemore Central, walking down past the old abandoned theatre building, The Regent, towards the bus station, six of them were waiting. In the darkness they took their turns with her before escaping into the night.

They left her for dead.

Susan didn't die, though; her body healed quickly. It was her mental state that concerned everybody. She wasn't communicating; she hadn't spoken since the attack. Deep trauma was indicated, according to the experts, and Susan was transferred to the psychiatric unit at Eaglesfield, a few miles outside Valemore.

Daz got bored with Penny and dropped her like a stone. He reckoned he'd had his money's worth, and he warned her to keep her mouth shut or else end up sharing a room with her sister - if she was that lucky. The police investigated, but never caught any of the six. If Carl had suspicions, he kept them to himself, taking them away with him to university that September. He gave up visiting Susan.

That was a boy for you.

Penny woke up. Her head was hurting. Perhaps it was all the bad dreams she was having. It was time Susan came home instead of messing about like a spaz on that unit. It was depressing having to make her way into college on her own every day; they were supposed to be a team. It was no good waiting for doctors and psychologists to sort Susan out, that lot were worse than useless.

It was well into the afternoon. Penny wondered if her parents had gone over to Eaglesfield to visit their *favourite* daughter. Sometimes she felt like reminding them that they had *two* daughters.

Despite the pain in her head, she could feel the ghost of an idea forming around the blurred edges of her mind. She'd been working hard at college lately, particularly in music. Susan had taken the lead for too long, and it was time to show where the talent in the family really lay. It would be another reason for Susan to show her more respect in future.

Yesterday's paper was still on the table at the side of Penny's bed. She looked at it again.

Daz Johnson. Dead.

A fight between local gang leaders, that's what the police were saying.

Yesterday, after reading about Daz, she had gone over to Eaglesfield, and made a curious discovery. Something had changed. Susan had been different, somehow, the difference subtle though unmistakable. Too much of a coincidence, she thought: Daz dying and Susan showing ... *signs*.

Penny's headache was getting worse. If she didn't do something, her head was going to explode.

She got dressed. The thought of going out for air became a compulsion to go into town.

A phrase was repeating, and had been for days.

Healing is sacrifice.

Penny left the house as darkness was falling.

CHAPTER ONE

Straw haired Penny, in carefully torn jeans and biker jacket, sat quietly sipping an espresso. She could feel the man in the tan raincoat, four tables to the left, watching her.

November, and the shopping centre was pumping the stale, air-conditioned atmosphere full of Christmas. There was not a spare seat in the café, and a multitude lined the walls, ready to play musical chairs, weary yet poised to strike as *Wizzard* became *Slade, Cliff, Bing, Mud*.

Penny was already wishing she hadn't made this rare pilgrimage into Valemore Central. A shadow stirring in the back of her mind had brought her here; a feeling to do something.

What, though? Buy Susan a Christmas present?

Penny hated Valemore Central, hated this shopping centre with its fake Christmas that started in autumn. She let the coffee burn her lips, and for no conscious reason flicked a look across her shoulder, before turning her head back quickly and once more raising the cup to her mouth.

Pervert, she thought. *They love this place.*

She drank the scalding, bitter sludge so fast it made her eyes water, all the time keeping the man in her peripheral vision, while focusing on the back of somebody's coat one table to the right of him. A coat of dark grey, dark blue - it might even have been black. It didn't matter. The corner of her left eye was doing all the work, establishing that the man was already getting it up over someone else.

Penny studied him: his expensive raincoat, slicked-back auburn hair and confident, ridiculous sideburns. Business man, late thirties, loaded; a neatly gift-wrapped package in his pocket to appease the little lady, no doubt, and something just as dirty in his trousers for any girl unable to resist the coiffured smell of money.

Getting up from the table, she let her gaze rest momentarily on the Brylcreemed hard-on, instantly realising her mistake. Penny quickly feigned interest in some imaginary object above his head, but it was already too late. Their eyes had locked for the split second it took to put a smile on his greasy face and a ball of vomit in the back of her throat.

She touched, as though for luck, what was hidden inside the zipped pocket of her leather jacket, and made for the exit. Without turning around, she knew that he was leaving, too. Her heart was thumping. Was this what she had come here for: blood and music, healing, sacrifice? *Good Susan, Bad Penny.*

Hurrying through the glass doors, she descended two flights of steps, feeling the first draught of cold air rushing in from the street outside. She could hear footsteps behind her, a man's footsteps, hard and heavy, and a moment later she was entering another world as surely as if she had walked through a wardrobe to find Narnia waiting.

The night air startled her. There would be a bitch of a frost come morning. Penny moved into the well-lighted street that ran alongside the monolith from which she had exited, moving purposefully though resisting the urge to run. She didn't look back until reaching the crossing, a hundred yards down the street.

He was coming toward her. Was that a wave?

She looked impatiently at the traffic lights, and tried to gain some perspective. Why shouldn't he be coming this way? This was the main route out of the centre, leading across town towards the cheaper car parks, the bus station, and the central taxi rank.

Was he the type to catch a bus, or walk for a taxi when he could whip out a phone? She doubted it. The lights changed, and Penny started to hurry across the road. The man was only a few yards behind her; out of the corner of her eye she saw him gesticulate. The thoughts were rushing around her head. Wild thoughts, filled with madness.

The centre was illuminated all the way to the bus station, except for the short stretch down by the abandoned theatre; the place where the horror had taken place; the site of nightmares.

Shoppers were still moving around the main drag, crawling in and out of the stores like dying flies. Christmas songs bleeding into the chill night and Valemore's hub still good for another hour of business at least. From Halloween to Christmas Eve you could shop until your soul ached.

Needing to be sure of what she was dealing with, Penny darted into the alleyway running parallel to the main drag. Halfway down, she glanced back.

He was still coming.

Penny emerged from the other side of the alleyway, footsteps echoing behind her. There were two options: take the quiet path down past the derelict theatre, finding the bus station in less than two minutes; or else take the longer walk past the multiplex, through the two car parks, arcing back around to the bus station from the marina. It would take closer to ten minutes, but there would be people and there would be street lighting all the way.

She could almost feel his footsteps beating on the pavement.

A couple were coming towards her on the other side, feeding each other out of a carton of chips.

A voice from over her shoulder: "Excuse me."

Penny didn't turn around. Her right hand folded across her chest, clutching at her breast pocket. It felt more comfortable there, stroking at the secret talisman hidden from the world. She picked up the pace, taking the short-cut down towards The Regent.

The streets were narrowing, emptying, running like thieves to the place of darkness. What was she thinking of, coming down here? There was still time to backtrack. Take the well-lit path, or maybe head back into the centre and call a cab. There were still options, and every one of them had to be better than this. Even a mobile phone seemed a good idea now, didn't it?

No way. Not for anything. She hated them. All the other students at college had them. The whole world had them. And every time they struck up with their trite little tunes it made her want to smack it across the owner's head. People were like sheep.

An old man wearing a large Santa Claus hat passed her, and she took the opportunity to glance back. The man in the raincoat was holding something, waving it at her. Ahead she could see the dark outline of The Regent.

The pulse in her neck began to thud. It made no sense to take this route. There was nothing but darkness down here, darkness and pain.

Turn back. Find the crowd. A police uniform - for all the good that might do.

The black shape of The Regent was pulling at her like a malevolent gravity that she no longer had the will to resist. Nobody in the world was coming up from the bus station, and nobody was heading down toward it. She crossed a side road littered with stationary cars, the only free parking in town. Maybe that was where the man was parked. Penny entered the shadows, falling into the dark gravity of the Leviathan that Valemore no longer wanted.

Was he still coming? Was his car one of the few parked for free? The council wouldn't let this gift run for much longer. Two sets of yellow lines and the street would be worth thousands a day. But what did a pedestrian care?

She was passing the side entrance of the abandoned building, the once magnificent Regent where her parents had first met. A matter of seconds and she would be out of the shadows of the derelict monster and stepping back into the light.

"Hey, Miss."

She stopped, her hand back across her chest, feeling inside her jacket; footsteps, loud and fast. A cough so close it brought vomit up from her throat and into her mouth. *A hand touching her hair - or just a breath of freezing night air?*

She spun around. The man was no more than a few feet away. "What do you want?" she shouted. The man held up his hands; *playing the innocent*. Even in the gloom she could see that he was grinning.

She was breathing hard, harder even than when she'd been out running, pounding the streets and the parks for hours, trying to get her thoughts in order. Even then her chest didn't burn like now. But running was for losers, she didn't need any of that shit. "What do you want?" she repeated.

The man pointed at the dark outline of the ruined theatre. "A tragedy, don't you think?"

Is he talking about Susan?

Penny began to move away, walking backwards, not letting him out of her sight; her feet feeling at the ground, knowing that to stumble might mean never to get up again.

"Wait a minute," he said. "I want to show you something."

Penny kept moving. "Yes," she shouted. "I bet you do."

He was holding something up in the air, but it was too dark for Penny to see what it was. She felt the intense chill of the night descending like a curse.

"Don't you want it?" he said.

A man used to getting his own way. He was close, too close, and still holding the object, whatever it was. "In the cafe," he said. "I noticed you."

"Why don't you get yourself a girlfriend," said Penny, still moving backwards. Keeping her eyes fixed on him and one hand across the breast pocket of her jacket.

He looked puzzled, or at least he tried to. Like he was pretending he didn't know what she was talking about. "You left something," he said. "Look."

She checked the front pocket of her jeans. *Shit!* "What do you want?" she said.

"To give you your purse back."

"Why?"

He laughed. "Call me Honest John."

"Throw it on the ground."

"You've been watching too many films." Throwing the purse down anyway, he took a couple of steps backwards, holding both hands in the air, making a lame stab at Jimmy Cagney. "I'm clean, I tell you; ain't carrying a friend."

She edged forward and bent to pick up her purse, checking the contents. Her money was there; house keys, too. There had been nothing in the purse giving away her address. Maybe she'd misread the situation. *No way.* He'd watched her in the café-bar and he'd left when she'd left, following her all the way down here. What did that add up to? And that jibe about the tragedy of the place - was that some highbrow theatre joke? It took one sick nut to crack a joke like that. *What if he had been one of them? One of the six - one of Daz's goons?* Or maybe he was genuine, kindness and public spirit coming to Valemore.

He wanted more than to return her property. But that made him a jerk, and not some sicko wanting to attack her and leave her for dead. Who was she kidding? There was no such thing as coincidence. This was the place. He was one of them. And she had set it in motion.

Bad Penny.

No, he was too old. Daz would have used boys not men. Six youths from out of town, wearing hoods and attitude, not tan raincoats when it wasn't even raining.

"Aren't you going to thank me?" He was laughing shamelessly, starting to come forward again. "You could at least let me buy you a drink."

The thought was ticking in her head like an unexploded bomb: *It could have been you, it could have been you, it could have been ...*

Putting the purse into her jeans pocket Penny felt again at her breast pocket. Then she turned, looked behind her, out into the empty darkness that stretched fifty yards down towards the bus station. She could turn and run from here, scream if she needed to. Over that distance she could outrun any kind of sickness. But what good would that do? What would that achieve?

She let him come towards her. Didn't turn and didn't run. He still had his hands raised in the air; still wore the cocksure grin that made her want to put a fist through his face. She let him come right up to her. There was no fear now. No fear left inside her. Fear had gone, departed, to be replaced by a force infinitely more powerful.

He said, "Can I put my hands down, please? I may work out four times a week, but a guy's arms can only take so much punishment."

Why not roll up your coat and ask me to feel your biceps?

"How about that drink?" he said. "You can't call the coffee in the last place a proper drink, can you?"

"How do you know I was drinking coffee?"

He laughed. "You're sharp, I'll give you that."

"I said ... how do you know what I was drinking?"

"Hey, take it easy. I was standing right behind you in the queue. And before you ask if I took the purse out of your pocket so that I could return it, you needed the purse to buy the drink, remember?"

"Who are you - Sherlock fucking Holmes?"

"You're funny."

"No," said Penny. "I'm hilarious."

He started to rub his hands together. "Let's continue this conversation over a drink," he said. "Otherwise, I think we're going to freeze to death. What do you say?"

"I'll miss my bus."

"Then I'll get you a taxi. You can't lose."

Somebody was walking down towards them, a man in a sheepskin jacket, looking like he had all the time in the world. How could she have been so foolish? They could be hiding - around the back of the building - in the shadows of the doorways … *six of them*. Daz setting the whole thing up before he died. Maybe he'd heard something, a rumour, and decided to teach her a lesson. Keep her quiet.

The man in the sheepskin jacket looked her straight in the face as he walked past. For a moment she thought he was going to wink at her, or at least say something. Instead he just stared, giving her the up and down like he was sizing a cow. She hated the way men did that, like they couldn't help themselves. He looked more of a jerk than the one standing in front of her, the one pissing about in the cold instead of hopping along home to the little lady and putting up the Christmas tree.

As if he'd read her mind, Mr. Raincoat said, "Come on, what's a drink? It *is* Christmas."

"Is it?" She shook her head. "I don't think so."

"Have you got a problem with me?"

The idea rose up, burning with a fury, thrilling and terrifying.

Healing is sacrifice.

"Problem?" she said. "I don't have a problem."

"Then what are we waiting for?"

She blinked, almost smiled. "Around the far side is more sheltered."

For a long moment he didn't say anything. "What are you talking about?" He looked shocked, but who did he think he was fooling? She knew what he was doing, weighing it up, trying to retain control of the situation.

"Have you seen what's around there?" she said. "Would you like me to show you?"

He started to speak, stopped, looked at the dark shape of the building, then back at Penny. "Come on," she said. "What are we waiting for?"

She started to walk, could feel him following, studying the way she moved. Penny took him all the way, to the far side, through the weeded-up car park and the broken glass and nothing much else except for the rats and the needles and the used condoms. It was unthinkable that the authorities had still done nothing about putting lighting down here, after what had happened. This was the place where nobody came unless they had the wrong reasons to come; the big expanse of nothing that was home only to vermin and the imagined echoes of muffled screams and the ghosts of terror and pain.

Penny walked carefully among the scattered debris of smashed glass and illegally tipped junk. The man was muttering something, though she couldn't quite catch it. She led him a few yards further on and stopped. "Bring back any memories?"

He shrugged. "I don't know what you're talking about."

"It does for me. I think it will for you, too, once we get started."

He frowned. "I think you've got the wrong idea."

"What idea's that?"

"Don't you think it's a little cold?"

"For what?" said Penny.

"Well, you know."

"No, tell me."

"How much? Not that I normally go in for this ... kind of thing."

"Of course not. But seeing as it's *Christmas.*"

"Can't we go somewhere ... more comfortable?"

His voice didn't sound so cocksure now. Cozy little hotels were more his style; handsome tips to the waiter.

"You don't like it here?" she asked.

"How much?" he repeated.

"Depends what you want, doesn't it?" She moved towards him and held out her right hand, touching his coat.

"You're serious?" he asked.

She moved her hand inside his raincoat, and watched his puzzlement turn into the promise of a smile. Moving her hand around the pocket of his trousers, she felt something nudging into life.

"I can't," he said. "For God's sake - not here."

"Coming back to you, is it?"

"I don't know what you're talking about, but we're going to freeze to death." He put an arm on her waist; she brushed it away, and in the same movement placed her hand back inside his coat and unzipped his trousers. "Cold?" she said. "I'll show you the truth."

She opened her jacket and unbuttoned the shirt underneath, before easing him out of his trousers. "Not so cold now?" He tried to kiss her but she moved her face to the side, all the time keeping a grip of his hard-on, while her other hand unbuckled his belt and unfastened the catch on his trousers, letting them fall. "Take off your coat," she said. "Take off your shoes, your pants, everything. I want to make you comfortable."

"Comfortable! You're out of your mind."

She let go of him.

"Okay," he said. "I'm doing it."

He took off everything, standing naked before her, his clothes, his shoes piled in the rubble, barefoot even amongst the broken glass and the dirty syringes. She eyed his erection and pitied men, so governed by such an inconsequential little thing stuck between their legs; a thing that could, despite its blatant absurdity, be so wilfully destructive. Naked, he didn't look anything at all; not dangerous and certainly not powerful. That piece of meat, gristle - isn't that what they called it? - stuck up in the air like a sad conjuror's wand. It made her want to laugh.

"God's sake," he said, the calm professionalism extracted from his voice, leaving the mere gruffness of manliness less sure of itself. "It's freezing."

As he spoke, she saw the air puff out of his mouth in clouds, like the caption spaces in cartoons. Without letting go of his swollen penis, Penny turned around; felt in her jacket pocket with her free hand. "You can leave anytime you want," she said. "Nobody's forcing *you,* remember that."

She took something from her jacket.

He was pressing against her, and it made her want to puke. But it was a part of it, part of the process. That vessel of destruction, how many women had it undone already? She had to feel its power to destroy, if the purging was to mean anything. If an offering was to be made that could affect anything.

A sudden stillness took hold of her and she knew it was beginning. A melody was forming. This was it, the moment of moments; her mind, her body, *on fire*.

His teeth were chattering, but his hardness against her was as resolute as an iron fist. My God, she thought. A man could be skinned alive before he would let a conquest go unconsummated. No, they were not to be feared, not in the final analysis; pitied, perhaps, under the right circumstances. His fingers were tearing at the waistband of her jeans, and she held her breath, counting out imaginary numbers, letting the melody, the immortal tune start to assume its shape and form, its skeleton taking life inside her like an unborn child.

The blade in her right hand did not glint in anything but her own eye; for that was where the light was, and he couldn't see the light. His eyes were somewhere else, and despite the intensity of the cold, it was clear enough from the numb fumbling of his icy fingers that he was still counting his pathetic blessings.

She tightened her grip around the bone handle of the knife, Susan's knife. It had belonged to a boy at school, a spoilt little shit's useless present from some South American business trip. But a kiss had made it Susan's, and she had seen its uses. "Could take a boy's tail off in one go." That was Susan, the *real* Susan.

He had taken down her jeans and her underwear. He was good to go. She tightened her grip of him. "Let me guide you," she breathed, savouring his final gasp of anticipation. He was close enough to ecstasy, ready for the few thrusts that it would take him to finish. "You haven't paid," she said, gripping him so tightly that it was hurting her fingers.

"Hey, go easy, will you."

"Not until I've taken my *cut*."

She turned back to face him, her right hand gripping the handle of the blade fiercely, swinging down in one clean action, more like a butcher wielding a cleaver than a young girl brandishing a knife. Her left hand never let go of the erect penis, not even when it was severed from the scrotum.

She watched him fall among the ruins.

When the blade had fallen for the last time, carving anger into every wretched inch of him, she held up that most afflicted part of the human anatomy like a trophy, before forcing it at last into the dying man's mouth.

Kneeling at his side Penny realised that her headache had gone, and her mind had cleared. "Quits, what do you say, sister? I went to town and I got you something. *Healing is sacrifice.*"

Using the dead man's clothes to wipe the blood from her hands, she got dressed.

*

As Penny Henderson sat perspiring in the freezing air, propped up against the cursed west wall of The Regent, she whispered, "This is the beginning, Susan. This is how it starts."

She checked her watch. Mum and Dad would be starting to worry. It was time she was getting home.

CHAPTER TWO

Philip Waters had the morning edition practically out of the paper-boy's hand. He didn't even notice the headline, moving straight to the private advertisements. By the time he had taken the newspaper through the short hallway and into the living room, he had found what he was looking for.

Calling all Composers!
£10 for a crack at immortality!
A new competition aimed at new talent!
The winners in each category will have their
compositions recorded professionally onto CD.
Categories: solo piano; and small ensemble (up to and including sextet).
A unique aspect of this competition is the opportunity to receive critical feedback prior to resubmitting material.
For more details ...

"Is it in?" asked Olive, entering the room, a towel wrapped around her wet hair. Waters beamed at her, his face appearing to hover over the top of his paper. "Want to take a look, Ol?"

"Some of us have jobs to go to," she snapped. "So what have you given as a closing date: twelve months - a couple of years, perhaps?"

"Does your job demand such cynicism all the time, Ol?"

"You mean the job of living with you?"

"The closing date for my competition, since you ask, is Easter."

"Suitably nebulous. Yes, very Phillip Waters."

"March 31st, actually. Precise enough for you?"

"I see," she said, rubbing her hair in front of the lounge mirror. "So not much chance of any assistance with the bills for at least another four months?"

He tossed the newspaper onto the coffee table. "At least I'm doing something. I'm trying, for God's sake."

"Of course you are, my sweet. But the phrases 'too little' and 'too late' spring to mind. Forget March 31st - April Fools has more of the Phil Waters about it."

"I'd explain if I thought there was any point."

"Ouch," she said, throwing the wet towel at him. "We are cutting this morning." She picked up the newspaper. "Anything else in, apart from your ad?"

She started to read the headlines.

"The hook, Ol," he said, "apart from the prize, of course, is the opportunity to resubmit. That's the killer. Everybody relishes a second chance. They won't wait until Easter, believe me." Olive carried on reading. "Are you listening to me, Ol?"

"Second chance, eh?" she said, not taking her eyes from the newspaper. "Who won't wait?"

"You see, most musicians, in my experience regard themselves as latent geniuses waiting to be discovered."

"Is that so?"

"The idea is that they write for more details and I send out information about my correspondence course. Profoundly simple: the essence of every great idea."

"Mmmm," she said, still reading. "I know what the idea is. I wonder what the reality will be."

"You really are a cynical bitch sometimes."

"Only sometimes? I must try harder. Anyway, it's what pays the bills. I'm paid to be cynical and it keeps the wolf from the door. Talking of animals, have you read this?" She looked up. "Phil, have you seen this?"

"What's that, Ol? Cutbacks in the social work department? New ways of saying 'men and women' without offending anybody?"

She gave him a look. "Actually, smart-arse, 'Man found in the early hours behind the old theatre'. The one in town – and a fag-end-throw from my office."

"What, dead or something?"

"No 'something' about it. Just dead."

"So?"

Olive sighed. "Oh, of course it can't compete with the launching of the Phil Waters *composer of the year* contest. Hell's bells, Phil: a man's been cut into pieces a couple of miles up the road, and you look at me like it's a pan fire in the Outer Hebrides."

"What do you want me to say? These things happen."

She threw the paper down. "I don't know why I bother," she said, firing up the hair dryer. "So, what's the agenda for today? Re-read your ad a few times, then a little stroll down to the local for your lunch? I'm sure Marcus Redfearn will be absolutely thrilled to see your ad. His idea by any chance?"

Waters smiled sardonically. "I thought I might sort out my work room."

"Dust off the piano, that sort of thing?"

"You know something?"

"Amaze me, Phil."

"You social worker types are just a bundle of contradictions."

"Is that so? What a man of insight. And is that the extent of your observation, or is there more?"

"How much can you take?"

"Let's find out, shall we."

"You talk a lot about 'empowering' and 'enabling' people, but when it comes to the crunch you're as full of shit as the next guy – only more hypocritical."

"Oh, I'm going to need a plaster for that," she said, laughing. "Little Phil not had enough praise for his ad this morning? Grow up, will you? I'm going to work. Maybe, if it's not too much trouble, you could get some milk and bread, at least."

He glanced at the station clock on the wall. "You'd better get a move on, Ol. Don't want to keep the ladies at the office waiting. They'll all have their theories on the front-page gossip. Busy morning ahead."

He listened to the door slamming, and switched on the kettle. Remembering that there was no milk in the house, he switched it off and poured out a glass of water. "Social workers," he cursed. "Self-righteous bitches."

He spent the morning re-organising his work-room and jotting down a few ideas for pricing structures. It made good sense, he thought, keeping the initial entry fee low and encouraging multiple resubmissions through a careful mix of praise and negativity.

This could lead to two possible developments: direct access to his thirty – or maybe thirty five - part correspondence course; or, alternatively, an almost endless process of resubmission as the hopeful composer sought perfection.

It seemed to Waters that he had amply deserved his lunch-time pint with Marcus Redfearn. And if Olive wished to maintain the higher moral ground, believing a pint with Marcus was one more example of pleasure coming before business, then that showed how little she knew outside the prefabricated walls of a council office. There was a lot to recommend, having the likes of Olive sharing your bed; but maybe there was something to be said too for the sexless world that Redfearn had chosen.

Marcus Redfearn taught music at Valemore College of F.E. The college was arguably the single remaining jewel in the town's tarnished crown. A couple of miles south of Valemore Central, the suburb of Little Valemore had slowly shrunk with the times to embody its name, becoming an almost invisible knot in the long thread of suburbia that ran down to Eaves End. There was talk that the local police station, the oldest in the county, was likely to close in the next round of cuts, and eyes were also on the college. Results had never mattered more and next year was election time again.

Redfearn seemed to know what examiners were looking for, and how to pass that knowledge on to his students. His success rates were too good to be ignored, and this ace-in-the-hole allowed him a certain leeway when it came to a lunchtime pint. Maybe, as Waters had pointed out, many times, Marcus Redfearn wasn't the town's greatest musical talent, yet what he did know he could pass on, assuring him a job, and a bloody well paid one at that. But it also meant getting up and going into work every morning, not to mention playing life by somebody else's rules. So let the Redfearns sell their souls in the classroom and leave the Waters of this world to a higher calling.

It had been a conversation along similar lines, over a recent lunch time session that had first ignited the idea of a correspondence course in musical composition. Waters recalled it happily as he headed, newspaper tucked under his arm, across the emptying sprawl of Valemore, down past the college towards the sacred Feathers.

The pub was half full. Close to the college, it maintained a residual clientele through most of the day. Lunchtimes though were largely food affairs at the Feathers these days, with most casual drinkers drifting back in when the plates cleared around two.

It was 12.30 when Waters arrived, and barely five minutes later when Redfearn came bounding through the door. Waters was a slightly built man, giving an impression of ungainly lankiness, while in contrast Redfearn, broad in the chest and heavy in the shoulders, gave an impression of athleticism well rested.

"Not bad," said Waters, looking at his watch. "Five minutes from the school bell to the first taste of the barmaid's apron."

Redfearn took the head off the pint that Waters had got in for him, and noticed the newspaper. "Scary stuff," he said.

"What - oh, the murder? Ol mentioned it."

Marcus Redfearn laughed. "How is the little lady?"

"*Little lady*! She'll have the language police on you. You know, an electrician once went into her office to change a light bulb, and happened to ask one of them to make a brew. He was nearly skinned alive."

Redfearn shook his head. "I'm no expert on relationships, but I'm not sure you two are exactly made for each other."

Waters smirked. "What gives you that impression?"

"You've been like cat and dog since the day you met. What do you get out of it?"

Waters tapped the end of his nose. "That would be telling."

"Okay, so she's a very attractive woman. But what's *her* excuse?"

"I guess it must be my piano playing."

"I'd watch it, Phil. She could be the one."

"Wash your mouth out."

"She's been living with you six months."

"Three, actually. Well, coming up for four."

"What about her house - solicitors still carving up the spoils? Where were the once-happy couple living?"

"Up in Cheshire with all the other rich types. He still lives in the house, apparently. Five bedrooms. Olive can afford to have strong socialist leanings."

"Don't suppose you want to live on your own patch doing his job - hers either, come to that."

"My sympathies are entirely with Mr. Roxburgh. The police get some bad press, and some of it justified. But if he put up for ten years with what I'm putting up with now …"

"Five bedrooms?" Redfearn whistled. "No kids?"

"Both committed to their careers. He's a detective inspector these days. Ol should get quite a slice out of him."

"I see."

"See what?"

"It all fits together. She lives with you in your humble semi and the judge says, Oh, dear, what a shame for the poor woman, slumming it like that. You're a pair together."

Waters handed him the newspaper. "If you've finished sticking your nose into my private life, perhaps you'd care to look at my ad."

Redfearn glanced at the headlines. "Wonder if Mr. Roxburgh is on the case?"

"Don't know about that. Ol certainly thinks *she* is. She'll be spouting her theories all morning at the office. Detective Inspector Olive Roxburgh of the Yard. You can run from her, but you can never hide."

Redfearn flicked through the paper, at last coming to the ads section.

"So what do you think, then?" asked Waters.

"Actually, Phil, I'm not so sure."

"What's wrong with it?"

"I don't know. I -"

"Come on, man, spit it out."

"It's just that – when I suggested a competition, I was thinking more of the students."

"I'm not following you, mate. If there's a problem, just say it."

Redfearn spent an uncomfortable minute trying to order his thoughts. Waters was tired of waiting. "The secret, Marcus, is to get them to see their work has the merit they secretly already believe it has, and then show them they're within striking distance of producing something special."

A look of disappointment settled onto Redfearn's face, as though his worst fears had been confirmed.

"I'm thinking of producing some leaflets," said Waters.

"For your correspondence course?"

"I've done them already. They'll go out with competition details. No, I mean flyers."

Redfearn took a good glug of his pint, paused for a breath, and then finished the glass. "I think what you're going to ask me next will go down better with another pint."

"Hey, I'm supposed to be the one who's out of paid employment."

"You want me to put some flyers around the college."

"Is that a problem?"

Sometimes, like now, Marcus Redfearn wondered what he ever saw in Phil Waters. They both had an interest in music and drinking beer, but that was about it. There weren't many friends in the life of Marcus Redfearn, and maybe that was the problem. People short of friends could find themselves at the beck-and-call of those who recognised another's need, and who were prepared to exploit it.

"I mean, if it's a problem," said Waters, "I'll ask elsewhere."

"If I'm being appointed Head of Promotions, then I'm nothing but honoured."

"Same again?" asked Waters.

"Looks like it."

As Waters trotted off to the bar, Redfearn hung his head in an aspect of shame.

By seven Olive still hadn't come home. Waters further adapted his work-room, re-tilting his computer screen, re-jigging books and documents from alphabetical into chronological order and then back again. He tried designing a flyer, even printed a few off, wondering whether Olive's opinion would be worth pursuing, if she ever came back.

He was playing a Lennon and McCartney song on the piano when she returned to the house later that evening. It was his own arrangement, and he had to admit that it was a fine one at that. When he heard the front door, he stopped playing. "That you, Ol?"

"Don't stop," she shouted up the stairs. "That's one of my favourites."

Waters smiled to himself, and picked up the melody again. Maybe that was the truth of it: that she was just a sucker for his playing. Finishing the song, he turned around to find her standing in the doorway.

"Play it again, Sam," she said. "After the day I've had."

He started up again, and in a moment felt her kisses falling like soft rain on the back of his neck. "Let's begin today again," she said.

He could feel the movement in his groin. It looked like being another interesting evening.

CHAPTER THREE

Penny got to college early. She'd been awake long before dawn, and the two mile walk from Eaves End had taken some of the edge off her restlessness. But that wasn't the reason for the early start.

The pianos at home, the old upright that had been in the Henderson family for at least two generations, and the Clavinova bought a few years ago had served both Penny and her sister well. Yet the arrival of the second instrument had still caused more than its share of ructions in the Henderson house.

For many years they had shared the upright, until eventually it was decided that the girls needed an instrument each. The idea had been to get rid of the old one and purchase two identical replacements, so that there would be no arguing over who had what. Then a four bedroomed property became available, outside Little Valemore, in the more prestigious Eaves End.

Eaves End was rumoured to have inherited the vigour and character that had seeped out of its tired neighbour. Though still part of the sprawl that constituted Valemore it was a little closer to the countryside than Little Valemore, and further away from the growing blot on the landscape that was Valemore Central.

Eaves End was a collection of houses, an estate marking the tail end of a snaking suburbia that had lost all shape under the shadows of its dull centre. A tasteful enclave almost lost between Little Valemore and the start of the farmlands stretching down towards the county line. The people of Eaves End had generally lived there all of their lives. The likes of the Henderson family sometimes broke through as a result of sheer hard work or good fortune, and occasionally a mixture of the two.

The house that fell vacant was modest by surrounding standards, and Mr and Mrs. Henderson had come to realise that while they had made it to the top division as far as Valemore was concerned, they had at the same time been relegated to the bottom of that division. Four bedrooms and a garden, the fourth bedroom earmarked for a future study, though precisely whose had never quite been established; a garden that nobody had the inclination for, other than occasionally looking out on and dreaming of a major project, possibly next year.

Mrs. Henderson worked as a psychiatric nurse in the community, and spent most of her days in the houses of Valemore Central. Mr. Henderson served the same people from his base at the Family Therapy Unit, not far from the social work office where the likes of Olive Roxburgh plied their trade.

The cost of moving to Eaves End was a challenging one, even for two professionals. Mr and Mrs. Henderson were going to have to make a few sacrifices to make their dream home a reality, and one of the sacrifices was halving the cost of buying two new pianos by keeping hold of the old one.

A family meeting had been called to discuss the matter in an open and honest way. *The Henderson way.* The upshot of the meeting was that Penny wanted the new instrument. Susan gave way. Soon after moving into the new property, the old piano was taken out of the living room and relocated into Susan's room, while the new piano was delivered straight to Penny's room.

In the weeks and months that followed, it seemed that Susan's playing was coming on in leaps and bounds, leaving Penny lagging behind. So Penny decided that she simply couldn't get on with an electrified version of a real piano, her progress hampered by "playing on a fake."

Susan agreed to a swap, and the Clavinova was moved into Susan's room while Penny returned to the old upright.

But still Penny couldn't settle to the arrangement, Susan continuing to improve at a rate that Penny couldn't match, regardless of what instruments they were practising on. And that's the way things stayed right up until Susan landed at Eaglesfield Psychiatric Unit, leaving Penny with both pianos to practice on, though neither seemed conducive to the art of composing.

Penny had a mind to try the college piano. At that time of the morning she could get an uninterrupted hour, no problem. The music inside her head had been haunting her, but it didn't sound right when she tried to play it on the pianos at home. Maybe the problem was nothing to do with the art of composition; maybe it was all to do with sound. This was big music; fine, subtle and ambitious music, and the college Baby Grand might bring it to life.

In the empty classroom Penny messed around with the themes running around inside her, giving the faintly gothic, melancholic melodies and counter-melodies half a dozen different harmonic settings. None of the treatments felt right though. It sounded best when she played it straight.

The main tune had come to her complete with a basic, simple arrangement, which in different circumstances might have been welcomed as a gift from on high; but now that only seemed to add weight to the likelihood that it was really some old favourite that she'd picked up somewhere and then forgotten about. Messing about with it at least disguised the steal a little, if it was a steal.

Hadn't McCartney had the same feeling when *Yesterday* turned up after a good night's sleep? Hadn't she read that somewhere? Or maybe it was something her father had told her. Her parents were Beatles fans, or had been, in another lifetime. They didn't seem to like stuff that had been written this century.

This wasn't a pop song, though. Pop music was the wallpaper that surrounded modern society, but not its substance. People called it art because they didn't know what art was. You didn't have to know much about music, or about anything, to have a hit record. Luck, and a good night's sleep, that's all you needed, apparently.

Penny played with the melody until she heard noises out in the corridor. The rest of the world was catching up with the day, and it was time to call it quits on the tune and head up to the library to find some peace and quiet. She had no classes until late morning, and all her projects were up to date. It paid sometimes to be a good student.

The library had a quiet room, and Penny took a couple of the freshly-delivered dailies into the empty solitude. She looked at the front pages of both papers with a detached curiosity, as though it was a faintly familiar story the details of which she couldn't quite place. It occurred to her that the nagging familiarity of the newspaper story was not dissimilar to that of the haunting theme, and she wondered if the two were somehow magically linked; if they could be brought together.

Her pulse moved in rhythm with the thought.

Putting the thought to one side, she settled to reading the tabloid and broadsheet accounts of how the body of a man, late-thirties, not local but on business in the town, had been found mutilated behind the derelict theatre down by the bus station. Details of the dead man's injuries were not given in either of the newspapers, and Penny's interest began to quicken. She assembled the remaining papers from the main library, taking them back through to the seclusion of the quiet room. But all she could find were repetitions on the same themes: street-lighting, policing policies, crime in general and the usual crap about the government.

She yawned. The police wanted people to come forward who may have been in the vicinity on the evening in question. It didn't look like they had much, though it wasn't always easy to tell. She rubbed at a pair of watery eyes and made herself a promise of an early night.

She really ought to visit Susan.

Would it wait another night?

In her mind's eye she saw Susan stand up, walking towards her in slow motion. Susan staring straight at her: intense, relentless, *accusing.*

Penny blinked the image away. No, tired or not it would have to be tonight.

With still half an hour until class, she checked through the advertisements in the local pages, faintly hoping that somebody out there might be selling a decent piano at an affordable price. Mum and Dad kept asking what she wanted for Christmas, and if she didn't give them some constructive suggestions soon she would end up being the only seventeen year-old in Valemore with the latest -

She saw it. The largest of the small ads.

Calling all composers.

Penny read the ad in disbelief, and then read it again. Was this guy for real? Some loser trying to make a living off the vain dreams of the poor, deluded and desperate - people like that needed a bullet.

Still, she kept the page open, and drummed her fingers against her bottom lip. Maybe it was the sheer in-your-face-audacity - it certainly wasn't the sincerity. Who was this creep? She was about to take the papers back to reception when it occurred to her: what if she sent him some material? He might at least recognise where she'd stolen the tune. And if he didn't, that might suggest that it was original after all. She ripped out the ad and slipped it into her pocket, before folding the newspaper, piling it on top of the others, and taking them back to the reception desk.

Walking down to the refectory to grab a coffee from the machine before heading to her late-morning class, Penny took the ad out of her pocket and read over it again.

She wondered why the word *sextet* seemed to leap out at her, tugging away at something, bringing the familiar melody back into her head with a vengeance. At the same time the association brought with it a flash of anger as she thought of the dead man, of the sympathy he would now be in line for and the damnation he deserved.

She would visit Susan tonight.

Yes, tonight.

Taking the plastic cup from the machine, she noticed that her hand was trembling.

Penny put the ad into the top draw of the desk in her bedroom. Later, when she got back from visiting Susan, she would send off for more details. The melody was back again, and she took it through to Susan's room, switching on the Clavinova. Susan often practised with headphones, but Penny couldn't see what there was to be secretive about. If Susan was as talented as everybody seemed to think, then why all the cloak and dagger?

Back at the old house in Little Valemore, the family piano had been in the small front room that also contained two easy chairs. Mum and Dad would often drift in and listen to the girls play. There was nowhere to hide in a room that contained only an acoustic piano and two chairs. No technology with which to fake anything. No facility for headphones. A test of character, stand or fall.

She picked at the tune, but the frustration was like a rope tightening around her. Maybe the tune wasn't right for the unaccompanied piano. It certainly wasn't right for this piano. It never needed tuning, this thing, but that was about all that could be said. It had, thought Penny, as much tone as a kazoo.

She went back to her own room and lifted up the lid on the old upright. It sounded even worse, like it needed tuning again. How could she achieve anything without the right tools? But then the piano at college hadn't provided the breakthrough, either. Penny tried imagining the melody performed by a string band, with a clarinet or an oboe to bring out the mournful top-line. She couldn't be sure. Questioning its originality was putting a block on everything. Until that was cleared up the thing was going nowhere.

So why not sketch out the idea as a piano piece, send it to El Creepo, the giver of immortality, and see what he thinks? Do it. Make a start. Do it now.

"Hello - anyone home?"

Her mother was coming in through the back door. Putting the lid down on the piano, Penny went downstairs to meet her.

Penny had a surprise lined up. Chicken casserole for dinner, with cheesecake for dessert. They would eat together as a family for a change, if Dad wasn't too late getting home.

Mrs. Henderson looked tired these days. She'd aged over the past months, and colleagues whispered that it was hardly surprising, considering what her family had been through. She never took a day off sick, though, and hadn't done in years. Work kept her going, said those who knew her; work and church.

Mr. Henderson was the same. He'd been a keen amateur musician, once upon a time, playing clarinet with a local jazz orchestra. A decent pianist, too, though these days he could go for months without playing a note. It didn't seem a priority to him. When the kids were young he would play for them; nurture their talents in any way that he could. He didn't want them to let go of their dreams as easily as he'd let go of his. Age was a creeping sickness that took no prisoners. A family and a mortgage didn't leave time for dreaming, and neither did grief.

Keith and Jane Henderson, older parents to begin with, were starting to look more like grandparents; the tragedy of what had happened to Susan eating into them without mercy.

Penny made a hot drink for her mother and told of her plans to prepare a family meal.

"No college work?" her mum asked her.

"Not tonight. I thought we'd eat and then I'd visit Susan."

Mrs. Henderson gave her daughter a lingering look. "What you mean is, why don't we all visit together?"

"Well, we could," said Penny. "There's no law against it."

"Your dad's not even home yet. You know he likes to visit at the weekend. He's so tired lately."

In the living room, Penny sat down next to her mum and placed an arm around her. She knew her dad visited Susan when he was supposed to be working. Mum did too. What was the big secret? The family was nothing *but* secrets. They were scared of letting on that Susan was still their favourite, like she always had been. "You and Dad need to rest," she said, relishing the prospect of seeing Susan alone. "I won't mention it when he comes home. I'll slip off quietly."

"What's so special about tonight?"

"Oh, you know ... just girl talk."

Mrs. Henderson laughed. "She'll be glad to see you, she always is. You're a good sister, and a good daughter, too, come to that. We have been blessed in so many ways," she said, looking into some imaginary distance where bad things didn't happen to good daughters.

When Keith Henderson got home, the evening news was coming on the BBC. He had missed the first two stories: a political headline and a plane crash; but as he walked through the back porch and into the kitchen, his nose twitching at the delicious smells coming from the hob and the oven, he caught the start of the report on the violent death of the business man found behind the old Regent building. The report was filtering through to the kitchen as Mr. Henderson took off his coat and shoes.

The door from the living room suddenly swung open. "Hi, Dad," said Penny, bursting in, kissing him before opening the oven door, taking out the casserole dish, and carefully spooning the juices over three chicken portions.

Mr. Henderson looked on in mock amazement. "Surely, Penny, you are not responsible for this?"

She turned, a little uneasily. Realising that he was referring to her cooking, she forced a smile. "Aw, shucks, you know - so many talents, Dad."

"Keith, have you seen this?" Mrs. Henderson was in the living room, sitting in front of the television, shaking her head. "I don't know what this world's coming to, really I don't. It isn't safe to be out of doors."

Mr. Henderson joined his wife in front of the TV. They watched and listened together as the news reporter made vague remarks that amounted to nothing that wasn't evident from the headline itself, while Penny listened from the kitchen, needlessly basting the chicken pieces for a second time before placing the dish back into the oven. Then she added a little more butter to the garlic frying gently on the hob, and took a couple of large mushrooms out of the fridge.

Penny enjoyed watching her parents savouring their meals. They didn't seem to savour much these days and it was a damned shame. Maybe they ought to recognise the good things that they still had - like, for instance, a remarkable and healthy daughter still under their roof!

After the washing up, Penny sat at her piano for a few minutes, improvising while her parents watched the regional news reports. Penny played quietly, all the time keeping the low muffle of television voices audible through the open door. She couldn't make out the actual words, but she sensed them, and could visualise her parents sitting below, shaking their heads in disbelief that another outrage had come to haunt their little world.

Without meaning to, Penny found that she was playing around with the mystery melody again. When she realised what she was doing, she stopped.

"No, don't stop."

She swung around to find her father standing in the doorway.

"What *was* that?" he asked.

"Oh, nothing much."

"It didn't sound like nothing."

"You don't recognise it?"

"Should I?"

"It seems familiar, that's all."

Mr. Henderson sighed, with sudden remembrance. "But you're hoping it isn't, right? The curse of the creative mind: does this belong to someone else?"

Penny smiled. "You're right, Dad." She played the melody again, not tinkering, not improvising; retaining the simple accompaniment with which the tune had originally arrived in her head. Without saying anything, she gently placed the piano lid down. When she turned around again she caught the look in her father's eye.

"I didn't mean to upset you, Dad. It's a lousy tune anyway."

"It is not," he said. "It's beautiful. But it reminds me, that's all."

"Reminds you?"

"Hearing you play. You and Susan, you would play for hours."

"I'm sorry, Dad."

"Don't be. I hear you're popping over to see Susan later."

Penny felt the need to justify herself. Her dad broke the tension. "Tell her that I'll see her on Saturday. I'll go for the day."

"I'll tell her, Dad."

"And I want you to give her something." Leaning forward, he kissed his daughter. "Pass that on from me. Look, give me five minutes and I'll run you there."

"No, Dad, chill out. You'd only cramp our style."

His expression became sorrowful. "Sometimes I think she doesn't want us there. Is it something we did, something we didn't do?"

"Dad -"

"If you knew, if there was something we could put right, you would tell us, wouldn't you?"

"There's nothing, Dad. I promise."

He shook his head. "You're two of a kind, do you know that. Always up to something. Remember this?" He leaned over the piano and tapped out the main theme from Chopin's *Funeral March.*

Da da-da da da-da da-da da-da da.

Penny's heart was thumping.

"I always knew the pair of you were up to something when I heard that tune."

The code. The secret code. The deepest code of all. It would always be there, between them. The thing they shared. The thing that could never be broken. When Susan played that theme, the two of them came together against the world. It was unshakeable. It would always be so.

Wouldn't it? Even now? In spite of ... this? In the light of what had happened? Of what had ... transpired? Had the code been broken? Could what was broken one day be restored?

Mr. Henderson wiped his eyes with the back of his hand. "I'd put cotton wool in your ears, if I were you. After today's news there's going to be some heavy sermons."

He turned to go, hesitating in the doorway. "Don't forget to give Susan that kiss. And Saturday, tell her. Hell or high water."

Penny put on her faithful black leather jacket and walked down to the bus stop, the warnings from her mother to be careful as there are such monsters running wild still ringing in her ears.

CHAPTER FOUR

Phil Waters matched a cigarette and handed it to Olive.

"Evening's over then?" she said, drawing deeply on the smoke.

"Needn't be," he said, lighting one for himself. "A refuelling stop."

They were both propped up on pillows against the headboard. Even with the central heating firing away, the bedroom was cold and Olive, not out of modesty, had already pulled the sheets up to her neck. Waters slid off the bed and walked over to the window. The bedside lamp was on, and he cautiously turned back a corner of the curtain and peeked out.

"Anything to report?" she asked, eying his nakedness with interest. "Or are you displaying your wares, looking for takers?"

He pulled his head back from behind the curtains, taking a pull on his cigarette. Glancing at her, he resumed his post at the window, while Olive's eyes remained fixed on his thighs. He's idle, she thought. Badly trained and too well educated for his own good. An intelligent fool, articulate enough to endlessly justify a wasted life. Full of stupid ideas that he still believes will make him rich one day. A well-spoken Del Boy with an ear for music, and an arse ... She giggled. *Phil Waters - the perfect arse!*

"Something funny?" said Waters.

She started to grind the cigarette into the saucer-ashtray. "I hope you're not looking for inspiration out there. There's something far more interesting in here, honey buns."

He didn't need a second invitation. As he turned back towards the bed, Olive's eyes widened. "So soon?" she said. Launching himself on top of her, the ashtray fell to the floor, spilling its contents, and earning him a meaty swat across the hide.

"I didn't think you social work types condoned violence," he said, climbing back under the sheets.

"Violence against men - we thrive on it. It's one of our favourite methods of control. Here's another." Her head disappeared beneath the sheets, and in a matter of seconds she could hear the deep moans coming from the surface, as Waters began his roll call of all the deities in his vocabulary.

When Olive surfaced, Waters began to kiss at her face like a hungry spaniel. This, she thought, is the moment of fusion. He and his kind would sign his soul over to the devil without a second's hesitation. *Putty in our hands and too dumb to know it.* If this could be preserved, bottled, there was not a woman alive who would fail to rule her world forever.

And then he did it; that thing that always took her straight to the ceiling. Turning the tables – oh, he was so full of deceit; to look at, who would have thought he had it in him to do so much so easily. Hidden depths - she almost moaned the phrase out loud. How quickly power could change hands.

She was losing control, as she did every single time. It was so powerful; close to unbearable. Lost inside it, cut loose from the world, the mere world of men on women, women on men; for now, in these nuclear moments, none of the politics mattered, and the eruption blew all of that and more clean out of the water.

The bed was beginning to rock beneath them. Was he feeling one hundredth of what she was feeling? If men could feel what she was feeling then they were not, after all, to be pitied. If they could feel this, in all its glory, then they were every inch as sacred.

The headboard slammed against the wall, and the mutual groans became the only fixed point in a wild black ocean. The first satanic shrieks were breaking out, building to a scream of release, then tumbling, as if through space, finally entering gravity and sinking into the numb depths of a silent sea.

Waters was flat out when Olive shook him. "I'm going to work," she said. "For some peace and quiet."

"What are you talking about?"

"I've made a drink for you, busy boy."

He sat up quickly. "You've made me a drink? Is it my birthday?"

"That was last night, lover."

"What do you mean, peace and quiet – I wasn't snoring?"

"I don't know what you've been dreaming about, but I'm glad I wasn't there."

"Where were you?"

"I'm talking about your dream, you moron. It sounded awful."

"I can't remember dreaming about anything."

"Routine nightmares? Can't live with yourself? Look, I'm off. Oh, and by the way, I'd stay indoors if I were you."

"How do you mean?" he asked, taking a sip of hot tea.

"There's been another killing. A man in his thirties, dick cut off same as the last one."

The tea spilled from his mouth, spraying across his chest, burning him. He rubbed at the hot liquid. "Cut his dick off? They actually said that?"

She pulled on a corner of the bed-sheet and wiped the rest of the hot tea from his reddened skin. "I'd put some cream on that if I were you."

"I'll be alright. So they said that on the news - about his ‐"

"Of course they didn't, you idiot. Well, not in so many words. They reckon they're after the same bloke as did the last one, though."

"How do they know it's a man?"

"Come on," she said. "It may be every girl's fantasy to go around cutting off dicks -"

"Is it?"

"Well, it might be at that. But I think it's more likely a male thing."

"What, gays or something?"

"Listen, Phil: don't ever get a job in a social work office, do you hear?"

"I wasn't planning to."

"Good. You'd get lynched."

"They don't go in for free speech much, do they?"

She glanced at her watch. "Drink your tea, put some cream on your chest, and try to stay out of trouble."

"Anything else?"

"As a matter of fact, yes, there is. If your dick's still attached when I get home, we'll recommence. See you later."

He went downstairs and switched on the television. One story was dominating the local news. Some businessman had been found out in the woods, a few miles up the road, his BMW parked in a lane close by. He was naked, multiple stab wounds, mutilation; the details were vague, as usual. The obvious suggestion was that they were looking for one person for both murders, though a copy-cat killing could not be eliminated at this early stage of the investigation.

Waters could feel his chest burning, and he went through to the bathroom to check out the medicine cabinet, finding nothing more than three plasters and a single paracetamol. He would have to call at the chemist - or then again, he could call Olive at the office and say that he was tied up and could she call for some supplies on her way home. It didn't hurt that much. He could wait.

After some deliberation, he called her, for the hell of it, and listened happily to some rich and colourful abuse about men being lazy, good-for-nothing bastards. He knew how she loved to put on a show, talking that way, particularly in front of a sympathetic audience. It must, he thought, be one sad outlook to be a man working in that office. The whoops and bursts of applause were coming down the line like gunfire. *One of these days those bitches really are going to lynch somebody.*

The excitement was beginning to die down, and he wondered if the boss had walked in. But what difference was that likely to make? If it was a woman, she'd join forces against the common enemy; and if it was a man – well, good luck.

Olive's voice was quieter now, deliberately calm. She had something important to say and clearly intended making a meal of it. When Olive told a story, she started at the beginning and then went back a couple of hundred pages. But she was coming to it now, unable to hold off any longer.

Waters listened, though he couldn't quite believe what he was hearing.

CHAPTER FIVE

The Eaglesfield Unit was situated on the southern rim of Grayling. If your room didn't face north, there was every chance of a glimpse at least of the surrounding countryside. North looked into the heart of Grayling, a factory land as dirty and depressing as Valemore Central itself.

It was late when Penny arrived. She'd make up for that at the weekend, with Mum and Dad there, too. Tonight was a bridging visit, or at least that's what she'd told her parents.

The truth was different.

This visit was vital.

There were things that she needed to say to Susan, private things that couldn't wait. Susan had to know what had started, or there was no point to any of it. That was the way the magic worked. Sympathetic magic. The founding stone of all hope. The beginning and end of faith itself.

Susan hadn't spoken since the attack, and she remained unresponsive. Still, Penny knew there were ways of saying what needed to be said; ways to get through to her sister, even in her present condition, whatever that was. Deep trauma, said the quacks, but what did they know? Susan would hear and Susan would understand. They were two of a kind, after all.

Mr. Henderson used to say that all the time; and that when they got an idea into their heads, it was like a fever taking hold. He also reckoned that their single-minded stubbornness would be the making of them, singling them out as special and marking them out for great things. Gifts come in many forms, he would say. Mrs. Henderson would laugh when he talked like that, and pass it off as men talking rubbish. Secretly, though, she loved it when he told her that their daughters were destined to make a big noise out there in the world one day.

Eaglesfield was divided into separate buildings that further sub-divided into smaller units: mental and physical, old and young, angel and devil. Susan was accommodated on the upper floor of the North Psychiatric Wing for Younger People. It wasn't a large unit; a dozen filled it. She had her own room, and for an institution it wasn't a bad room, despite the view. It could have been a room in a university hall of residence, except for the quality of the furniture and the fact that the nocturnal sounds were not fuelled by alcohol and sex.

There were film posters on the wall taken from Susan's collection at home. Penny had chosen the ones she thought her sister held most dear, and Mrs. Henderson shook her head every time she looked at them. Why young girls wanted to be reminded of other people's nightmares all the time was beyond her. There were photographs in the room, too: Mum, Dad, Susan and Penny. No grandparents still alive and no cousins to augment the little family unit. Two only children falling in love, getting married and creating twins.

The physical injuries Susan had sustained in the attack had proven to be the least of her problems. Within a handful of days she might, under different circumstances, have been leading the life of a normal teenage girl once more. Yet here she was, months later, still languishing in the crazy world of psychiatric fantasy, where men and women in white coats and painted smiles and frowns made up theories and treatments for want of a better way of passing the time, and waiting for the healing to come.

And so the Eaglesfield mantra: these things take time.

It astounded Penny the way so-called professionals never tired of reminding them of that same old wisdom.

Like they had invented it, or at least discovered it. The mind, they repeated, at regular intervals, and in long and tiresome meetings, is a very strange and complex creation. It can even perplex the experts – *apparently*. Baffle the most senior health care professionals – no shit! Yet the Henderson family learned to bear the fatuous reminders, and to endure the painful and pompous soliloquies on the limitations of the country's finest medical minds, delivered on occasions *by* the country's so-called finest medical minds.

Though Susan hadn't spoken since the accident, she had, once or twice, written down short and indecipherable phrases at the request of the various therapists whose visits filled her days. The doctors confirmed categorically that no brain injury had been sustained; that Susan's mental state was clearly and irrefutably the result of severe trauma. It was entirely curable, though nobody could put any kind of time on it, or was willing to do so.

So it was back to faith. Faith in time the great healer; faith in a daughter and her doting twin sister to overcome the obscene thing that had been done and that could never be undone. And if faith wavered in the hearts and minds of Mr and Mrs Henderson, as Penny knew that it did, then she alone must be its truest keeper.

Penny found her sister in the first of the two general lounges. Susan had been reluctant to leave her room during her first months on the unit, but recently her ventures into the communal areas had been more forthcoming and generally less brief. She had eaten with two other young women that particular evening, and was sitting in front of the television watching a travel programme. It looked as though they were starting off in Southern France, and Penny wondered, fleetingly, if one day they might take off and enjoy a good holiday together.

She stood for a few moments in the doorway, watching her sister; trying to weigh-up whether or not she looked more responsive today. Of course, she could simply ask the staff on duty for a full-report; but then nobody knew her sister the way she did. When the real change came, she would see it first; for she would inaugurate the process of healing and it could not be any other way.

One of the staff asked Penny if she would care for a drink, but she declined. Her plan was to make small-talk with Susan until her television programme finished, and then see about organising some privacy for the remainder of the visit. The show was done with France already, zipping across the Atlantic to an impossibly white-beached resort in Florida. Penny thought she liked the look of France better, and it seemed like a good enough way to break the ice.

She took one of the plastic seats over to where Susan was sitting, and placed it next to her sister, careful not to obstruct anyone's view of the television. Susan continued to stare blankly at the screen, betraying no visible emotion. At last Penny said, "Okay, Susan, where are we going then, France or Florida?"

Susan didn't appear to register her sister's presence. It went this way sometimes, most times, and it never failed to make the members of the Henderson family burn with guilt and frustration. As though Susan was punishing them for not visiting more often; for not abandoning their lives completely and moving into the unit themselves and done with.

Penny said, "I say we choose France. That Florida sand doesn't look real to me. I reckon they imported it from the chalk works down the road. I wouldn't like to spend my holidays lying on chalk dust, would you? No, if you ask me, it's France, up to now."

She always did this. Chattering away like she was born to it. Hating herself for it, but unable to stand the silence, that sinister, accusing silence that Susan exuded.

After the adverts the show moved on to the Channel Islands. Penny reckoned that France still had it. She asked Susan if she fancied going back to her room, as there was something that she wanted to tell her. Susan didn't respond; she sat watching the screen until the credits were coming up at the end of the show. Penny tried again, and when Susan still didn't respond, she made an unnecessary visit to the bathroom, giving her sister a little more time and space. This had worked on a couple of occasions, Susan betraying the subtlest suspicion of a response. No doubt the professionals had a phrase or two to explain it.

When Penny returned she asked again about having a little private time together. "Mum and Dad will be here at the weekend," she said, "so we can forget the real talk then. You know how it goes when they're here. But this can't wait," said Penny, her voice becoming a whisper. "You see, I made a start, Susan. I made the first sacrifice."

Susan turned slightly and smiled, weakly.

Penny glanced around the lounge, but nobody else had seen it, she was certain of that. "Good girl," she said. "I'll get a nurse."

In Susan's room, once the nurse had left them alone, Penny took her sister's hand. "I heard this story. You see, there were six crows, and they were doing everything they could to ruin the farmer. They didn't really want the farmer's crops; they just wanted to show that they could ruin her. Power, that's what they wanted, and the farmer, one day, got sick of cursing nature and decided it was time to take it upon herself to sort things out, once and for all. The only way to save the farm, you see, was to kill the crows."

Penny, all the time that she was talking, stared into her sister's eyes. Susan was registering all this, Penny was sure of it.

"Well, anyway, the farmer, she's made a start already. There were six crows, once upon a time, but now there are only five. In no time there will be four, then three – and before you know it, the farmer will take her land back, every square-inch of it. You see that, don't you, Susan? You believe me when I tell you that it will be so."

Penny could feel the trickle of a tear coming down her cheek, and brushed it quickly away. "I'd better be going," she said. "Let you get some rest." She stood up, still holding Susan's hand. As she started to gently ease her hand away, she noticed a weak sign of resistance. Penny looked down at Susan's hand, then at her flushed face. "What is it? Don't you want me to go yet?" She sat back down. "I'll stay as long as you want me to, you know that."

Susan was looking straight at her, her grip even stronger now.

"Susan, trust me. Leave it all to me." Penny looked into her sister's eyes for as long as she could bear it. The silence was coming down hard, taking on the quality of malevolence. She felt Susan's hand withdrawing ... then tightening again.

Almost an hour later, the nurse suggested that it was time to let Susan rest. Every time Penny had made to leave, Susan's hand had squeezed into hers with increasing strength. The nurse agreed that it was a most encouraging sign. "I don't know what you've done," she said, unlocking the key-pad so that Penny could exit the unit, "but a little more of it might be just what the doctor ordered. I believe that your sister's going to be okay."

It was well after nine when Penny reached the bus-stop. She'd missed one bus already and estimated at least a twenty minute wait for the next one. There was a pub a couple of minutes down the road: The Cheese Makers. A drink would kill the time.

The restlessness inside her was making her fingers buzz, and the tune forming in her head, she knew, meant no sleep that night. So what was the hurry?

Penny walked away from the bus stop, Grayling behind her; heading in the direction of home, drawn towards the one dirty light burning in the darkness.

The pub was busy for a Wednesday evening. It was a lousy hole at the best of times, but midweek found it chock-full of Grayling business-men stopping off on the way home. The area had built up a reputation over the past few years, and seedy legends proliferated. Penny knew to get the bus straight there and the bus straight back. She was neither stupid nor naïve, and never had been, not even as a child. An old head on young shoulders, Mrs Henderson used to say.

Just like Susan.

Penny walked through to the bar, well aware that a biker jacket and torn jeans would send an unequivocal signal out to the shit-for-brains who came in looking for something more than a pint and a stale baguette. She touched the chest pocket of her leather jacket, and felt re-assured at the bulge as she made her way through the maggot-filled den, patting the hidden talisman like it was her oldest and most trusted friend.

She was halfway down the Britvic when she felt eyes moving over her. Particular eyes. *Maggot eyes.* Then she smelt him. Body-odour – he smelt like a skunk.

"Can I get you another of those?"

She looked up. My God, she thought, they're cloning them. He could have been the brother of the last one. The same standard-issue outfit, more or less, and the same cocksure grin plastered across his arrogant chops. *Susan's type, oh yes. She would approve of him.*

"Okay," she said. "Thank you."

A drink later and he was offering her a ride in his BMW.

And she was accepting.

There was a place she knew where things could get *interesting*. Turn off here, and head for the woods. Wasn't Christmas meant to be a time of fun and gluttony? Where's your spirit, man? Could be you're getting old before your time.

He was game enough, no question. She could almost smell the semen boiling up in his balls. All the time he was driving he kept reaching for her thigh, and all the time she kept one hand across her chest, feeling at the re-assuring metal that lay just beneath the zip.

In no time they were abandoning his car and entering the woods on foot. He could hardly contain himself; a child on an adventure. He insisted on taking out his wallet and sorting out what he called "the business side of things." She wouldn't hear of it; there was plenty of time for that later. He had to keep his mind off the money and on the job in hand. Sex, she explained, is not worth a fuck if you don't keep your mind on the game.

He was so excited he could barely walk straight. But he still couldn't seem to take his mind off the money. It was bugging him, and he couldn't let it go. He had his way of dealing with things, and any other way was going to cause him an ulcer.

Penny was going to save him from the whole unpleasant business of ulcers.

She told him to relax; loosen up, enjoy himself. There would be nothing he couldn't afford. The important thing, she insisted, was *satisfaction.* You couldn't put a price on that.

Inside the wood, in the deeper part of it, it didn't seem so cold. She didn't feel the penetrating bitterness, and once she'd started getting him acclimatised to the situation, neither, it seemed, did he. Not even when they started undressing. Not even when he was lying in the soil, the blood leaking out of him, his mouth twitching like a dying rabbit, giving to the ghosts of the night the impression that he was sucking on his own blood-soaked scrotum.

CHAPTER SIX

Phil Waters spent most of the day in his work-room, getting next to nothing done. It came easy, creating the illusion of purposeful activity, tinkering on a computer, and by lunchtime he was ready for a break. Out of a perverse sense of duty, he idled through until Olive came home at six-thirty, looking suitably exhausted.

He hadn't given any more thought to the second murder, not since putting the phone down after Olive had told him about the meat-and-two-veg-in-the-mouth stuff that had been hinted at on the radio. When she'd told him, he hadn't been sure what was the more disturbing: the sheer depravity of the act itself, or the humour it appeared to have generated around the office.

They were crazy bitches, those social workers, and more depraved than any man. Perhaps the killer was a woman with a vendetta against men. It was some sick world, he thought.

There had been developments throughout the day, and as Olive crashed on the sofa, clutching a stiff drink, she brought him up to speed. Waters couldn't help but find it disconcerting that she should be so well informed.

"Been in touch with old 'Roxburgh of the Yard'?" he jibed.

She gave him the evil eye. "I will, this once, let that comment go."

"Very generous of you, Ol. Hard day listening to the radio?"

Despite his truculence, she was too bursting with news-reports to storm off into a sulk. Interested or not, he was going to hear every last detail.

As it turned out, the senior detective on the case was, indeed, none other than Nigel Roxburgh. The man Olive had spent ten years with. The extent of their current communications, though, she insisted, was entirely conducted through solicitors.

The police had issued a statement suggesting that a young man wearing a light green waterproofed coat had been seen in the vicinity around the time that the latest murder had taken place. The man was of average height and build, with dark brown, possibly black, collar-length hair. Police were eager to speak to the person answering that description, to eliminate him from their enquiries.

"They reckon he's gay?" asked Waters, switching on the TV and searching for news. "Sounds like it to me," he added, with a tone of certainty that made Olive smile.

"So, Columbo: who do you reckon's gay - the killer or the victim?"

"Isn't it obvious?"

"Not to me. But then you're the senior armchair detective in this house."

"Both," he said. "That's what they're like."

"Phil, pardon my ignorance, but what the hell are you talking about?"

He gave her an exasperated look. "Come on, Ol. They're always strangling each other or doing something obscene. It's a different code of ethics. I think the police should let them get on with it, as long as they don't bother the rest of us."

She blinked, for the moment unable to find suitable expression for her disbelief.

"Of course," he went on, "I don't expect you to agree."

"And why would that be? Because I haven't just stepped off Planet Zanussi! Hell's bells, Phil, who *do* you like?"

"What?"

"You don't like social workers, you don't like gay people; you're not keen on students and - except when you're in bed with them - you don't seem to like women."

He sniggered.

"What do you see in me, Phil? No, second thoughts, don't answer that."

"We're two of a kind, Ol."

"How do you work that out?" She held up her hand. "Don't answer that, either."

He turned up the volume on the TV, after suggesting that even the news reports had to be better than "feminist sermons."

They listened to an excitable reporter treading water over the brutal slayings of two men within a few miles and a couple of days of each other. The police were keen to apprehend the young man whose description was zooming around the country, ensuring infamy regardless of whether or not he turned out to be the killer. "Looks a bad lot," said Phil Waters, when the police-artist's sketch came up on the screen. "Just look at those eyes, will you. Look at those eyes and tell me that he isn't the man."

"He isn't the man," said Olive.

"What's that?"

"I said: he isn't the man. Open your ears."

"Are you trying to be funny? Ring your old man – give Roxy Roxburgh a call. I tell you, Ol, he didn't make d*etective inspector* by not knowing an evil face when he sees one."

"Is that so?"

He squinted back at her. "Then again …"

For that ill-considered remark he earned a smack around the ear that for a moment left him seeing stars. "I thought you lot were supposed to be pacifists," he said, and less than a second later his other ear was ringing in sympathy.

"And there's plenty more where that came from," she warned him.

He grinned at her. "You're turning me on, Ol."

"What doesn't turn you on?"

"How about it?" he said, taking her hand as he stood up. "How about an early doors?"

"What's with you? I haven't eaten yet today."

"You're about to, Ol."

By the time they reached the top of the stairs, both of them were naked. They didn't make it as far as the bedroom, not the first time. When they finally fell asleep, the TV still repeating downstairs, adding nothing and subtracting nothing, they resembled the spirits of warring nations who had at last found the road to peace. Coiled together, and still basting in each others' juices, they might have been the perfect couple. That they loathed each other, and spoke a different language most of the day, didn't seem to matter. If anything, it seemed to intensify the charge of electricity that broke out between them at ever-diminishing intervals.

Olive went in late the next morning. She had some lieu time to use up. She'd heard Phil muttering in his sleep, and turned to him. He was lying on his back and making low, groaning noises. She'd eased back the sheets and gazed lovingly at the mighty erection he was sporting. It had seemed a pity to waste it.

After a pause for phone calls and tea-making, activities had then resumed, and the two of them at last lay in a dreamy half-sleep, listening to the postman trying to negotiate the overly-aggressive letter-box.

"That thing's too stiff," she muttered.

"Thank you," he muttered back, earning a lazy slap on the arm.

"How's your chest – still sore?"

"I've got sorer bits."

"There's only one part of your body that concerns you, do you realise that?"

"Yes," he said, drifting. "The same part that concerns you."

Olive pulled herself up, eying his chest. The redness of yesterday had virtually disappeared. He was such a baby, making a fuss over nothing, as usual.

"I'll make another drink."

"You do that, Ol."

"Do you want this one over your head or your chest?"

"Think I'll soak my nuts in it."

"Don't tempt me," she said, getting out of bed, wrapping herself into a yellow cotton dressing gown. Then she slapped his head once for good luck, and headed downstairs.

Waters lay there, mildly cursing her, wondering if the postman had brought anything interesting. For a moment he pictured a small mountain of manuscripts, hopeful entrants responding to his ad; wanting him to turn them into the Beethoven, Bach, or – if all else failed – the Lloyd-Weber of the day. And all at a most reasonable and affordable price!

He let the daydream fade into the more concrete dream of Olive's breasts, and almost immediately he felt the usual, predictable stirrings accompanying the image. "Don't you ever rest?" he complained, proudly. "Can I not sneak a thought past you – can I not contemplate the Roxburgh arse without having to stir myself from peaceful slumbers to mount the wretched thing?"

"Charming!"

Tea had arrived for the second time. He looked up to see her standing over him, holding the steaming mug menacingly.

"Talking to it now, are you? Let's see it, then. Let's see if it can take its medicine."

"Ol, I was kidding -"

"I'm not." She tilted the mug, letting a drop splash onto his bare chest. He jumped up, rubbing at where the scalding liquid had landed. "You're crazy, do you know that?"

"I must be," she said, putting the mug down by the side of his bed, "for waiting on a turd like you hand and foot. There's some post."

His eyes widened. "You've brought it up?"

"Don't push it." She softened. "As a matter of fact …" She handed him a bundle of letters. "The top one looks interesting," she said.

The envelope at the top of the stack was handwritten. He tore it open, and punched the air. "Yes!"

"About your competition for losers?"

"Listen to this, Ol."

"Just the gist, if you wouldn't mind."

After silently reading the letter for the second time, he said, "Upshot is: Mr Alan Barclay, music student at Bride's College, Hampshire, would like further details of both the compo and the correspondence course."

"Is that it?"

"Could be the beginning of a beautiful friendship, Ol."

"Spare me. Aren't you going to open the rest?"

"Didn't think you were interested."

"I'm not."

"Surprised, then? A little curious, possibly?"

"Come out from up your own backside, Phil. There's a world out here."

She read a magazine while Waters opened two more handwritten envelopes, both bearing out-of-county postmarks.

It seemed that both Mrs. Kate Evesham, retired music teacher, and David Beecham, aspiring rock star with "one eye firmly cocked towards the film-score" wished to join the elite band of hopefuls in the race to secure the Phil Waters seal of approval and guarantee of artistic immortality.

The rest of the pile consisted of the routine round of circulars and loan offers.

The one at the bottom of the stack, however, looked intriguing. Like the first three, it was handwritten. Unlike the first three, it bore a local postmark. The brief letter came with a single sheet of manuscript paper, folded over to meet the requirements of the letter-sized envelope.

"This one's keen," he said, unfolding the manuscript page.

Olive smirked. "That's it? That's the entry? Doesn't take a music teacher to see that we haven't exactly got a symphony there, does it?"

Waters gave the manuscript page his full concentration. Then he got out of bed and pulled on the pair of unwashed jeans that Olive had kicked along the landing earlier that morning.

She watched him in amazement. "What's wrong with that tea?" she said.

Ignoring her, he picked up a discarded shirt from the doorway and left the room, still clutching the manuscript page.

"Charmer," she said, picking up the letter that had accompanied the page of handwritten music.

Dear Mr. Waters,
Please send further details re. Competition. Enclosing idea for sextet. SAE attached.
Thanks,
Penny Henderson (Ms)

A melody struck up from the next room. He certainly had some talent when it came to music, she had to admit that much. It amazed her that anyone could look at a page of music and play it straight off the bat. Not much of a tune, though, she thought.

A few minutes later, after he'd finished playing the thing through for the second time, Waters came back into the bedroom. "What do you think of that?" he asked, drinking down his cold tea in a single gulp.

"Nothing special," she said. "You're not going to tell me that we're witnessing the arrival of a new Mozart?"

"Not quite," he said. Then he turned straight around, went back into his work-room and played the piece over while Olive got ready for work.

CHAPTER SEVEN

Marcus Redfearn didn't believe in too much preparation. In fact he didn't believe in preparation at all. If a class was scheduled to begin at nine-thirty, then that was the time to arrive. Not nine-fifteen and certainly not eight-forty-five.

Yet the practice existed and it never ceased to baffle him. Colleagues, for some reason unknown, felt obliged to work a dawn shift, messing around for an hour before the class even began. Time that could be better spent lying in bed staring at the damp patch on the ceiling, and threatening to spend a slice of the summer holidays decorating instead of swilling ale. Well, next year, maybe, or failing that, definitely the year after.

Urgency was not a word to be found in the Gospel according to Marcus Redfearn. And as for the mythical practice of using evenings to prepare for classes, that kind of foolishness could get a teacher a bad reputation. Evenings had another reason for being, and it had absolutely nothing to do with classrooms. Evenings were what pubs were invented for. Evenings and weekends came under the sacred realm of the public house, and accordingly should be dedicated exclusively to the consumption of fine ales.

Friday morning, nine-thirty, was not one of the highlights of his week. For starters, there was the inevitable hangover. Thursday evenings were a glorious invention. A reason to believe that the human race was not the forlorn endeavour it so often appeared to be. The promise of the weekend viewed over a Thursday evening tipple produced a kind of ecstasy that was best fuelled with an early arrival and a couple of large ones to cap it off around closing time. A well planned and executed Thursday evening could kick off a weekend magnificently, though the consequence of all of that magnificence was the torture chamber of Friday morning.

It wasn't solely the hangover that was responsible for his apprehension, however. Friday morning, nine-thirty, held another demon. The weak spot. The part of the curriculum in which he most certainly did not excel.

In every other respect he did what he did as well as anybody; he knew his business and he could communicate his abundant knowledge in a style that was stimulating and effective. His pass rates were becoming a phenomenon, and to achieve that consistency and burgeoning excellence over his first four years in the job defied the jealousy-driven, hare-brained theories of luck and good fortune that arose every now and again in this and every other educational establishment up and down the land. Still the weak spot though. And it came around to stare him full in the face every Friday of term-time at exactly nine-thirty, lasting all the way to lunch and always requiring a solid couple of pints to wash the worst of it away.

Composition.

What was it that troubled him so much? He could talk about the process until hell froze over; blind a spellbound class with endless theorizing on the subject of creating original music; yet to actually do it, well, he could more easily walk on water.

Pity, then, that the examining board had gone to town in recent years on exposing Mr. Redfearn's weak spot. Compositional theory was down to thirty-five percent, leaving a long way to free-fall. They wanted original music on the page, not clever ramblings on finding formulas to produce it. And it was, at least to the compositionally-challenged Marcus Redfearn, a shame. He would comfort himself with the knowledge that he didn't have to be able to do it, only to teach it; that his job was to provide five hundred years of background and countless examples, and not to actually produce the notes on the page. Still, it made him feel like a fake.

There were fourteen students in his class this year, and not one of them sat and froze at the keyboard the way he did when confronted with the task of pulling a melody out of the ether. Some of the students this year were good, remarkably so, in his opinion. And he envied them; couldn't understand why he could not do what they could do.

Of course, he had found ways to overcome the problem that meant that the class could actually proceed and not have to sit watching him twiddling his thumbs for three hours, bemoaning his inadequacies. Teaching anything, after all, was largely about resource and wit, and in both respects his reservoir was never less than full.

One of his favourite tricks to get the class started on a Friday morning had been borrowed from what transpired during the legendary meeting between Mozart and Beethoven.

Beethoven, wanting to impress the master, had asked Mozart for an idea on which to extemporise. And Mozart, so legend has it, trotted over to the piano and bashed out a theme, leaving the younger man to make of it what he could. Beethoven then set the room on fire with his dazzling extemporisation, impressing even the great Austrian.

And so Marcus Redfearn would begin the class by playing a short theme taken from some obscure manuscript buried deep in the archives of musical history, asking his students in turn to improvise on the theme for a couple of minutes. The class would then discuss the improvisations, Redfearn coming into his own with analysis and suggestions. Not once did he perform the exercise himself. He simply could not. He'd even seen a hypnotist about it, though it hadn't done any good. Fifty quid down the drain.

Money that could have been put to better use down at the Feathers.

At times it infuriated him and at other times it saddened him. It was a form of impotence. In his heart he longed to create music, to express himself through his passion, and he admired beyond words those who had the gift. He played the class a short theme transcribed from an aria he had dug out from one of Handel's lesser-known operas. He played twice through the four-bar theme, before inviting the first student to take it up.

The first student, as always, was Garcia. She wasn't the most inventive student in the class, though generally she maintained a solid sense of structure, rarely losing sight of the stated musical idea. Listening to her tackling the theme - a little awkwardly, a little stiffly, perhaps - made Redfearn wish that he could be half as good.

When she had finished playing, hitting the home run with her usual flourish, suggesting greater things than had indeed been delivered, Redfearn opened up a discussion on the performance, inviting the other students to comment. When the best had been extracted from the discussion, he restated the theme on the piano and invited the next student up onto the platform to take their turn. This process usually exhausted the first half of the three hours, and most of the students seemed to enjoy the challenge, as well as the opportunity to discuss each other's contributions in a constructive way. The last student, that particular Friday morning, was Penny Henderson.

Penny was an unpredictable student. Her work could be excellent, it could be poor, and Marcus Redfearn was still a long way from weighing her up. She seemed to him to be a complex young woman, who maintained an air of mystery that intrigued him. He knew of the tragedy that had hit her family. What had happened to Penny's sister was awful beyond imagining, and would naturally impact on anybody close to her. Whenever Penny appeared distracted and inattentive, he would remind himself that she must have a lot to deal with. Even sitting at the keyboard in front of class, she could sometimes give the impression that she wasn't in the room at all. Once or twice, performing the Friday morning exercise, she had strayed into another piece of music altogether. On one occasion she had somehow arrived at the national anthem, much to the amusement of the rest of the class. It hadn't appeared to have been an intended piece of cleverness on her part, for when the laughter had finally broken through her distraction, she'd stopped playing, returning to her desk bearing a look of humiliation.

Redfearn watched carefully as Penny seated herself at the keyboard. She was wearing her customary jeans, and a plain, well-worn polo-neck sweater. The colour of the top clashed with her straw hair, but she still managed to look more stylish than just about any other student on campus. There was something very different about this girl, he thought.

He observed her hesitation at the keyboard, though even in this he noticed a poise and tranquillity. In her presence he always had the feeling that something remarkable was about to happen. Still, she hesitated, and Redfearn felt a familiar knot of nerves threading from his throat to his stomach. It seemed to tie in with his own inadequacy. Invariably, when watching an anxious student prepare to extemporise, he would hold inside the same impossibly long breath that accompanied him long ago, watching a circus acrobat attempt the high-wire, apparently without a safety net.

At last the tension broke, and Penny Henderson began to play, at first repeating the theme as stated, repeating it flawlessly before moving on from the theme, building in small blocks, returning to the theme, creating another block, and back to the theme, and so on. 'Theme and Variations', is what the text-book would have called it, and she was handling the form beautifully. After the fourth 'variation', she restated the theme and finished there. It was easily the best performance of the morning, and way above her previous efforts.

The class was generally appreciative, except for Garcia. "I think it was a cop out."

Redfearn frowned. "Perhaps, Garcia, you could expand a little on that."

"I think it was just a repetition of the theme," she said, sharply. "There was too little improvised material."

He asked Penny if she wished to answer the charge, and she declined. She was never the most talkative of pupils, and resolutely avoided discussing her own musical contributions. The downside of a sensitive nature, thought Redfearn.

Garcia pulled him out of his thoughts. "Don't *you* think it was too heavily reliant on the given theme, Mr. Redfearn?"

The teacher looked at Penny for a moment, and then turned to Garcia. "I think that we have been given a valuable lesson today. But I'm keen that we draw out, between us, what exactly that lesson might be." He scanned around the class. "Most of you have been quite appreciative of Penny's performance this morning, but I'm not sure that we have ascertained exactly what made it so special."

Garcia again interjected. "It's easier if you just stick to the theme. Anybody could have done that."

"Could they?" he asked, beaming at Garcia. "I think you're close to what I'm getting at." Again he wrested the initiative away from the indignant Garcia, scanning around the other faces in the classroom. Penny, he noted, had long lost interest in the discussion. He walked to the whiteboard behind the piano and wrote:

LESS IS MORE.

Then he turned again to the class. "Do you see?"

Garcia again chirped up, determined to win the day. "How can it be? Anybody could have done what -"

"But they didn't! And that's the point. Penny kept it simple and she used the material at her disposal to the full. She grasped the theme and showed what could be done with it. She gave tantalising glimpses, rather than beating the thing into the ground. Penny engaged the listener, calling on the listener's imagination. Economy is a great thing in artistic expression. Excess always produces second and third-rate work. While Penny was playing there was a sense of expectation in this room, a tension."

Redfearn stopped, suddenly aware that the atmosphere in the classroom had changed, becoming quiet and still. The students appeared to be looking at him as though they had never seen him before. He coughed, nervously, and suggested that it was time to take a break. There was a lot to get through this morning. Much to be done before the beer could start flowing again.

He watched the students troop out of the classroom. It occurred to him that he wasn't teaching fourteen students at all. Thirteen plus one added up to fourteen, but it still wasn't the same thing.

That evening, Marcus Redfearn sat alone in the bar of the Coachmakers. He was mildly drunk, though lacking any of the exuberance that usually accompanied him on a Friday night.

It was a strange start to a weekend, almost unique in his experience. Instead of relishing the opportunity of forty-eight hours of excess, he found himself already - and unaccountably - looking forward to Monday morning.

He returned home earlier than usual that evening. No curry, no late bars, just straight back to the small house close to the college, where he lived alone.

On the chair in the living room was his briefcase, hastily dropped off on his way out to the pub. From it he extracted the manuscript containing the theme by Handel that he had used in class that morning, taking it over to the piano that took pride of place in the centre of the room. He sat down and played the theme through a couple of times, and then tried to develop it. But almost as soon as he tried to create something, his fingers crawled to a halt, the impenetrable bricks piling up into a huge stone wall in his mind. He gave it up, making himself a coffee and switching on the television; but quickly the restlessness returned. He went back to the piano and played over the Handel theme again. Then he had an idea.

He tried to recapture what Penny Henderson had done in class. If he lacked the ability to extemporise, he compensated with an extraordinary gift for memorising music, even after a single listen.

He got the first variation almost perfect the first time, and it didn't take him long to knock the other three into shape. In a matter of a few minutes he had the whole thing down, and played it over with the energy of a teenager learning a rock and roll song for the first time. Before he realised what he was doing, he was writing it out. He didn't need to; he would never forget it. Still, he wrote it down, taking almost an hour to do so, checking and double-checking that he had every note in its rightful place.

When he'd finished he went up to bed, taking the completed notation with him. He got undressed and squeezed himself into the cold single bed, naked and alone. It was no longer an early night, yet he felt as sober as a Monday morning in term-time.

He went over the notation a dozen times as he lay propped against the coverless pillow, quietly humming the music as he read it. It got better every time, revealing new qualities. It was quite extraordinary.

When at last he switched off the light and nuzzled into the darkness, the music was still flowing like a fantastic river through his mind. With an effort of will, he tried to turn his attention to how he might spend the rest of his weekend. But as his thoughts at last faded into the twilight world of sleep, he felt the pull of the coming week gathering forces around him, taking him back to the classroom.

To the one who stood outside the thirteen.

CHAPTER EIGHT

Phil Waters and Olive Roxburgh spent the first part of Saturday morning heartily engaged in their favourite activity. Olive, driven by thirst and the urgent need to visit the bathroom, got up first.

She was walking back up the stairs, carrying two mugs of tea and wondering if it would take a military operation – or perhaps even a surgical one – to get that lazy bag of bones out of his pit and making *her* a drink for a change. Stopping halfway up the staircase, startled on hearing the music strike up, and then rolling her eyes as she recognised the tune, she muttered, "Will you change the tune, Phil!"

It was like him to get obsessive. He was like a kid with a new toy. And it wasn't as though this was some newly discovered masterpiece, rather some hopeful student who had chanced her arm to win a lousy competition. What was the big deal? It didn't sound a big deal, no matter how many times he played the thing over.

"Here's your drink," she shouted, before continuing along the landing to the bedroom. Waters finished playing the piece through on the piano, and immediately started it again. "Phil! I've made you a drink!" Ignorant cretin, she thought. *Make your own drinks next time.*

The piece finished. Olive waited. It promptly started up again.

She finished her drink, and then picked up his. Her mouth was on fire, but she drained the second mug all the same. "If he plays it through again," she snarled, "I'm going to go in there and break his fingers."

She listened as the piece came to its end. She could feel the tension building in the seconds after he stopped playing, amazed to find that she was holding her breath. He was moving around in the adjacent room, coming through to the bedroom. "I've drunk your tea," she announced, proudly.

"That's good of you, Ol. Cheers."

"What is it with that lousy tune?"

"Good question," he said. "Not keen, then?"

"I mean, it doesn't go anywhere, does it?"

"You don't think so?"

"Do you? It's like some student suicide note set to music. I tell you, Phil, it's doing my head in. Why don't you lighten up and play me some funeral music instead?"

He sniggered. "That's very funny, Ol. Very witty."

"Glad you think so." She held up a fist. "Care to hear the punch line?"

He kissed her. "I love it when you get angry, Ol."

"I can see," she said, looking at the bulge in his shorts.

"It's got something, though."

"What has?"

"It's only a sketch of an idea, not even the finished thing. Matter of fact, she suggested a *sextet* in her letter. So who knows where it will go."

Olive caught him a good one across the side of his head, and Waters was on her.

That afternoon, Olive went shopping. Phil Waters, meanwhile, sent out information to his respondents, and enclosed a brief note to Penny Henderson, suggesting that the idea she had sent had some potential and that he would be eager to see more material as soon as she was able. He threw in a couple of technical comments, to show that her money would not be wasted if she wished to have her work more thoroughly critiqued, and then he signed off. The letter was deposited into the post-box before the ink was dry.

He took the rest of the day off, calling in at a couple of pubs, thinking that he might run across Marcus Redfearn. He wanted to see how his newly appointed Head of

Promotions was getting along. But Redfearn clearly had business elsewhere or else was laid up with the flu. Teachers were always getting sick; it wasn't healthy spending all your life in a classroom. It would have to be the mother of all flu germs, though, to keep old Marcus from his weekend traditions.

Early that evening, when Olive had returned from her shopping trip with what looked to be enough shoes to kit out a football team – not, observed Waters, that many goals would likely be scored with the things she put on her feet – Waters suggested they go out for a few and "round it off with the Holy Trinity."

"Don't know about the movie part, Phil, but I'm game for the curry and sex."

They stayed local, and Waters was surprised to find that Marcus Redfearn was still nowhere to be seen. He hadn't been in any of the locals all day, apparently. "Perhaps he's in love," suggested Olive, tucking into a large brandy and coke in the last pub before the curry house.

"Marcus?"

"When I say 'love' … he's got a dick, hasn't he?"

"Don't think he's that interested in women."

"Maybe it's not a woman," said Olive, with a swirl of mystery in her voice.

"What do you mean by that?"

Olive, watching the dawning outrage spread across Waters' face, started laughing. And the more she laughed the more indignant he became, each feeding off the other until, barely able to look at his purpling rage a second longer, she put down her drink for fear of emptying it all over the leopard-skin dress that she'd bought to go with her leopard-skin shoes. "Oh, Phil, you're such an arsehole sometimes." Then she leaned forward and put on the cheap air of intrigue again. "Maybe he does like women, but has, you know, some kinky habits that he doesn't like to talk about, especially to an old prude like you."

"Prude?"

"Well, suppose he likes to keep them tied up in his basement? It's always the ones you least suspect."

"Cut the crap, Ol."

"You know something, Phil? You don't have the first clue about this world you're living in."

"What's that meant to mean?"

"Look at you - you don't know what to believe."

"I only believe what you tell me to believe, Ol."

She held a straight look. "Then believe this: I reckon your mate is the dark horse of Valemore. I reckon Redfearn is doing it as we speak. I bet he's got one the size of -"

"I said knock it off, Ol, will you."

Her jaw was trembling. "College classes are full of horny teenage girls, Phil. You want to think seriously about a career change." Her voice trailed off into another explosion of laughter.

Waters got up and stormed to the gents. Getting on top of the laughter, Olive shouted after him, "Perhaps he's staying behind – showing them how to play the flute."

He could still hear her laughter as he stood at the urinal. He didn't really need to pee, but he made the effort and took his time about it. As he stood there, pleasantly drunk, unpleasantly irritated, it occurred, as he looked down, that he held the key to his own doom literally in his hand. I don't much like her, he thought. Sex, that's all it is. But she's good, the best, top division. She turns me on, and the more I get the more I want. She's got the best body I've ever seen and the filthiest mouth – not to mention the most appalling taste in clothes. He smiled. And the most shallow appreciation of music.

He belched a couple of times and then farted.

She has the capacity to make my life hell, but she leaves my dick up in heaven. A wise man, not led by what's in his trousers, would steer well clear of the Olive Roxburghs of this world. But have I the strength?

Addressing his genitalia directly, he said, "What do you have to say on the matter, any thoughts?" He smirked, then placed the silent member safely back into his trousers. "Not a great conversationalist, are you? Don't know why I bother talking to you."

Ignoring the look from the beefcake now standing next to him at the urinal, Waters walked back into the lounge bar. He watched Olive for a moment, sitting there, still bouncing in her chair with the last dregs of laughter, and it occurred to him what a wise old owl Detective Inspector Nigel Roxburgh really was. To rise above the need for a woman like her, to escape. The rare gift amongst men: to gaze on the most divine body and say: *I can do without it.*

Phil Waters had a severe hard on most of the way through his Chicken Tikka Madras. Olive was well practised eating with one hand, after all. It was times like this that he almost believed he could love her; times like this when he would gladly give all that he had that she might stay with him forever.

Times like this that he thought Inspector Nigel Roxburgh the biggest fool in Christendom for not still having this to look forward to when he came home at night.

Old Roxburgh would doubtless be out now, pounding the midnight streets, looking for the pervert who was slicing off the privates of the business world. With a godforsaken job like that to do, what fool would shun the promise of a woman like Olive to comfort you and distract you when you came home tired and weary and sick to the gills hunting psychos and scumbags.

Sextet

They took a last drink and Olive gave a last and promising tweak to what stirred inside Waters' opened flies. Then it was away from the Balti Palace and out into the freezing night with the best of the weekend still waiting.

Olive was truly inspired that night, as though she had read the private thoughts of Phil Waters and wished to show old man Roxburgh, through the telepathic medium that she imagined connected all males, just what he was missing.

On the second circuit of their Saturday night marathon, she gave a flesh-made prayer to Marcus Redfearn, demonstrating with zest how to play not simply the flute, but virtually every instrument in the orchestra, capping this display of virtuosity with an extraordinary act of ventriloquy. And whilst in the act of climactic fellatio, she sang the tune that Phil had spent the morning playing; sang it even as he climaxed, too weak and helpless to reprimand her in any way.

As he lay there in the aftermath, his mind gloriously emptied of all earthly considerations, something occurred. He couldn't imagine why it hadn't occurred before. The postmark on the letter from the woman who had composed the 'sextet' piece had been local. And there was something distinctly youthful, student-like, about both the letter and the music – even Olive had picked up on that. So ... could it be? It was possible, surely. What if ...?

He smiled as he lay in the darkness, coiled next to the temporarily satisfied sex-goddess.

What if she attended the college? A student of Redfearn?

Lying there, prostrate, his hand slid from Olive's breast. The thought filled him with amazement. The running of the universe might not, after all, bear every sign of dereliction of duty. Coincidence and fate was everywhere; it merely took some event to make you wake up and notice the patterns.

A grin unfolded, and the next thing Olive was nudging him out of the delicious borderlands of sleep, wanting to know what was so amusing all of a sudden. Was premature ejaculation something that a man should ever have the face to laugh about?

The next morning, in the hour before the sacred tradition of Sunday lunch out, Waters tried to ring Marcus Redfearn. Three times he tried, because three certainly seemed to be his lucky number these days.

"Like I say," said Olive watching as he placed the phone down for the last time, "the man's found himself a tasty morsel."

Waters glared at her before abruptly turning away.

"What was that all about?" she said, scratching the back of her head. "Men!"

Olive bought lunch and Phil Waters was temporarily reminded that it wasn't solely the sex that made her such compelling company. When she was buying they ate that much better and swilled the finer wines that much longer. The social work probably just about paid for her shoes, and granted her license to have a well-developed public conscience; but the better things in life, he had no doubt, were still provided for off the estate of the now eminent Nigel ("you may call me Detective Inspector") Roxburgh.

They left the Italian restaurant mid-afternoon, and Waters was all for doing a quick tour of the locals. Olive's eye twinkled. "There's a beer or two in the fridge. We could take it upstairs."

My God, those eyes, he thought. They're irresistible. "Perhaps just a quick one in the Coach," he suggested.

She raised her eyebrows at that, and they both smirked. "Okay, let's go and see if your chum is in there boasting about how he's shagging the little arses off his students. And don't frown at me like that, Phil, because it makes you look a bigger pervert than he probably is. Coming?"

Redfearn was not in the Coachmakers and hadn't been in all weekend, which seemed mightily strange as Sunday afternoon was his favoured slot in the Coach. Waters left a message behind the bar for him to ring if he came in later, and was ready to leave and take up Olive's offer of beer in bed, when she changed the game plan.

"You've made me walk all the way here, the least you can do is make it a double."

"True," he said. "We have walked about two hundred yards, but what the hell. Large brandy with coke and ice," he said to the barman. "Pint of Stella, while you're at it."

He turned to Olive and smiled. She kept a straight face. "Then you can book a taxi, Phil, because these heels are not for walking."

The barman put the drinks on the counter. "The price women pay for fashion," he said. "The wife would rather cripple herself than put on a pair of trainers."

"Sensible woman," said Olive. "People who wear trainers outside a sports hall ought to be beaten to death in the market square."

With that she took a seat in the corner, the two men watching her go. "Don't worry about her," said Waters. "She's a social worker. They're not very tolerant."

"So I believe," said the barman. "Nasty lot, if you ask me. I mean, take my son, for instance. Four kids and every one of them taken into care. I mean, I know he couldn't exactly take them into the nick with him, and the mother was nothing but a smack head, but still you'd have thought they could have sorted something out. Stress of it sent him right off his nut. Social workers – they were the undoing of him, I tell you."

"Do us a favour, mate, and sort us out a taxi. Twenty-minutes?"

The barman nodded. "No probs," he said, glancing over towards the corner. "I can see you've got your hands full."

When Waters handed Olive her drink, she asked him, "Should my ears have been burning?"

"Just the usual banter about my hands being full."

She pushed out her chest provocatively. "I'll show him a handful."

"Impressive," said Waters, licking his lips. "But I think he was referring to your occupation."

"How did that come up?"

"He was telling me about his grandkids going into care when his son went into the nick."

"Where was the mother?"

"Dead," said Waters.

"What happened?"

"The lad cut her head off and left it on the church steeple."

"Phil!"

"The last thing you need after that is some social worker taking your kids off you."

She shook her head. "You talk some bollocks."

He lifted his pint. "To bollocks," he said.

They spent the next half an hour arguing the toss over the merits of various singer songwriters, Olive extolling numerous virtues and Waters doing his best to sound like a ninety year old piano teacher who thought Elvis to be the apotheosis of the Marxist revolution. They were looking at their watches, when the barman gestured over to them. "Looks like our taxi," said Waters.

The barman was coming over, and shaking his head.

"What's rattled his cage?" said Olive.

"Probably just forgot to make the call. Or maybe he wants you to put in a word for his son."

"I think you'd do better walking," said the barman. "Police have blocked off the roads."

"Since when?" asked Olive.

"Since now."

Waters got up and walked to the door. Outside it was already turning dusk, and what was left of the sky suggested that something heavy was about to fall. There was no traffic, nothing moving at all. He could make out flashing lights; the sound of sirens coming from every direction. Olive came up behind him and placed a hand across his shoulders. "See anything?"

"Not much. What do you reckon?"

"I reckon it's your round. Like I said, I'm not walking another yard in these shoes."

"Not even for a shag?"

"Not even for that."

"You're just a nosy parker, aren't you," he said. "You think the police are going to come here and then you can start interrogating them."

She winked at him. "Don't worry," she said. "We'll make up for lost time. Champagne, though. Abstinence makes the heart grow fonder, didn't you know that?"

"Do you mean what I think ..?"

"What *do* you think? And while you're working it out, Einstein, I'll stick with the large brandy. Now get yourself up to that bar and get some drinks in."

And so that's what he did. And ten minutes later, when the first unsubstantiated rumours started to trickle into the lounge bar, he did exactly the same thing again.

CHAPTER NINE

Monday morning, Penny Henderson eagerly tore open the letter waiting for her on the mat. It wasn't so much the content as the timing that impressed her. This Waters guy was saying some generous things about her music, and he made one or two suggestions that might prove worth thinking about - but his timing, wow!

It had been a full weekend. The whole family had spent Saturday afternoon at the unit, and everybody agreed that Susan seemed a little more responsive than usual. It was in her eyes. They were brighter, more alert. And she appeared a shade more animated, too. *Like she was slowly coming back to life.*

Even Mrs. Henderson who, when she put her mind to it - as she frequently did these days - could be the world's greatest pessimist, commented on the difference. There was an upbeat mood running through the Henderson family, with genuine smiles replacing the painted ones that, Penny reflected, were doubtless as transparent to Susan as they were to each other.

She stayed a little while after her parents had left. Mum had started her usual, "It isn't safe out there alone," but Dad had countered with enough good-natured ridicule to ensure a points decision in Penny's favour. No, of course she wouldn't be late. Two sisters sharing some girlie time together - it was the best medicine of all and Mrs. Henderson knew it.

Once their parents had left Eaglesfield Penny stayed less than fifteen minutes. She told Susan that the second part of her project had been completed, and that she was hoping to bring it to the halfway stage before the weekend was over. She took her sister's hand. "After all, what good's a Christmas present on Boxing Day?"

She told Susan about her change of plans. "What I had in mind was too ambitious. I could never get it done in time. I orchestrate like a leper takes a bath. I'm going to speed things up. It isn't fair on you to drag this out."

Penny smiled. "Do you remember that time you said it would take a *Song Without Words* to get me over Chicken Pox? You had it written in a couple of hours. Mendelssohn would have been proud, and still you said sorry for taking so long. And it worked, it really did. But how did I repay you – by giving *you* Chicken Pox! You didn't complain, though – you just told me another *Song* would do the trick. But my *Song* wasn't as good as yours, and it took you forever to get better. You were always the writer, Susan, but I'm doing my best. I'm working hard and I'll make things work out this time, I promise."

She squeezed Susan's hand. "So what do you think about this: a sextet for the piano. Six pieces thematically linked. The first's done already, it just needs tweaking. And I have my material for the second. I'll have that done by the start of the week, the whole thing by Christmas - how about that?"

Penny surveyed the blankness in her sister's eyes. "I'm not going to stop until it's finished, Susan. I won't let you down, I mean it."

She felt it. Subtle pressure at first, as Susan's grip tightened. Penny pulled her hand away, panicking; feeling the force of her sister's stare as it settled upon her.

She took the bus, but not to Eaves End. Coming this way into Little Valemore took her along the park route that ran behind the college, and up towards the single, shop-lined thoroughfare that the locals called High Street. As the bus passed the park gates she wondered where exactly Mr. Redfearn lived. Quite a few of the lecturers at the college lived around this part of Little Valemore, and as he didn't appear to have a car and was never seen at the bus stop, she could only assume that his journey into work was a short one.

She thought about Waters, too. His address wasn't far away; the other side of High Street. Penny wondered what the creep looked like, and what kind of place he lived in.

It was getting on for seven when she entered High Street. She wasn't known in the shops around there, and most of them were closed at that time on a Saturday evening. The off-licence was open one side of the street, and a late-shop further down on the opposite side. It occurred that she might run into Mr. Redfearn down there, though he'd more likely be in one of the pubs getting stewed. It seemed a shame that a nice guy like him should feel the need to drink away his leisure time like he did. A couple of students living close to the park had seen him out a few times, and by all accounts he was always getting well-oiled, and usually alone. That made it even sadder, she thought. In a world full of weirdos it was always the decent people who had trouble finding happiness.

Wasn't that why magic existed in the world? A remedy for those who believed; an opportunity for justice and meaning?

Waters might be knocking around. If only she had a photograph. She imagined a weedy guy with eyes that wouldn't remain still. No, she didn't need a photograph. The type stood out a mile.

Penny went into the off-licence. There was a melody inside her head, a strong one. A man in a raincoat was in front of her, buying cigarettes. From the back he looked perfect; a walking tune, made for her sextet. His hair was lacquered, by the look of it, and his hand was clutching a dark brown attaché case. He smelt strongly of scented soaps and his nails were immaculate. She stood closer to him, hearing the smoothness riding out of his educated voice, her instincts boiling over. How easy it was to find them, everywhere, in every part of every town. Like a plague, an infestation.

What if this was him? *Waters.* Was that likely? Little Valemore was still a sizeable suburb. And anyway, the smell wasn't right. This man, buying cigarettes, turning around to leave, he didn't fit the part. This one had bigger fish to fry, and wouldn't be wasting his time on competitions and postal courses. Postal was old school, and the man standing in front of her was not that. He was less weasel and more shark. He'd made enough for this week, so why not take a drive into town, find an easy pick up?

What about a change of plan? A nice fresh college girl to celebrate your lucrative week?

He looked at her as he left the shop, raising his eyebrows unnecessarily. She held his brief but speculative look, and out of the corner of her eye she saw him turn around and look back. *Bull's eye.* She turned around, smiled; watched him hesitate.

"Can I help you?"

The girl behind the checkout, no older than herself, was addressing her.

"What's that?" said Penny. "Oh, right – sugar free gum?"

Penny left the shop, tucking the pack of gum into the side pocket of her leather jacket, her fingers catching the re-assuring solidity of the blade beneath. She stood in the doorway, looking both ways along the street. No sign of him now. She waited for the sound of a car, stopping outside the shop, the window coming down, and the smooth voice asking if she needed a ride.

The young girl behind the counter was watching her through the glass, and looking nervous about it, too. Why should the girl look nervous? The danger, at least for her, had already passed. So why was she looking at her like that? *What had she seen?*

Penny smiled at the girl and quickly moved on. The man was not coming back. And now *she* was loitering around, putting the fear of God into an innocent girl trying to earn a living on a Saturday night.

She walked towards the late-shop, merely to keep moving. She'd blown it. She couldn't have aroused more suspicion if she'd sent out advanced notices. If she acted around here, the girl in the off-licence would remember her, and give a good description to the police. That's how it worked. Fear was good for the memory cells. So that was that, her work over for the evening before it had even started.

She walked into the late-shop without realising what she was doing, and found him there.

What was he looking for that he couldn't get in the off-licence?

He was over at the far aisle, looking through the magazines. There were one or two customers dotted around the store, mainly women buying bread and milk, and one arty guy who had to be a student – *or a music-competition organiser?* – weighing up some cheese, putting it back, picking it up again, moving on to the cooked meats and scratching the back of his head like he was dealing with something insurmountable, something requiring thinking time and possibly advice from the two assistants decked out in green-check uniforms.

The man in the raincoat turned around, catching Penny's eye, and raising his eyebrows again. They sold cigarettes in here - cheaper than in the off-licence? She looked at his hands. No visible nicotine stains. Perhaps he used something to scrub them away, adding to the deceit, the false charm of the clean and wholesome; biding his time; the cat watching the mouse.

He moved towards the till, a magazine in his hand. Penny moved in behind him, watched him place the magazine down on the counter, a car magazine. He was taking out his wallet. Did men like him never have change in the pocket? It always had to be a note taken out of a leather wallet and handed over with an ambiguous twinkle in the eye, every transaction an opportunity to practice, to rehearse the steps. Fine-tune the *act*.

She watched the face of the assistant. A middle-aged woman already lost to the world of the living. Her face came alive in his presence. What was he doing? What kind of smile was he giving her? She was saying, "You haven't got anything smaller?" She was flirting. A minute ago and she had looked ready to audition for a zombie movie. Now - look at her. Twenty years younger at a stroke, wishing somebody like this had come into her life all those years ago. How different things could have been with a man like him giving her the sparkling-eyes treatment. Look at the stupid woman, fumbling in the till, trying to change a fifty pound note.

He was turning around, the remains of a grin on his face. He was shameless. Penny wanted to say: *Look, everybody knows that you've got a pocketful of change nestling up against your hard-on*. She held his look; remembered why she was here, and why she had made this journey.

Because once a little girl had six boyfriends all at the same time.

She returned his sick smile and he looked about to say something. In spite of her will to follow this through, Penny found herself turning her head away, watching for a few moments as the arty guy picked up the cheese again, before placing it back and returning to the cooked meats and starting the dumb charade all over.

"I seem to be causing a queue."

Penny turned back. The man in the raincoat was beaming at her. "I do apologise," he said. "Are you in a hurry?"

"Got it now," said the woman behind the counter, and she started to count out fifty pounds in notes and change, minus the few quid for the magazine. "Sorry about that," she said, more than a little flushed. But the man had no interest in her now. The rehearsals were done with. It was time for the real thing.

He moved to the side of the counter, carefully walleting his change. Penny was surprised he didn't leave the coinage as a tip. She watched intently as he performed the mundane action with all the deliberation of a stage-hypnotist setting up a trick, dimly hearing the assistant asking if she could help, and the man looking up from what he was doing.

"Can I help you," repeated the assistant. Penny looked at her blankly, and could think of nothing to say. She eyed the shelves of sweets and tobacco behind the assistant, looking for something to leap out so that she could utter its name. Nothing did. She felt the panic building. "Are you alright?" asked the assistant.

"Gum," said Penny. "Please."

Then she heard the man laugh. "Nothing so simple these days," he said.

Penny looked at him. She had no idea what he was talking about.

"May I make a suggestion?" he said. "Sugar free. Peppermint. Orbit. You will *not* be disappointed."

"Okay," she said, and saw as though in a dream the assistant take a pack from the shelf and place it on the counter.

"Allow me," said the man, placing a coin on top of the pack. "It was my suggestion, after all."

"No," said Penny. "I couldn't."

She heard footsteps behind her, and turned nervously. The arty-type was holding onto a small block of cheese like it was something he had spent a lifetime seeking. Penny let the assistant take from the coin, watched her giggle with her eyes as she handed the change back to the man in the raincoat. Then he was holding the door for Penny, and she was going through it, out into the night.

She looked back at the assistant, who was already busy taking for the cheese. Somebody else to remember her?

What the hell.

She spent Sunday writing the next two parts of her piano sextet, and making minor adjustments to the first part. Her juvenile fumbling in those two shops had annoyed her, though still proved usable in the end. She wondered if it hadn't, after all, added an extra dimension to her writing: the detail of the humdrum world bringing a heartbeat to the abstract, the sublime. Reflecting her uncertainties; translating them into musical feelings, and kicking off the third part of her *magnum opus* with a delicious tension. Quickly the music had become more focused as she wrestled back control, taking charge of the night.

He had been eager to check that she was okay, even offering to run her home. Reckoned he was some sort of doctor, though that didn't ring true for Penny. She accepted the lift, walked with him to his car; felt a sudden crisis, a lack of confidence. Control had slipped again, and boiled over into the music.

She asked if they might walk awhile, and he said that he understood. He enquired if she was warm enough and she had smiled at him and asked if they could walk a little way down towards the college. There was, she said, a bar down there where she knew some friends who would run her home.

How cool he had played it, making out that if that was what she wanted, fine.

They turned down from High Street and soon approached a small chapel with an encircling graveyard. It was starting to spit with rain and she asked if they might shelter in the doorway of the church before heading to the bar. He kept asking her questions and she told him what she guessed he wanted to hear. That she hadn't been well. That her sister had been involved in an accident and that she was still feeling the stress of it all. He responded by telling her that she would come through it.

As if he knew – as if he knew about Susan.

She asked what he was doing around town, and he surprised her, saying that he had a practice nearby. Coming out with it so boldly had wrong-footed her, and yet it was an easy enough lie. How could she prove otherwise at that hour on a Saturday night? And what would he be doing there at that hour on a Saturday night? Doctors knocked off for the weekends these days, at least that's what Mum reckoned; and she was in the same business, more or less. So what was he doing hanging around buying cigarettes in one shop and car mags in another? When she asked him, he laughed and then apologised. "I don't mean to mock you, it's just – I'm not used to being followed, particularly by young and beautiful women."

This man knew how to lie and he knew how to turn it on.

So she had found again what she was looking for.

"Followed?" she said, feeling inside her jacket. She could tell by his eyes, their increasing industry, and by his general agitation that he was getting ready to make his move. In preparation she took a breath, deep as a grave but giving nothing away. He was indeed a fine, fine liar; an arch deceiver; yet he had not the faintest idea of the company he was keeping. She watched him take out the carton of cigarettes, breaking them open, offering her a smoke like he was offering it to a blindfolded prisoner awaiting the bullet.

Sextet

*

Sunday evening, television on. There was a murder-mystery starting at nine, and they were warming up the set – an old superstition that ran in the family from the days before the transistor had kicked out the valve.

Penny had come downstairs to join them; she had three movements of her sextet written. She would go and see Susan mid-week and give her the news. It didn't matter what the competition creep thought now; the die was cast. Susan was improving, the magic was working. It was all beginning to happen. When this thing was done, what did some lousy recording of it matter anyway? No, she wouldn't send him any more of her work. After all, how could he possibly appreciate the gravity of it?

Mum and Dad were sitting in front of the television already, though it was only quarter to the hour. In a moment they would be up on their feet, racing around like scratching cats, performing the usual fidgets: brewing up, making a last minute sandwich, drawing the curtains and running upstairs to switch on the electric blankets. They were always breathless by the time their intended programme came on, the sense of occasion assured by their dizzy rituals.

They hadn't watched television much of late, apart from the news, of course. Penny couldn't imagine what they could want with a murder-mystery when they were living in the middle of one. Mum had stopped reading those kinds of books, the forensic thrillers that she had thrived on before Susan was attacked.

Tonight was different. They didn't even acknowledge her as she entered the room. They were sitting in front of the screen as though the main feature had started early. The news was on again and featuring another local murder. A mutilated body found late on Sunday afternoon. The body had probably been there since the previous evening, said the reporter. The churchgoers at communion, earlier in the day, had doubtless walked past it, unaware. The body had been tipped into a gravesite that had been prepared for a burial on Monday. Mrs. Henderson turned to her daughter. "Do you see what I mean, Penny? Are you listening to me?"

"Yes, Mum. I'm listening."

"You were out until gone ten last night. I tell you – I don't like it."

Mrs. Henderson started to cry, and Mr. Henderson comforted her with an arm and a kiss.

"That could have been you in that grave, Penny. Are you listening to me?"

"There, there," said Mr. Henderson. "There, there."

CHAPTER TEN

Marcus Redfearn had taken the late train back to Valemore on Sunday evening, before jumping into one of the taxi cabs parked outside the station. The taxi driver had to manoeuvre a little, due to the police blocks positioned around the town, promising that he'd get him back in time for a drink before closing time.

It hadn't even occurred to him to call for a drink, and it struck him that the taxi driver was an astute guy, knowing his habits so well. Maybe he *would* call for a drink. Catch some of the speculation and gossip that would be flying around the local pubs. He thought of Waters, and wondered which pub he might be in, before concluding that he wasn't in the mood for drinking any more than he was in the mood for the company of Phil Waters. This whole competition business didn't feel right.

He'd woken up on Saturday morning, played over the transcription of Penny Henderson's improvisation another dozen times at least, and decided, on the spur of the moment, to get out of town. Clear his head; gain some perspective, distance ... *distance from what? From a weekend drinking with Phil Waters? From something else - somebody else?*

Boarding a train, he'd visited his mother in Chester. A visit that was, he had to admit, somewhat overdue - and hadn't she reminded him!

Old Mrs. Redfearn lived in a small warden-controlled flat close to the river. He spent Saturday afternoon with her, gazing down at the swans, trying to steer the conversation away from why he hadn't found a nice girl and settled down and was she ever going to become a grandmother. If she hadn't the power these days to make him blush with that line of questioning, she could still make him feel mightily uncomfortable.

His mother's flat was too small for him to stay the night, and so he had checked into a small B&B a few hundred yards down the river. He had ear-marked a couple of pubs for later in the evening, though when the time came he hadn't felt like drinking at all. Two pints had sufficed, which, added to Friday's abstinence, was fast making this the driest weekend on record.

He took his mother out for Sunday lunch, finding a place with a conservatory looking out on the water. Within a few minutes she had resumed questioning, pausing only for the occasional mouthful of roast beef and sips of cold coffee. "You have got somebody, Marcus. You have. I can tell you have." She tapped her nose. "A woman knows these things. We never lose it."

"Oh, Mum, really."

"Don't you 'Oh, mum' me, young man. A woman knows, and a mother especially. There'll be a new hat for my wardrobe this summer - I can feel it in my bladder." The bill arrived. "Aren't you going to tell me her name?"

"Mum, really – there isn't anybody."

She grinned at him, unpeeling his chocolate mint, and crunching it whilst carefully folding up the foil wrapping. "Have it your own way, Marcus. Have it your own way. But mark my words."

"Yes, Mum."

"Yes, Mum indeed."

He hadn't taken the transcription with him on the journey, but as soon as he got back home on Sunday evening he took it out and played it through on his piano a few more times.

He wasn't thinking of *her* - not physically, of course; only her music.

That's what he reminded himself as he lay in bed, looking over the manuscript one last time before he turned out the light. And an hour later he was still lying there, not sleeping, the music turning around and around inside his head; letting it play, trying not to think about her.

He thought of what the taxi driver had said, about the mutilated corpse found in an open grave in the cemetery off High Street. "The whole town's talking about it, mate. Third one, this is. It's no joke. People will stop coming out. I'm starting to wonder if it's safe me being out doing this job."

The driver was an Asian man, not much more than twenty years old, by the look of him. He said a strange thing, or at least it seemed strange to Marcus Redfearn as he lay in bed thinking about it. "There's too much girl-power around these days, mate. It's what they teach them these days in college, and I'm paying tax for it. A guy looks the wrong way at a girl these days he ends up without anything to piss through." The driver laughed when he said it, if a little nervously.

As Marcus Redfearn lay sleepless, suffocating in the darkness, snippets of conversation and fragments of images kept drifting into his mind. The driver's use of the word *college* had struck a peculiar note. He tried to let it go, but he couldn't get Penny Henderson out of his head.

On Monday morning the class started promptly as usual. Arrive on the button and kick straight in - that was the Redfearn way. The students got used to it and generally they were prompt too. It was a matter of setting out your stall early on and keeping to the rules that you had created. But as the clock ticked one seat in class remained vacant, and there was no sign of Penny Henderson. That hadn't happened before.

He was thinking about the police and the mutilated body and all that had come to the quiet town of Valemore over the past few days. Then he thought again of Penny's absence. Maybe she was ill. He could check it out at break, pop over to administration and see whether a call had come in.

He started off the class, the History of Music, with a barrage of dislocated facts about the great Baroque composers; aware of the wildness of his presentation though unable to get a grip. Perhaps it was lack of sleep, because he was certain that he hadn't caught so much as a wink of it the whole night.

The students were turning from one to another, whispering behind the backs of their hands, while others looked awkwardly at their desks; wondering, no doubt, if their teacher hadn't been overdoing it a little with the sauce over the weekend.

Penny Henderson's improvisation was in his head again. He was thinking that he was going to have to set the students some work while he got his act together, when the classroom door opened and in she came. Full of apologies, of course, but he didn't need to hear them. They were of no consequence. All that mattered was that she was here.

His thoughts quickly began to settle down, allowing him to take back the reins and open up, in front of their very eyes, the period of musical history that ran from Henry Purcell to George Frederick Handel. By break time he was leading his students toward Handel's great *Messiah*. They would be back early from break, he had no doubt. His brand of classroom magic was up and working again; the crisis had been brief, already a trivial footnote in a forgotten history.

He smiled at Penny Henderson as the students began to make their way from the classroom, and she returned his smile. She didn't appear to be in any hurry to leave the room.

When the last of the others had left, she approached him at his desk. She was wearing those torn jeans again, the ones she generally wore. The ones she was wearing in the dream – or at least for part of it. Maybe she had a wardrobe full of them, all torn the same.

Better not to think about student wardrobes, he thought. *Better not to look too long or hard at those jeans.*

"Sorry I came in late," she said.

"Don't worry about it, Penny."

"I got busy with this piece of music I'm writing. I got into it and didn't realise the time."

"Like I say, don't worry about it."

"It's this competition. I sent some material off. I wasn't going to."

"Competition?"

"Probably not a very good one," she said. "Probably a bad idea; but I'm excited about this music and I kind of wanted someone else to look at it."

"It never hurts to get feedback," he said, "as long as it's informed and constructive. Do you mind me asking ... which competition?"

She told him. It had crossed his mind already. He felt a flash of anger. "I wouldn't mind looking over anything that you've written," he said, as casually as he could. Her face lit up. "Really?"

"It's my job, more or less. Bring some of your work in. I'd love to take a look." Her smile faded, and a look of shame clouded her pale skin. "Penny," he said. "The class don't have to see it, if that's what you'd prefer." His heart was thumping. He watched the awkward smile stumble around her face. "Just bring some material in and leave it for me. Leave it on my desk. Nobody else need know."

Already the class was trickling back from break, doubtless eager to hear more about Handel's *Messiah*.

Penny left the classroom quickly.

For the rest of the morning Marcus Redfearn thought about little else than the prospect of looking at Penny's music. He thought, too, about Phil Waters and his competition.

It wasn't right, taking money to feed some baloney about immortality, and sending back trite, useless comments, stringing vulnerable students along and getting his own gravy train running. This girl was desperate for genuine, constructive, critical feedback, and at the same time clearly lacking in confidence. Waters was out to exploit that. The whole business was a scam; the man nothing but a phony.

Redfearn's fingers curled into his palms, and before he knew it he was making tight little fists under the desk.

CHAPTER ELEVEN

Penny spent most of the evening sitting in her bedroom, at the small desk at the foot of her bed, going over her compositions and making slight amendments to the versions that she had posted out to Waters earlier in the day. It was good of Mr. Redfearn, offering to look over her work, and to be so discreet about it. Now she was assured two pieces of criticism, and Mr. Redfearn wasn't even going to charge her. Surely that suggested that he was genuinely interested in her music.

Choosing to disregard Waters' clearly-stated, clearly exorbitant charges, she had enclosed only her manuscripts. If he wrote back asking for money, he could go hang. If he didn't bother to write back, then balls to him. He could keep the manuscripts, and when she became famous he could look back at what he'd missed - and use them to wipe his greedy backside on, for all she cared.

There was a knock at her bedroom door. Mr. Henderson walked in.

"Oh, hi, Dad. How's it going?"

He pointed to the end of her bed. "May I?"

She moved the chair closer to the wall, so that her father could perch on the bed. He was looking at the manuscript pages piled up on her desk.

"Anything special?" he asked.

"Take a look."

He picked up the sheets of paper filled with his daughter's hand-written notation. "Looks impressive," he said. "I can practically hear it coming over the radio."

She laughed. "That would be a compliment if the airwaves weren't so full of crap."

"Fair point. All your own work?"

"Afraid so."

"Will you play it for me?"

"You've heard some of it already. It's what was playing the other day."

"Oh, yes," he said, thumbing through the pages like it was a book of mysterious incantations and magical spells. "All this paper for that one little tune?"

"Three tunes, actually. Three out of six. I'm working on something for a competition."

"What's the prize?"

"Immortality."

"Just you - or does that include the family?"

"Dad!"

"Oh, now I see," he said, drily. "*Musical* immortality. And there I was thinking we were all going to live forever." He continued flicking though the pages, as though the secrets contained inside them might reveal themselves without a medium. At last he said, "When it's finished, will you play it for me?"

"Of course I will," she said.

He placed the pages back on her desk, and stood up, kissing her. "That's my good girl." He looked at his watch. "Not too late now. Many great composers died young because they never got to bed at night."

"Is that a fact?"

"Ask your teacher."

"I'm nearly done for tonight, Dad."

He stood up and touched her forehead, brushing the hair back from her face like she was his little girl again. "Goodnight, Penny," he said. "God bless."

"Say goodnight to Mum for me, will you? Is she okay?"

"She's okay."

"Goodnight, Dad."

He closed the door and left her alone. She could faintly hear the television downstairs. Some crime series full of violence and brutality? A young teenage girl getting raped and strangled and Mum getting all misted up, an extra brandy or two and falling asleep on the sofa, Dad staying downstairs with her until she woke up feeling cold, then letting her have her little cry before getting her upstairs to bed?

No, not these days, Penny reflected. Mum didn't do crime thrillers now, preferring to watch dull shit that could still make her cry. A couple of drinks and anything could make her cry. Penny could tell when it was likely to happen; evenings when she was more reflective, less absorbed by the mundanities of the daily round.

She looked again over her most recent composition. It occurred to her that she had never done anything with so little effort. The melodies had come out of nowhere – unless they really were the stolen remnants of stuff she'd heard and then forgotten about. The shape of the music, the structure - it was falling into place so naturally, as though she had glimpsed the architecture in a lost dream.

Not so long ago she used to marvel at the way composers produced work that was both varied and at the same time unified. The great contradiction: finding variation within unity. Yet that was precisely what she was accomplishing now. Penny Henderson, constructing a single musical edifice, and at the same time six independent pieces; the shape not merely suggesting one linear tower, but rather a pyramid structure: three blocks, two blocks, one. Giving it strength; giving it power. And out of that invisible, radiant power, lay the hope that could sustain her, sustain her family, and bring her sister back from the darkness.

It was around midnight when she finished working on her manuscript. Her parents had already gone to bed. It seemed she had got it wrong this time. Barely an hour after she had asked Dad to pass on her goodnights, Mum had appeared at her bedroom door, a little red in the eye, but no more than that.

"I'm turning in, sweetheart," she said. "I'm whacked. Shouldn't you get some sleep yourself? You don't want to overdo it, love." Dad standing behind her in the doorway, saying, "She's turning in now, isn't that right, Penny?" Dad winking, ushering Mum to trim the speech and cut to the kiss. Mum doing that, but lingering, a sob building up and Dad coughing from the doorway, Mum swallowing and saying, "Yes, I'm coming now." Then a final round of goodnights, awkward shuffles, unnecessary nods, embarrassed smiles; the door closing at last, the muffled sounds of the sexless goodnight ritual issuing from the adult chamber, until finally the house fell into its soulless and pitiful silence.

Penny placed the hand-written copies of her work into an A4 envelope and carefully printed the name, Mr. M. REDFEARN, on the front. With the quietness of foot that a soldier might employ on tour in the jungle, she got herself ready for bed. These days she didn't expect to fall asleep.

It went like this: lie in the dark for an hour, trying to control your breathing; trying to remember the old days when the magic was first discovered; when it had worked to break fevers, before developing, progressing, appearing limitless in its applications. The time that Susan brought the dead sparrow into the house, composing its funeral march; putting an end to two solid days of diarrhoea and vomiting. How Penny had cried in gratitude, praising her sister for maintaining faith when her own had deserted her.

Lying in the darkness, desperate to once again retrieve the vital spark of energy and belief; attempting to leave behind the pull of the glory years and move into the present, visualising Susan getting better, coming out of the unit, smiling again, laughing again; Susan playing the piano, Susan writing music - the spark, the energy and the belief returning home where it belonged, and the two of them together, composing together, performing their masterpiece on the stage *together*. Mum and Dad in the audience, overcome with tears, clapping and clapping.

Holding onto the visualisation for as long as possible, though never long enough; the mental effort required to sustain the images - literally mind-blowing. The inevitable mad chattering of the demon's teeth coming to tear down the thin fabrics spun in her own mind to protect her, tearing them down with such mocking ease that it made her want to give up the ghost and let it be over with.

She could not do that. And so instead would place her hands over her ears, to keep the demon out that way; but it would find a different route, come clawing into the no-man's land at the edges of her focus; and she would snap back, biting, kicking and scratching, holding off the enemy within for as long as she could sustain the strength and the courage. But the forces kept coming, hungry, relentless; and the panic would hit, swelling inside her chest, breaking into the cavity, reaching into the pit of her stomach, taking all that could be conquered before marching north, invading the four corners of her brain, finally engulfing her.

She would sit up in the darkness, struggle to get back on top of her breathing; and start the whole thing round again until, exhausted, far into the night, she would find some wretched oasis of rest, waiting for the nightmares to kick in again – but not every night, not even most nights now.

Yet still not knowing when they would come; not knowing if tonight would be the night. How much worse, a thousand times worse, making her crave for those early days when at least she had the certainty of knowing that her nights would always, *always* climax in raw-throated screaming and the sounds of her parents' feet stampeding along the landing in their terrified eagerness to get to her and comfort her.

This limbo; this good-night/bad-night torture, with its cruel glimpses of peace twinkling out at her like daggers of broken glass - tantalising remissions, juicing up her nerves, and making them fresh and succulent for the next descent.

She was asleep before the first round of visualisations had ended. Dead to the world, dreaming of the competition, winning it; Mr. Redfearn applauding wildly and congratulating Mr and Mrs Henderson on producing a daughter of undisputed – no, of *unrivalled* brilliance. Brilliance? *Genius.* But somebody was missing. There was a black hole in the dream through which everything of worth was draining. No Susan in the dream. No Susan on stage and no Susan in the audience. No mention of Susan in the flamboyant and emotional thank you speech. And then suddenly Susan *was* there. Standing up, coming towards her. But the look – "No, Susan, I haven't forgotten."

That look in her eyes. Like in the horror-movie posters that adorned her walls.

"I'm going to heal you, Susan. I'm going to make you forgive me. We were a team and we will be again."

Waking up; startled, shivering, crying. The room pitch dark, draped in the thick heart of the night. Clutching at her pillow; sobbing into it. Her bedroom door opening, the shadow of light cutting into the darkness; her father trying to comfort her, then her mother, taking her turn, crying a little herself – perhaps, who knows, silently rejoicing that tonight wasn't her turn again.

Then the family filtering back into its respective and private oblongs of despair; praying for the morning to come and rescue them from the bottom of this living grave.

CHAPTER TWELVE

Phil Waters opened the A4 envelope with a sense of great expectation. Olive was racing around the house like a mad thing, late for work as usual, and blaming him like it wasn't as much her fault that she needed sex *twice* on a Tuesday morning.

She was out of the shower, mincing around the bathroom and muttering angrily to herself when, like a little boy bursting with news, he took the package through. "Look at this, Ol."

"Phil, can't you see I'm in a hurry?"

He watched her towelling herself; watched her take the silk underwear off the back of the bathroom chair. For a moment he was torn. He loved to watch her dressing; it was second only to watching her undressing. But the contents of the envelope were tugging at him, too.

In the end he struck a compromise: he watched her slip on her pants, his eager member responding like a single eye flapping open at the turning on of a bedroom light, and then he stepped purposefully, manfully, out of the bathroom, flicking through the pages of the manuscript as he walked along the landing to his office.

"Phil?"

He heard her call, but he kept on walking. His first impulse was to sit down at the piano and play through the whole thing. Instead, he forced himself to read the brief accompanying note, hand-written in a youthful scrawl.

Dear Mr. P. Waters,

Thanks for your comments and further details of your competition etc. I've decided to write a piano sextet, although I realise that technically there is no such thing. I want to write six linked pieces for piano, and I want to call it a sextet. Anyway, I have now completed the first three parts and would be glad of your thoughts on the work so far. I can't really send you any money at the moment and I hope this isn't a problem.

Hope to hear back from you soon.
Yours,
Penny Henderson.

"Wouldn't you know it - a freeloader!"

Olive ran along the landing and into the bedroom to finish getting dressed. Despite her race against time, she found a moment to poke her head around the office door. She had been about to say something provocative, but noting the expression on Waters' face, she hesitated. "You look like you've found a fiver and lost a tenner."

"See you later," he said, abruptly taking himself over to the piano.

"Love you too!" she said, banging the door shut behind her. "And you have a nice time at the social work department, Olive," she added, heading down the stairs. She was still mimicking him as she dried her hair and put on her coat, slamming the front door so hard on her way out that she instantly looked back to check that the glass hadn't shattered. Mildly disappointed that it hadn't, she climbed into her VW Beetle, and tore off down the street with the radio turned up *loud*.

Penny Henderson had clearly made some alterations. They were small ones, mainly, and none apparently inspired by any of his suggestions. What was the point of him giving advice if she wasn't going to heed it? And if she didn't want his advice, why send him more of her stuff? Was she so hell-bent on winning the competition? That wasn't the way this was supposed to work. Advice was good; advice was lucrative and fed on itself. People quickly became advice junkies. You could foster them for a lifetime once you developed their taste for it. They would be ruined, of course; totally incapable of ever flying solo, but that was hardly the point.

He played over the first piece half a dozen times, checking it against the original. There was no doubt about it; all the changes were good ones. She had taken a strong idea and tightened it where it needed tightening, expanding it where it lacked development. If he had been a teacher, and this had been a graded exercise, he would have had to give top marks. There was nothing to criticise. Of course, there would be much that he *could* find to say, there always would be. What, after all, was the point of offering a critique service if you couldn't consistently come up with anything critical?

He played the second part through, reaching the end before realising that he had been totally immersed, and unable to think of a single negative. It was beautiful. Haunting, like the first piece. He played it four, five, six times. She had done something here; something extraordinary. She had created two pieces of music, self-contained, technically accomplished and musically … well, really quite astonishing. And at the same time, independent as the pieces were, they fitted against each other like twins in a womb.

Of course, that kind of accomplishment was not uncommon through the pages of musical history. But then neither was the word *genius*. A little nervously, he turned to the third piece. Could the disparate cohesion be sustained, he wondered; because this kind of thing got harder to pull off the longer it went on.

After a half dozen runs through the third part – as stunning as its predecessors on every level – he played through the three parts from beginning to end before leaving the room, scratching his head. The architectural unity had been sustained without needless repetition. The invention was quite remarkable.

He went back into the room and played the three parts over again. Either the insatiable Olive was sapping his critical faculties, sucking it all out through his dick, or else he had discovered a student of such remarkable compositional skill that – that what?

He needed a second opinion. Checking through his address books he made the surprising discovery that he did not have Marcus Redfearn's phone number. Yet he'd phoned him only last week! He cursed Olive; it had to be her fault. One of her tidy-ups, rare but invariably intrusive. The creatures couldn't resist them, not even the social-work types. It was in the blood, in the genes.

He looked at his watch. Marcus would be teaching now. He would pop down to the Feathers and catch him for a lunchtime pint. Phil Waters smiled. The prospect of revealing this discovery to his old drinking pal was a fine one. At the same time he could check how Marcus was getting on with promoting the competition at the college.

What if this Penny Henderson was a student at Valemore?

That thought again.

Someone so amazingly talented - Redfearn would have mentioned her.

Or would he? He could be a dark horse sometimes could Marcus.

He checked the time again, and then sat back down at the piano, playing through the three pieces a couple more times, leaving him with a curious mix of feelings. On the one hand, an almost paternalistic sense of pride, as though a talent he had discovered and nurtured was coming of age; and on the other, the pervading possessiveness of a jealous lover not wanting to share his remarkable treasure. *Pity the silly little bitch doesn't think that all this attention and time deserves payment.*

*

At around noon, he put on his jacket and headed down towards the college. Redfearn's time was twelve-thirty, and Waters fancied a warm-up pint or two to celebrate the official arrival of his first bona-fide postal student - and not just any student.

The Christmas season was building to its usual, though still distant, climax, and people who would never usually be found dead inside a pub were coming in for their seasonal lager-shandy or apple juice or whatever the non-drinkers were drinking this year. He took his pint over to the far corner of the lounge bar. There were a couple of seats going spare, and he laid his jacket across one and opened his newspaper.

There was a lot in about the latest killing, though it didn't seem that the police were any closer to arresting anybody. They seemed confident though that it was one person responsible for the three murders. Forensic science was a wonderful thing.

On the second page of the paper was a small photograph of Detective Inspector Roxburgh. Roxy, as Olive called him. Roxy was re-assuring the public that the police were working twenty-four hours a day to find and apprehend the perpetrator of these evil crimes. He was also asking for the public to be vigilant. Somebody must know this person.

"You don't say," Waters muttered.

There were a few tips from one top-notch professional to the great amateur sleuth that was the public at large: look for changes in behaviour, bloodstains on clothing or skin that could not be accounted for, the usual stuff. Some small detail, easily over-looked, but that might prove vital to the investigation. That might result directly or indirectly in an arrest. Anybody with any information please contact your local police station, or call immediately on this number. And remember, above all, somebody, somewhere *must* know this person.

"We'll remember," said Waters, before taking a gulp out of his pint.

No doubt Olive's office would be buzzing with speculation. She'd been full of it last night in the pub, and they'd ended up staying for an extra three drinks – or was it four? – while the tittle-tattle came blowing in off the street. Even at that stage, when it hadn't even been confirmed that there had been another killing, people were drifting into the pub with accounts of the latest in the series of horrific mutilation killings. A serial killer: here in Valemore? It seemed as likely as an infestation of killer tomatoes, thought Waters.

More people were coming into the Feathers now, and Waters looked at his watch. He found himself ear-wigging on the conversation going on around the table adjacent to him. One of them, a college lecturer, by the look of him – how did he get in here ahead of Redfearn when there was beer on the menu? – was holding court with a few of his students, conducting an informal seminar on the differences between violent crime on the two sides of the Atlantic. He sounded full of it; a lot of sociological distinctions but nothing that added up to anything. Of course, the nodding dogs around him, careful to show that their minds and their politics were in the right place, smiled, grimaced and generally drank to the horseshit that the older man was steaming out.

Phil Waters wanted to ask the man a question. He wanted to turn to the table at which he was holding them spellbound with his wisdom and insight, and wise up all those hollow sycophants by asking Ironside why he wasn't working for the FBI. Why he wasn't down at Roxy's office, showing them how they do it Stateside. He was even faking a mid-Atlantic drawl. Waters caught the man's eye and turned away, looking again at his watch. Marcus was cutting it fine.

When Ironside and his disciples left it seemed that lunchtime had peaked. The only people still in the pub were the long distance types settling in for the afternoon. The seasonal tipplers and the college crowd had thinned out completely, and it seemed a safe bet that Marcus Redfearn would not be coming out to play. Maybe Olive was right about him doing one of the students.

Marcus and Penny Henderson?

Waters laughed at the thought. Then he drank another pint down, a fast one, and headed home.

Olive came in close to six and she was full of it again. It was twenty minutes before he could get a word in, and when he did it wasn't appreciated.

"You're a sarcastic sod, Phil, do you know that?"

"So you keep telling me. But, it seems to me, Ol, that your lot down there might as well get a job at Police HQ, because you don't seem to do anything other than talk about these murders."

She looked at him incredulously. "You're not the least bit interested, are you?"

"It's a bit morbid, Ol."

"Morbid! Three people carved up on your doorstep and you think it's all just a bit morbid?"

"Hardly on the doorstep, Ol."

"The last one was. Are you not comprehending the situation? Three, count them, *three* violent murders in one town, *our* town, in a handful of days, and still you couldn't give a damn. What's the matter with you?"

He started to laugh.

"Come on," she said. "Let's hear it."

"I was just wondering ... that's all."

"Wondering?"

He licked his lips. "If death and mutilation make you feel a bit, you know, horny?"

For a second she looked puzzled. Waters licked his lips again, this time exaggerating the gesture. It earned him a punch on the arm and a slap across his left ear. Still, it worked its usual magic, and in no time Olive was propping herself up against the headboard, and lighting her first post-coital smoke of the evening.

Later, after a small argument about tidying up and throwing out important telephone numbers, Waters told her that he was going to take a walk down to a couple of local pubs in the hope of running into Redfearn and did she want to come with him. But then the phone rang and it was evidently Roxy, and she wasn't intending on cutting him short by the sound of things. Putting on his jacket, he headed out into the night.

Around ten that evening, having got himself more than a little drunk popping back and forth between the usual co-ordinates of three or four pubs, he decided to take a walk down past the college. He had been to Redfearn's house once previously. They'd been tanked up in the pub one evening – or was it a lunchtime? – arguing over who'd written some song or other. They had sung it through the streets like a couple of alley-cats wailing for a fight, making a ten-quid bet on who was right. When they got to Redfearn's house, they had tried the elusive melody on the piano, a few right notes here, a lot of wrong ones there, and laughing so hard they thought that they were going to need an ambulance.

A phone call to the local radio station had sorted out the bet, though. It turned out they were both wrong.

It was starting to rain. Waters was feeling the cold, and he thought about turning around and heading back. It would be easier calling at the college, perhaps tomorrow, and asking admin for a quick word with Redfearn. If he wasn't off sick.

Marcus Redfearn was never off sick. He was a company man, of sorts.

Company men didn't sleep with their clients. Their *teenage* clients.

Crossing the road on the point of looping back towards home, Waters found himself turning right into Ellgate Street, south of the main college complex. "Stone me," he said, in the face of the wet and funnelling wind. "Redfearn Towers!"

CHAPTER THIRTEEN

Tuesday had been a strange day for Penny from the start.

She'd got into college early. *Symphonic Development in the Nineteenth Century*. Not exactly her favourite part of the week. Yet that particular Tuesday morning she must have seemed curiously keen as she walked through the grounds, and through the main glass doors of E block, which housed the music department - or at least the part of it that comprised a classroom with a piano. All the technology, the studio hardware, was up in the annexe, unused and gathering dust. There were rumours that a music technology teacher was to be appointed after Christmas. Not that Penny was interested. Music was about learning an instrument; about writing. Twiddling around with toys was for kids.

Mr. Redfearn seemed to be of a similar opinion. Once or twice he'd made a joke about being the music technology teacher. He was alright was Mr. Redfearn. There was something different about him, refreshing.

One or two of the keener lecturers were milling around, and that guy who taught Humanities was eying her as she ascended the staircase. She'd noticed him doing that before with some of the other girls, and it always made her blood run cold.

Once Penny had reached the top of the staircase the tension began to ease, and she moved along the corridor more freely. There were eight classrooms on this side of the building on Floor One, and a couple were already occupied with eager lecturers making preparations for the day ahead. Penny scuttled past the two occupied classrooms, noticing one of the teachers - a history type, she thought - writing up notes onto a whiteboard. The other - could be a geologist - in the adjacent classroom, was sitting at his desk chewing into a dark and overgrown beard and poring over some marking by the look of it. Both far too engrossed in what they were doing to notice this early arrival to the still silent music department.

The music classroom was situated at the far end of the corridor. Along with the desks and chairs there was a piano and a few other assorted instruments, with a small studio section at the back that had been screened off and soundproofed, and which, until recently, had contained all of the recording and mixing equipment that had now been transferred to the annexe. One of the students had asked why that stuff had been moved and why they couldn't use it. Mr. Redfearn had merely raised his eyebrows in response, before qualifying his gesture with a short speech about the college still striving to define its views on what exactly music consisted of, and whether that elusive definition required a separate room in an annexe and a new member of staff, or whether such expenditure was meant to somehow justify the money that had been spent on a lot of unused and rapidly dating equipment.

Penny had liked the way he put it. There had been an edge to it. And he'd also suggested that the soundproofed area might be used as a practice facility for his students, adding, with that edge again, that the sale of a lot of unused technology might provide a decent second piano for that very purpose. He'd even tried to get the students to write to the principal – or get their parents to write – but lethargy, the curse of Valemore, was holding sway.

At least he cared. At least he was trying.

But for the time being, when there wasn't a class in progress, the classroom piano could be used by the students to practice on. Penny was one of the few who ever did, though rarely.

She entered the classroom and glanced up at the large clock on the wall above the whiteboard. Twenty minutes before the class was due to start. She looked back down the corridor, but there was nobody else coming this far.

Why would there be? Redfearn was never early. In his book, punctuality may have been a virtue, but early was a fool's pastime.

Penny unzipped her leather jacket and took out the folder from underneath her polo-neck sweater. From the folder she extracted an A4 envelope bearing the legend: *For the attention of Mr. M. Redfearn.* She placed the envelope on the empty desk and made for the door.

She skipped down the staircase to where the coffee machine stood unattended. Most of the drinks tasted awful, but it was one of those appalling college rituals, and most of the class took at least one shot a day from its grim, overpriced offerings. She put in her money and waited for the obscene noises to die down, before leaning over to retrieve the scalding plastic cup of sewer-water from the still steaming orifice.

"Taking one's life into one's hands this morning, I see."

She stood up so fast that the boiling liquid washed across her hand, causing her to let go of the plastic cup, which exploded across the floor. Mr. Humanities brushed furiously at the leg of his trousers, cursing under his breath as Penny put a hand up to her mouth and shot back up the staircase. For once she couldn't sense his vulture's eye gluing itself to her.

She made her way for the second time that morning to the first floor of E block, hurrying along the corridor, past the almost empty rooms, one teacher still scratching away on the whiteboard, the other still chewing at his beard and marking books. Walking back into Mr. Redfearn's empty classroom, Penny's eyes settled on the A4 envelope on the desk. She looked at the clock, stuffed the envelope back inside the folder, and waited for the others to arrive.

At the end of the lesson, Penny hung back while the rest of the students made their way to the sewer-water machine to wash down cigarettes and crisps. She eyed Mr. Redfearn, sitting coolly at his desk, not looking at her, not giving anything away. *He knows what I'm doing, though.* She could sense his awareness in the shuffling, uneasy movements that betrayed his glaring self-consciousness. Taking the A4 envelope out of its folder for the second time that morning, she walked out to the front of the otherwise empty classroom.

"The work I promised you, Mr. Redfearn."

With a returning wink, a draw of his desk was opened, and the envelope tossed inside. "Take a break," he said.

And so it was done. Only the two of them knowing what had taken place. But something momentous *had* taken place, she knew that. It was one thing to take this ... *thing* that had been born out of the sacred magic, and to post it off to some faceless entrepreneur. But to hand it, in person, to someone *interested* – well, there were implications.

For Penny Henderson the world had changed.

And for Marcus Redfearn too.

Penny noticed that Mr. Redfearn didn't accomplish his now-you-see-me-now-I'm-off-to-the boozer ritual that lunch time. He remained at his desk, looking through her work. How genuine did it get? No bullshit there, not from Mr. Redfearn. He didn't notice her peering around the door; so consumed was he in checking out her music. For ten minutes she watched him, before heading back along the corridor and down the staircase.

Mr. Humanities was in his doorway at the foot of the stairs. A nice stain on the bottom of his pale grey cords, if less of a twinkle now in his lecherous shit-brown eyes. His vulture's eye was on her, though, and she could feel it as she left the building for some much-needed air, remotely wondering if he wouldn't make an excellent subject for the next part of the healing work.

She left college late in the afternoon, feeling restless and edgy. Perhaps it was that creep with the shit-brown eyes; perhaps it was knowing that Mr. Redfearn was looking at her music, and wondering what he would make of it.

Needing to work off some energy, she took herself down to the canal side, and walked along to Grayling and then on to Eaglesfield. On arriving at the unit, she used the pay-phone to ring her mum, lying that she had taken the bus there.

"I don't know, Mum. I feel like she needs me here, that's all. Of course I'll be careful. No, I'm not getting a taxi back. I'm not made of money, and neither are you. Murders? You're kidding! When? Okay, okay, I know: sarcasm is not becoming of a *young lady*. No, I won't be late, I promise. Look, with so many police around, it's never been safer. Yes, and you know I love you too, both of you. I'll see you later. Bye, Mum."

The doctor was with Susan. The nurse in charge reckoned fifteen minutes, and suggested Penny use the guest kitchen to make a drink while she waited.

The kitchen was a small auxiliary room, with facilities for making tea and coffee. Penny picked up a mug advertising some unpronounceable medication, and spooned in some coffee, pouring on boiling water from the dispenser. It couldn't taste worse than what came out of the sewer-machine at college. She was about to check the fridge for milk when she stopped, placing the mug down carefully onto the metal work surface and slowly turning around.

A man was standing in the doorway. A man with a grin plastered across his face.

"Can I help you?" she asked.

The man didn't answer. Instead he kept grinning.

Penny turned back around, went over to the small fridge and took out a carton of milk, splashing some onto her scalding coffee, not wanting to keep her back turned on the guy in the doorway for a second longer than she needed to.

"Think I might join you," the man said, entering the room, the grin still dominating his bleached and pock-riddled face.

You look like the child-molester in the TV ads. Hope you don't burn yourself.

"Friend or family?" he said.

"What?"

"Are you here visiting a friend or – you don't work here? I'm here visiting my cousin."

"Oh, really," said Penny. "I see."

It was time to take her drink back along the corridor to civilisation. But the man – *was she imagining it?* – was blocking the doorway. "Evelyn," he said. And now he didn't seem to be obstructing her at all. He wanted to say something. Penny felt a faint stirring of curiosity.

"Evelyn is a lot younger than me," he said, taking a cup and making a drink. "I haven't seen her for a long time. I've been away."

"Is that right?"

They still send child molesters to prison, then?

He finished making his drink, and then he gave her his full attention. In the stretched collage of moments that followed, Penny felt the chill trace her spine, leaving her finger-ends tingling as though they had been plunged into ice-water. His eyes - they turned you to stone. But there was something else.

Possibilities.

He looked her up and down and said, "I've been away, but it's okay now. Evelyn must have missed me a very lot. It wasn't my fault, you know."

A *very* lot, thought Penny. That's *some* missing. She backed out of the room, nodding, smiling awkwardly, reassuring this poor? sad? strange? dangerous? *retard* that his Evelyn would be glad to see him.

What girl wouldn't?

Penny walked back to the nursing station. "Shouldn't be long now," said the nurse on the desk. "A few minutes and Susan's all yours. Are you okay?"

"Can I – use your toilet, please?"

"Use the staff one – just along the corridor."

Penny entered the nearest of the two cubicles that stood opposite two sinks. She sat down, surprised to find that she was trembling. Taking a few deep breaths, she felt at the knife inside her jacket.

Then the outer door burst open.

Two female voices:

"You know who *that* is, don't you? It's only *him* - you know ... Sidcup."

"Not -"

"*Yes*, Norman Sidcup."

"You're joking."

"They reckon Evelyn was on holiday in South Devon with him – and he's her cousin."

"No way!"

"Quite what they thought they were doing together in a caravan is beyond me. You can't begin to fathom how that sort live."

"But - I heard this Sidcup went back to the caravan and caught a stranger raping Evelyn."

"And you believe that? You've spent too long on the night shift. It's affecting your faculties. Our Mr. Sidcup ended up in hospital with a fractured skull, and there's no sign of this stranger, whoever he's supposed to be. And anybody who's got an ounce about them reckons that it was him what was raping his cousin but that she managed to whack him one. And out of shame that it had been her own cousin that was doing the raping, she made up the stranger so as it wouldn't be so embarrassing for the family. Makes you think, doesn't it? But he won't get away with it."

"You reckon?"

"You can pay, you know. There's people who'll do anything for money. They'll kill anyone you want for less than a week's overtime - cash of course - you ask my old man."

"And you think -"

"Mark my words: someone will do for our Norman Sidcup. If I had the spare cash I'd organise it myself. My old man knows the contacts, oh yes."

Penny heard the door to the adjacent cubicle open and close.

"Anyway," said the voice from outside the cubicle, "I'd best be off. He's picking me up. Isn't safe getting the buses, not at the moment. Have a good shift."

"A good what?" A loud fart rang out, echoing still as the voice outside shouted back, "You dirty mare. I've been mopping those up all day. See you later."

Susan was tired, and so Penny didn't stay long. She tried to tell her sister about the music, but Susan was lethargic and unresponsive. She appeared to have taken a step backwards, and to Penny it was like a punch in the stomach. She felt an urge to lash out, to ease the helpless anger of watching her sister losing the fight all over again. Where had all that faith and courage and mystical power gone? How was it possible that she had believed in that hokum for even a childhood second? She wasn't witnessing miracles, but merely gazing hopelessly into the pathetic eyes of a broken sister.

It wasn't meant to be this way. *A lesson was all.*

Before leaving, she kissed Susan. Without realising what was happening, she let a teardrop fall, splashing against her sister's cheek.

God, I can't let her see this weakness.

"I'm going to speed things up," said Penny. "I'm going to have you out of here by Christmas. You're going to hear this music – you're going to dance to it by New Year."

The words were sticking in her throat. If Susan was hearing, and understanding, she would recognise the bullshit.

Penny stood out in the cold, watching the tail lights of the missed bus disappear. It was twenty minutes at least before the next one.

She saw the car go past, then turn around and come back. Watched it pull up, the window come down, and the grotesquely pocked face with the fuckwit smile lean out and ask if she needed a lift.

Why not, she thought, the music rising inside her.

Norman Sidcup asked her a lot of questions as he drove her, the way she directed him, down towards the college. Most of the questions were about who she was visiting, and what had happened, and if her sister was getting better. Penny answered everything; she was never more candid; letting it all out for the first time, the pain and the hurt. What it was like to always live in the shadow of your own twin sister. What it was like to be second best and loved second best. What it was like to see your own parents spending all of their thoughts and tears and energy on the other – *on the beloved*.

They were close to the college when she let out a howl of anguish, like a wolf baying at a harvest moon. He asked if she was alright, if she wanted him to pull the car over. Penny didn't answer, continuing to rage, tears coming down like she had saved them all her life; saved them for this night.

Not having the faintest notion of the Pandora's Box that he had opened, Norman Sidcup pulled his car over to the side of the road, and sat helplessly, looking at Penny and not saying anything.

"... There were six of them. It was down by the old theatre, across town. *Six of them.*"

His hand hovered in the air for a second, as though he wanted to comfort her. It hovered and then fell back at his side.

"They know that much because they found six lots of semen inside her body. There were no witnesses. None were ever caught, though three are dead – did you know that?"

She stopped crying, and turned to look at the pathetic little man sitting next to her. *He doesn't know whether to smile or start screaming.* "Why did you give me a lift tonight?" she asked him. "Did you think it was unsafe for a young woman to be out alone with all this killing going on?"

"Evelyn …" he said. He looked like he wanted to say more. Penny waited. There was no hurry. *Take all the time you need, you're not going anywhere.*

It was his turn to start crying.

"If you want to tell me about Evelyn, go ahead," said Penny. "I'm a good listener."

It was like drinking from a stone, and she could feel her rage building again, making time seem precious and mean. This tortured brain-dead, keeping her company on this dark and freezing night. What had he done to Evelyn? What had he done to turn his own cousin into some fucked-up vegetable? Had he got it in him to confess? Was this his moment to unload?

They both needed the act of confession; it was good for the soul, so they said. Mum and Dad went to confession, but what did they have to confess? What had they ever done wrong beyond creating a monster and proclaiming an angel?

Did she really believe that? Some days, yes. It was the truth, after all.

So they should confess, it was right and proper.

Everybody had something to confess; some dirty little secret.

In spite of the cold, Penny started to unzip her jacket. "Did you fuck her?" she asked him. "Evelyn – did you fuck her?"

Norman Sidcup blinked, and a nervous grin curled his lips as he urgently shook his head. "She's my cousin," he said.

"I know who she is and I know what you are. *Did you fuck her?*"

Penny's jacket was open, and she studied his eyes as they focused on her chest with curious bemusement.

She looked down to see the strange shape beneath her sweater and, laughing, removed the folder that had only that morning housed her envelope full of music, and which now contained a mere side of notes taken from the day's classes. She laid the folder on her lap.

"If you want to see what else I keep up there, maybe you'd better drive around to the park side. If you know what I mean."

He started up the engine, and drove the car past the main college entrance. It wasn't seven yet, and most of the evening classes hadn't started. Quiet time in the park; the humping in the bushes usually kicked in later. The cold winter nights didn't seem to dent enthusiasms, and darkness clearly offered its own comforts and consolations.

He cut the engine at the far side of the park, as Penny had instructed him to do. The gates weren't locked. The council couldn't afford such luxuries as a park-keeper, not even a set of padlocks. She said that a walk would do them both good, and he seemed happy enough to oblige. She asked if she might leave her folder in his car, and he said that was fine. It didn't occur to her that he was going to lock the wretched thing. Funny how insignificant car-crime seemed in the face of more *pressing* matters.

She led him into the park.

The park stretched around the back of the college, offering a labyrinth of tree-lined paths. It was a place of choices, lots of choices. There were paths leading down to a small lake, paths leading outwards to the large playing fields up at the top. Penny and her new companion walked first around the near-side perimeter, where the perennial bushes infamously gave cover to the nocturnal love-makings of generations of students, and not only students. She asked him a thousand questions, impatient to hear the real story of what had happened to Evelyn. It all seemed locked inside Norman Sidcup.

Needing to come out.

They began to zig-zag down towards the lake. It was getting colder by the minute, though dry at least. Penny took his hand and said, "What must you think of me? Do you think I'm asking for trouble? Am I not breaking all the rules of how a young and vulnerable girl should behave if she doesn't want to end up on a cold slab?"

She stopped walking, and looked at him. Closer to the lake it seemed a little brighter, a little less bleak; the college lights a quarter of a mile away reflecting back off the water, illuminating the solitude.

When he didn't answer, she asked him, "Have you seen my Susan?"

He shook his head.

"She's the beautiful black-haired girl who doesn't talk. You should have known her before all of this. She was quite a person to know."

"I ..." he began. "I – I'm sorry."

"Sorry? Yes, I'm sorry, too. My mum's sorry. My dad's sorry. A lot of people on the unit are sorry. A lot of people I pass on the street are sorry. But everybody seems to get a little less sorry as time goes by. Funny that, isn't it? But not Susan ... and not me either. I'm as sorry as I ever was - and getting sorrier."

"I'm sorry," he repeated.

"So you say. So what about Evelyn? Happen recently, did it?"

"Hospital," he said. "She was in hospital more than a year. Moved her to the home, and then to there. It's nice there. It helps there. I haven't been able to visit not until now."

"You mean they wouldn't let you out?"

"I wasn't well."

"Of course you weren't. But you're better now, aren't you?"

"I'm getting better. These things take time."

"They do. And nobody knows that better than me. But there's something that I don't understand. I'm wondering what you were thinking, bringing me here to this park, all alone. What do you want, Norman?"

"I - I'll take you home ... if you're ready."

"Simple as that?"

"I'm ... getting cold now."

"Are you lonely?"

There was muffled, or else distant, laughter. Penny turned to listen. "Sounds like the evening's getting underway over there."

She was going to have to hurry things along before they both died of hypothermia. "You want company - female company? You want to take me into the bushes and have your way with me?" He was shaking his head. "You know what we were talking about, back in your car? You knew what you were getting into. You don't have to play little boy lost for me. I've become a woman of the world and I know what you need from me. Same thing you needed from Evelyn, isn't that right?"

"No, I don't, I don't ..."

"It'll cost you, though."

"But I haven't got -"

"I don't want your money. What kind of girl do you think I am? I want to know what happened to Evelyn. I want to help you put that right. I want to help you, don't you see? And help Evelyn. And help Susan, too. There are so many things we can accomplish tonight, and we start by unburdening ourselves."

He took a step backwards. "I don't know what you're -"

"Talking about?" She moved toward him. "Six into one won't go, I've learnt that much." He was still backing off when laughter, louder this time, rang out from behind them.

"I think I want to go home now."

"You don't want to fuck me, is that what you're saying? Am I so hideous? Or is it the truth about your cousin that you can't face?"

He turned, trying to walk away.

Penny followed. "Lost your bottle, eh? You come to the park with some young girl that you don't know - what were you thinking of? Were you thinking what it was like with Evelyn? I was thinking what it must have been like for Susan."

She moved on him.

Norman Sidcup turned back, raising his arms, tripping backwards, falling hard to the ground. Penny stood over him, taking the knife out of her jacket, holding it to his face. "Come out in this freezing night for some air, did we? An innocent little stroll? A cozy little chat? *What did you do to Evelyn?*"

The tune was raging like a symphony in her head. It had taken its time, but it was here now and more haunting than the others; and more troubled. It was going to be something when it was finished.

"Take your clothes off," she said.

He was cowering and at the same time holding his arm, which had taken the weight of the fall.

"Your clothes, I said. Take them off."

She inserted the blade into his nose and eased it against the flesh of his nostril. He began undressing, wincing from the pain in his arm and the sharp feeling of the blade in his face. Penny eased back and watched as he took off the rest of his clothes. Then she knelt on his chest, the blooded knife pressed once again into the softness inside his nostril. She asked the same questions: what had he done to Evelyn? What did he know about Susan?

His arm and his nose hurting so much that he wanted to scream. "What have I done?" he said.

"That's what we're here to find out."

When the knife punctured his lower abdomen, a hoot of laughter exploded simultaneously behind them. It had to be coincidence, but it didn't seem so. It seemed that the world that had taken the best of Evelyn and left little more than a carcass to live out its remaining days - that same callous, incomprehensibly cruel world was allowing another of its monsters to perform the unimaginable, and for no better reason than that the devil's work had to be done.

He pleaded for his life, out in the freezing park, yet still he wouldn't say what had happened to Evelyn. Penny made him plead quietly, cutting him carefully, humming the tune as she went about her work. He was unlike the others, and a frenzied end would not have been appropriate. The music would end poignantly this time, not violently; a reflection and not a confrontation. In the greater scheme of things it didn't matter, not really, that at the end he failed to make his confession and tell the truth about his cousin.

Penny knew enough, and could work out the rest.

As for her own confession, she had made a start on that, too. This sad wretch wasn't worthy to bear the full weight of all that she had stored inside. Her real and true confessor was still out there, and she would find him, there was no doubt about that.

At the end she closed his eyelids and held him, rocking him. And then she started to cry, softly, soothingly.

As Penny walked back along the perimeter path, the bushes seemed alive with rustles and whispers. Peak time, she thought. She had left Norman Sidcup on the bank of the lake, an offering to the pain gods. She had briefly contemplated a marine burial, but there was no point in making things more dramatic than they needed to be.

His car keys were in her hand, and when she reached the car she realised that it was late. That time had flown again. Mum and Dad would be getting worried. They would have contacted the unit and might even be ringing the police. She had intended retrieving her folder and catching a bus home; it seemed a better idea to take the car. Norman wouldn't be needing it now.

Her Dad had given her a few driving lessons, and so she knew the basics; knew enough to get home. If she drove carefully there was no reason that she would be stopped. There were police everywhere, of course, but a young girl driving home in the late evening - what could she know and how could she possibly assist them in their enquiries? As clear as an eyeball stuck on a needle, she was not what they were looking for.

Penny got into Norman Sidcup's car and drove cautiously down towards the main road. It could be abandoned close to home, leaving a nice little mystery for the police to brood over, another piece of the jigsaw to make their days more interesting. She abandoned the car four streets from home, close to where the bus usually dropped her. Leaving the keys in the ignition, she didn't even consider anything so melodramatic as wiping away fingerprints. Nobody had her prints in the first place, and why should they? Killing was easy when you kept your nose clean and came from good stock.

Penny walked home quickly, as any decent, intelligent, law abiding young woman would do when there was a killer on the loose. Time was of the essence. There was music to write.

CHAPTER FOURTEEN

Valemore was still holding on to its police station, and over the past few days it had become the second home of Detective Inspector Roxburgh. He peered through the one-way glass into the interview room. The man sitting across the table from the two guards was smoking a cigarette and looking agitated. He had been brought in the previous evening, found walking from the direction of Valemore Park, and in the act of turning into Ellgate Street. He'd been drinking, though had not been charged with a drink-related offence. He hadn't been charged with anything. Still, he wasn't going anywhere, not for a while.

Officers had brought him in because he had been unable to give a reasonable account of what he was doing in that part of town at that particular time. Under normal circumstances this would hardly have constituted a reason for hoisting a man off the streets and keeping him overnight in the cells. But that evening local police officers had not been operating under anything like normal circumstances, and less than an hour before Phil Waters' arrest, a man had been found dead in Valemore Park, discovered by two young students who were, to use their own words, "out having a stroll."

Most of the college traffic had cleared before the police started to block off the area. By ten there had been few people on the street *not* wearing a uniform. One man, however, had been walking away from the park, and refusing to say where he was going and why. "I'm walking to clear my head," Waters had told the officers who had picked him up. "Is that an offence now - walking? How about you leave me alone and lock up some criminals. You can start with the sick nut going round cutting off dicks."

D.I. Roxburgh had spent much of the night at the murder scene and talking to scene of crime personnel.

He'd grabbed a couple of hours to keep body and soul together, and by late morning was preparing to interview the suspect at Valemore Police Station.

As he entered the interview room, Roxburgh found himself to be uncharacteristically tense. It wasn't the increasing public pressure to find and apprehend the person responsible for this unprecedented spate of violent murders in the area that was bothering him. He could take that in his stride. It was the challenge of keeping the interview on a professional level; of not allowing personal feelings to enter into the equation. The man in the interview room must remain nothing more than a person helping police with their enquiries. He may prove to be a man who had killed once, or even four times – *but he must not, on any account, become the man for whom my wife gave up ten years of marriage!*

D.I. Roxburgh pulled up a chair and launched into the statutory procedure expected of an officer when interviewing a suspect. Waters, in turn, made no attempt to lighten the leaden air, making reference to the private life of the man bearing down on him.

For the first twenty minutes of the interview, D.I. Roxburgh found himself wanting to put a chair leg through the face of Mr. Waters. Not merely on account of personal circumstances, but on account of the man's extraordinary stupidity.

For twenty minutes, despite the fact that Waters was being held in connection with a murder - and quite possibly a series of murders – the man insisted on being obtuse in the extreme about where he had been going and why. In the back of the detective's nine-parts focused and professional mind, a little voice was whispering: *Look, shit-for-brains: if you're cheating on Olive, you want your balls cutting off. But this is a murder-investigation. So if that's the truth, let's get it out and done with so that we can get on and catch this psycho before he cuts up his next victim.*

The man wasn't being cool, and he most certainly wasn't being clever. He didn't look far from nervous collapse - but still he was refusing to co-operate. Roxy settled in, prepared for the long-haul. There was no need to turn up the heat. He would let Waters do the work.

"I was trying to find a friend."

"Do you have the name of this friend?"

"Marcus."

"Is that a first name or a surname?"

"Marcus Redfearn."

"And what is the address of this Marcus Redfearn?"

Pause. "I'm not sure."

"I see. Had you visited Mr. Redfearn's house previously?"

"I think so."

"You think so?"

"I mean ... yes."

"Once, twice – every Tuesday?"

"Once, I think. Yes, once."

"But you don't know his address?"

"No."

"When did you last have occasion to visit Mr. Redfearn's residence?"

"A while ago."

"And what do you call 'a while'? Last week, last month?"

"A year or two."

"And did he know you were calling to see him yesterday evening?"

Waters shook his head.

"Is that a no, Mr. Waters? Please speak for the tape."

"It's a no. He didn't know I was calling to see him."

"A social call, was it? Or business?"

Another pause, longer this time.

An hour passed and still this absurd, stubborn reluctance from Waters. All the years of police work told Roxy that though this man was capable of deceit – *leading Olive up the garden path, and some distance beyond* – he was not ticking the box marked 'cold-blooded killer'.

Let Olive cut his balls off; she would in time. As for allowing him to waste another minute of police time ... It wouldn't hurt, though, letting him spend a second night in the cells, while certain lines of enquiry were followed up.

Marcus Redfearn was quickly located, and his lesson on techniques of baroque counterpoint, with particular reference to Johann Sebastian Bach, interrupted. The police it seemed wanted a word regarding a friend of his.

Redfearn had no idea that Waters had been trying to find him the previous evening, and he told D.I. Roxburgh that much from the Spartan comforts of the Valemore police interview room. Yes, Waters had visited his house previously. No, Waters probably wouldn't remember the address, as he was drunk the last time, they both were - unless Waters had written the address down. "Wouldn't it be better to ask him yourself, I mean, directly?"

It was an honest question; an innocent question. A question you might expect from an honest and straightforward man, which Mr. Redfearn appeared to be. So what did he see in a rat like Waters? Reading between the lines, D.I. Roxburgh was tending to believe that Marcus Redfearn wasn't overly enamoured, and that had to be a mark in the man's favour.

When the interview had finished, Redfearn was returned to college to resume his duties, while the detective pondered what to do next. It seemed positively rude not to extend the hospitality of a second night's bed and board to Mr. Waters. After all, there was one line of enquiry that really ought to be followed up. *Olive.* As senior investigating officer, failing to follow up such a clear line was unthinkable. He could not on any account let personal matters get in the way of his investigations, or to cloud his professional judgement. It was nothing more than going through the motions, but still it had to be done. Mistakes like that were guaranteed career wreckers.

It was mid-afternoon already. Olive would be at the office, or out making calls; serving the community for good or ill. It's what she did and what she enjoyed doing. At least, one of the things she enjoyed doing – though best not to dwell on that, he thought. He would not disturb her in the execution of her daily round. He would wait for the evening. Visit her at her new address. See what style she was growing accustomed to these days.

D.I. Roxburgh called on Olive Roxburgh at the address of one Mr. Phillip Waters. He stayed a little short of an hour, establishing quickly that Waters had an alibi for at least two of the murders; and given the time Waters was seen leaving the pub, it was virtually impossible that he could have been responsible for the most recent killing. Still. It was interesting talking to Olive like that, and it tied up the paperwork beyond any future reproach.

Olive, bless her, didn't seem at all protective of her boyfriend. Perhaps the joys were wearing off. Perhaps she was realising the errors of her ways. Coming to understand exactly what she was giving up, *the sheer extent of it.*

The following morning, a telephone call from D.I. Roxburgh to Valemore Police Station procured the release of Phil Waters. By the time Waters returned home, Olive had already left for work. She had, however, thought to leave him a note, on the off-chance that he was a free man again.

CHAPTER FIFTEEN

Penny had been in class when the principal came in asking Mr. Redfearn if he could leave his students with work to be getting on with for a couple of hours. He was discreet, of course, though she didn't doubt for a second that it was all tied in with the events of the previous evening.

What could they possibly want with Mr. Redfearn? They could not, in a million years, imagine that he had anything to do with it. The world was all twisted up. Men like Mr. Humanities, they were the ones who ought to be hauled away to help the police with their pathetic enquiries. No, she thought. Not even that. In a truly just world, Mr. Humanities would be helping enquiries from underneath the forensic scalpel.

She had been relieved to see Mr. Redfearn back in class before the day was done. It went some way to restoring her belief in at least the possibilities of justice.

Most of Penny's evening was spent going over the fourth part of her sextet, making slight amendments here and there. The process seemed more painstaking than usual, and it didn't help that she was constantly wondering what Mr. Redfearn thought of her work. She wasn't going to push it, though, not after the day he must have had. If she knew him at all, he wouldn't be long in getting back to her.

As for Waters ... he would no doubt be writing back before long, wanting his money. He might have to be disappointed. Perhaps he would work harder and give more of himself if she withheld the favour that vultures like him craved. *Money*. Wasn't that one of the two great motivators of men? Susan had said that once, or something like it. About the principles that dictated their actions being the keys to their doom. What was it now? *Give to them and prepare to be deceived; withhold and bleed them to the bone.*

That was Susan. That was the *real* Susan. Not the little angel that Mummy and Daddy knew about. *Or thought they knew.*

Penny sat back on her bed and took a break. There was too much swimming around in her head; too much noise and distraction. It was easy to get sidetracked, when what she needed was focus. She thought about healing and about sickness, the two sides of the coin. Sure enough, the disease, the sickness was the dark wand that men waved. The evil thing they had done to Susan. But ultimately this wasn't about men, it was about Susan, and that had to remain paramount. Beyond mere vendetta lay the core, the healing, and the cure. Susan home again. A family at peace again. Forgiveness and reconciliation. Magic, healing and sacrifice.

It was the weekend when the Hendersons' next went to Eaglesfield together. They'd gleaned from news reports that the latest victim had been visiting the unit on the very night he was killed. All of the staff had been interviewed by the police, yet according to the newspapers little or no progress had been made. It didn't seem that they were any closer to catching the killer or even identifying him. The police had questioned a local man, but at a press conference it was confirmed that nobody was currently helping them with their enquiries.

Murder seemed to be the sole topic of conversation on the unit, and Penny wondered if they were going to have to draft in extra staff, as the regulars didn't seem to have time to get any work done for gossiping about stuff that didn't concern them, and of which they clearly knew absolutely nothing.

The family left early, passing, as they went, a man who Mr. Henderson recognised from the television. A man with piercing green eyes, and who Mr. Henderson thought looked in need of his own television series.

Penny lay in bed, her mind circling around three things. First: the letter.

Mr. Waters hadn't returned any of her manuscript, though he had taken it upon himself to suggest that a piano sextet was not a good idea. Not for his competition, anyway. Too confusing a notion, he explained. A sextet was a musical composition for six instruments, regardless of how many sections made up its structure. Like she didn't know that! Was he for real? Why didn't he simply suggest that she change the title?

Because that was hardly advice he could charge for. He had to wrap up his prejudices in a form that could justify payment.

And as for his critique of the actual music - it was junior school stuff. He hadn't wasted ink on it, but that was his only saving grace. His ink had been used up telling her about his correspondence course.

Some chance, Mr. Waters.

She wanted her work returning in any event. Didn't want the creep keeping hold of it for whatever purpose might emerge in the future. She would send a brief note. *Give it up, arsehole.* Or words to that effect.

That idea rankled, too. She wasn't stupid, could read between the lines. This guy *loved* her stuff. It wasn't her being an ego-maniac, he loved it, and Penny knew she could win the competition and get the CD recorded; her work immortalised and dedicated to Susan.

Could she let that go? How much would it cost to get it done? There was the recording equipment at the college that nobody ever used. Maybe Mr. Redfearn could sort something out. A course-work project, paid for by the college. It seemed a promising idea, but still the glory of winning a competition, even one run by a weasel, was a hook that wouldn't easily shake loose.

Then there was the second thing.

During her latest visit to Susan, she had managed a few minutes alone with her sister. Susan hadn't been at her best, there was no doubt about that. She had looked even more vacant than usual. Nevertheless, Penny had told Susan that the fourth part had been completed, and had even hummed the tune for her.

Susan had turned away. She had never done that before. And when Penny stopped humming, Susan turned back. So Penny tried again and, sure enough, as soon as she kicked in with the main melody, the same response from her sister.

Weirdsville.

And then the third thing.

In the car coming home, after Dad's quip about the policeman, detective, or whatever he was - about him needing his own TV series - Mum had started banging on about "that poor girl Evelyn" and how she didn't seem to get many visitors and wouldn't get any at all now that her cousin had been killed; and how some people never had any luck in life. She was going on about all this, not really saying anything in that Mum way of hers - and then, out of the blue, "I feel sorry for him."

"We don't really know the facts, dear." That was Dad, ever the cautious one.

"There's too much violence in this world to begin with, without adding to it. To be attacked like that, it must have been one of these vigilante killings."

"We don't know that."

"A woman knows these things."

"Don't talk so -"

"And I think it's a woman responsible."

"A right little Miss Marple tonight, aren't we?"

"Somebody wanted him dead because of seeing poor Evelyn in that state."

Mrs. Henderson's line of reasoning had rarely been so compelling. They had arrived home, but for a few moments the family remained in the car. "I reckon, for what it's worth, that somebody who visits the home saw her like that, heard the gossip that always goes around when you get a place with so many women in it …"

"Oh, Mum, for goodness sakes!"

"No, Penny, I'm sick to death of all this political correctness. Nobody can tell the truth. When it shields a truth then I think it's going too far."

"What are you talking about, Mum?"

"Women gossiping, that's what I'm talking about. Getting it all built up in their heads. I reckon somebody from the home, or visiting the home, killed that poor man. And what's more, I think she got it wrong."

"Fascinating," said Dad, at last opening the car door. "And why, *Miss Marple*, must it be a woman?"

"It's the same person who killed the others. And that was a woman, too."

"Of course," said Mr. Henderson, throwing up his arms, and smiling back at Penny. "How could we all have been so stupid?"

Penny climbed out of bed. Sleep was as far away as the morning, but her mind was made up: a copy of the fourth part of *Sextet* to Waters and a copy to Mr. Redfearn.

She tip-toed downstairs, made herself a hot drink, and switched on the radio. There was soft jazz playing, and it was soothing enough. Her mind drifted with the music and, without realising it, her thoughts settled on last Friday, late in the afternoon, the class packing up for the weekend. Mr. Redfearn had caught her eye, suggesting in that incredibly discreet way of his that he wanted her to hang back when the others left.

She waited around in the classroom for a minute or two, but one of the other girls wanted a word with him, and so Penny had made her way slowly across campus, glancing back occasionally, imagining Mr. Humanities' face pressed against a window in E block, watching her, scanning her for clues with his dick in his hand. Pretending that she had forgotten something, she doubled back. Mr. Redfearn was coming out of the building, but he wasn't alone. The other student was still talking to him. Penny felt a sudden swell of anger, and turned back around, unsure what to do.

Then she heard a voice behind her. The other student had gone. Mr. Redfearn walked with Penny towards the bus stop. He didn't say much, as it turned out. He would talk to her next week.

She thought he had appeared uncertain, as though he was battling to contain his own excitement. Like he wanted to say something but didn't know how. Maybe his discretion knew no bounds. They parted with nods and smiles, awkward gestures that adolescent lovers might have been ashamed of.

As the bus pulled away, she had looked back toward the college. College and home seemed worlds apart; the weekend had become a bridge that stretched forever. A curious feeling, almost like ... no, that was stupid.

It was nothing at all like being in love.

The soft jazz broke back into her thoughts, and Penny yawned. Perhaps if she went back to bed she could rescue the night. But the dragon wouldn't let her. More than once, and long before morning, Mr. Redfearn stepped onto the battlefield, dressed in shining armour.

CHAPTER SIXTEEN

On Friday afternoon Phil Waters came face to face with Marcus Redfearn. He'd taken the only course of action left: a stroll down to the college, helping himself to the worst cup of coffee in history, burning his fingers in the process. He knew that Redfearn finished bang on four on a Friday, he'd sat waiting for him to come bursting into the Feathers at five-past-the-hour often enough.

Waters arrived at E block in good time, expecting to see people leaving in dribs and drabs, half the college population already on its way. But it seemed that Valemore had tightened up its act, and was no longer the favoured haunt of time-wasters putting off getting a job. There was an atmosphere of industry about the place, even so late on a Friday afternoon.

It had not always been so, not in the good old days when he and his cohorts had filled their carefree days smuggling moonshine and marijuana joints into the library. One of his favourite anecdotes related how, the year after he'd left Valemore for a three-year binge at university, the college tried to clean up its image, starting with signs in the library proclaiming that smoking, consuming alcohol, and gambling were strictly prohibited. He climaxed the tale with the favoured observation that the college should have gone the whole hog and issued a prohibition against "banging the arses off the hairdressers."

At four, and not a moment earlier, E block came alive as the first wave of students filled the corridor and swamped the staircase. Then a second wave, smaller, less bubbly, not the real swots yet, merely the aspiring ones; and then finally, to no fanfare, the dribble, the coalescence of the righteous and the terminally misplaced; the swots and the clods in swots' clothing, reconciling themselves slowly, painfully, to two whole days away from their desks, if not their likely wasted labours.

And still no sign of Marcus Redfearn. Must have missed him, thought Waters. How was that possible? Maybe the man was ill. Why hadn't he checked? Why hadn't he taken the trouble of walking into reception and checking whether the oaf was even here?

He watched the students passing by, the range of ethnic diversity faintly irritating him. The 'trooping of the colours' was how he'd once put it to Olive. It was good to pass the irritation on sometimes, particularly to a paid up member of the PC army. It was probably Asian flu that had got hold of Marcus. Asian flu would explain a lot of things lately. You got a good enough dose of that and you didn't care if you never saw a pint again.

Waters started walking away from E block, already pondering whether to risk another stroll down past the park, and another stab at finding the humble abode of his old mate. Lightning, surely, couldn't strike twice - not even the type conducted by D.I. Roxburgh.

The thought made him spit decisively. Sober, he was certain that he could find Redfearn's house; piece of cake. He smiled, licking his lips at the sudden, slaking burn of anticipation. It was, after all, fast becoming late Friday afternoon; *sacred time*.

As he made his way back across campus, his eyes feasting greedily on the plethora of nubile teenagers surrounding him on all sides, he thought back with pride and self-pity to the glory days at Valemore College of F.E. Savouring the memories of the past alongside the sights of the present, he had no reason to glance back to see another man, a few yards behind him, likewise deep in thought. Marcus Redfearn, equally engrossed, equally unaware, walking alongside a young woman who, it would later turn out, owed Phil Waters a little money, a little respect, and -

was it, yes it was - *three* more pieces of that remarkable music.

The day's diluted sun was burnt out already, and the gloom looked set to get dirtier before the yellow milk-ball came around again. The girl had left the campus heading for the bus stop, Redfearn heading for the park entrance. Home for the teacher was a five minute walk, ahead of him a thinning pedestrian traffic of students, though he wasn't even noticing them. He was thinking about Penny Henderson, thinking about her as he passed the park entrance, past a hesitant man in a raincoat who seemed a little unsure of his bearings.

The two men stopped and looked at each other. "Marcus! Where've you been?"

"I've been to London to see the Queen."

"You might as well have. I've been looking all over."

"Really?" said Redfearn, a little awkwardly.

"It's going to piss it down. Let's get that coffee."

"Coffee?"

"You've still got a kettle in that hovel?"

"But …"

"I know, it's strictly pub time. But you've got to take it easy. That Asian strain can be fatal."

"What are you talking about?"

Waters was already walking on. "Come on," he said. "I was joking about the coffee. But I'm not joking when I tell you that it's better to have an alibi at all times when you take this route."

Redfearn caught up with him, and together they walked away from the college lights and into the darkening void.

Olive was leaving the office early for once, taking back a slice from that mountain of time that was owed to her. It was a short walk from the derelict-looking council building to the public car park, though not always a comfortable one.

She had a permit saving her time, trouble and the expense of the ticket machine, but still it was a walk that the staff tried to make in twos, and always with their keys ready. Lately, the tourists had taken to gathering around the far wall of the car park, to get a look at the glass-strewn waste ground behind, and maybe a snap or two of the old abandoned Regent theatre. But nothing else had changed. Women were considered wholesome pickings around this part of town, according to statistics.

Olive had her keys in her hand before she had even left the building, and she was moving at a purposeful gallop towards her blue VW. The day was falling into blackness, and what was left of the sky didn't seem to know whether to send down the rain or the freeze. She didn't always feel like somebody was watching her when she made this short journey alone, but she felt it now. Her eyes were busy as she moved quickly towards her month-old Beetle. She couldn't see anybody around, but her instincts were screaming *danger*.

Reaching her car, Olive instinctively looked back over her shoulder. There was nobody there. Feeling a little easier, she turned back to put her key in the lock.

"Not skiving off already, are we?"

The breath caught in her throat, preventing the scream.

"Nerves bad, eh?"

A familiar face was grinning at her from the other side of her car.

"Nigel?"

The figure rose up into a standing position. "Who else would dare approach a female social worker in the darkness of this car park? Another man might have lost his prize possessions by now."

"Don't push it, you still might," she said. "What do you think you're doing?"

"I was hoping for a lift."

"Where's your car?" Her eyes narrowed. "Lift where?"

"Oh, I don't know. Your place?"

"You need to speak to Phil again?"

The detective shook his head. "He left the house thirty minutes ago. He's gone back to school."

Olive's mouth fell open. "You mean – you've got him under *surveillance*?"

"Procedure, Olive. You know how it is."

She eyed him. "You're the policeman. I suppose you should know how to run a murder investigation."

"Who said anything about a murder investigation?"

"I hope, Detective Inspector Nigel Roxburgh cum Chief of Police cum OBE cum Lord of the Universe, that I'm not understanding you correctly."

"It wouldn't be the first time. Now, am I getting this lift or not?"

"Get in," she said, unlocking the doors.

The detective signalled to the unmarked BMW a few yards away, watching it immediately move off as he climbed into the passenger seat of his estranged wife's car.

On the drive down towards Little Valemore D.I Roxburgh listened intently as she told him of the honourable mentions he was getting from the mouth of her lover. "He hasn't talked about anything else. He's convinced that you hauled him in out of spite." As she said this, she flicked him a glance. "I mean, even a rat like you wouldn't stoop to that."

"Kind of you to say, Olive. You always were my staunchest supporter."

"He keeps talking about making an official complaint. I told him to do it."

"Thanks again."

"Nothing personal, you understand."

"I understand."

She laughed, bitterly. "He won't, though. I told him to do it just to shut him up. He's too idle to go through all the rigmarole. But he's convinced that you're teaching him a lesson and he's even gone so far as to suggest ..."

"Suggest what?"

"That you might be ... wanting me back."

She sneaked another look out of the corner of her eye. "See how you've upset the man?"

"Just doing my job," he said, and they both laughed.

"Do you love him, Olive?"

"What kind of a question is that to ask your wife?"

They were pulling into Waters' street. "I'm still not sure where it went wrong, Olive."

"I could tell you - if you've a couple of weeks going spare."

"You haven't told me whether you love him."

She pulled up outside the house. "I wasn't aware that I *had* to answer. Like you said, this isn't really about a murder investigation, is it?"

"Dangerous words."

"I know."

The two of them looked at each other for a long moment. Then she blinked, breaking the spell. "So what are you saying – that Phil is still under suspicion?"

"Sorry, Olive. Some things are still confidential."

"Hardly worth you coming in then, is it? Sounds to me like you've said everything."

The sound of a ringing phone for a second startled them both.

The detective took the mobile out of his coat pocket. He asked a couple of questions, but mostly he listened. Then he put the phone back inside his coat. "Sorry about that," he said. "Where were we?"

"You'd better come in," she said. "But I want to know what's going on."

She made a drink while he perused the house, not touching anything; just a man come in for a coffee, doing what people do, admiring photographs, checking out bookcases. Nothing requiring the formalities of a warrant. An accommodating woman was Olive, when she had a mind to be.

"So where is he at this precise moment?" she asked, placing two hot drinks onto the living-room table. "Can't you put him up on a screen? A day in the life of Phil Waters – I could come round with the choc-ices."

"You always did make me laugh."

"I'm a funny girl when the mood takes me."

"Not a bad place this. I wondered if I might take a look around upstairs - you know, out of curiosity."

"Like you might want to buy the place, you mean?"

"I'm going to need somewhere to live by the time your solicitors have finished. We could satisfy each other's curiosity."

"Is that right?"

"Has he been acting suspiciously?"

Olive spat out another bitter laugh. "What, before or after you took him in? Look, Phil is Phil, and apart from taking your name in vain day and night, his only other current obsession is playing the same music over and over."

"You don't approve?"

"It's doing my head in."

"Anything I might know?"

"Nothing by Britney Spears, no."

"I didn't deserve *that*!"

"Perhaps you didn't." She sighed. "He's started running a postal course in music composition."

"Postal?"

"That's Phil for you. Likes to do things *Phil's* way. Hasn't had much response - as far as I know."

"So he's playing to death the stuff he has had?"

"Sad, isn't it?"

"Heartbreaking.""Nothing else I can tell you."

"I see. Care to know where he is right now?"

"As long as he's not coming back along this street. You two aren't destined to get on – and you can put that in your notebook if you need to."

"That won't be necessary."

"So where is he?"

"How about I tell you while you show me the rest of the house. I'd love to see where a great musician hangs out."

"You could always try the Mozart house in Saltzburg. It's amazing."

"He's walking down past the park again. He seems to love it down there. Perhaps he's gone to look up this old friend of his, Marcus Redfearn. Have you met him?"

"Have you?"

"Come on, Olive."

He stood up. The phone was ringing again under his coat. He answered it, listened, and then told whoever was calling to pick him up straight away. He ended the call. "Got to go, I'm afraid. Still time for a quick look upstairs, though - what do you say?"

She shrugged, pointing to the stairs. "Do I have to hold your hand?"

"After you," said Roxy. "You know that a perfect gent like me always insists on ladies first." He followed her up the narrow staircase. "Most edifying, that short climb," he said, as they reached the top. "You always could wear trousers."

She pointed to one of the doors off the landing. "Phil's work room," she said. "Two minutes."

"Don't worry. I won't touch a thing."

On the desk, next to a page of handwritten musical notation, a handwritten letter was partially covered by a music dictionary. Two words at the left margin read: ... *your spell.*

He looked back at Olive, standing in the doorway watching him. "Looks like the makings of an interesting letter," he said.

"I wouldn't know. I don't snoop."

"And you a trained social worker? You should hand in your badge immediately."

"I think your lift's here."

"Do me a favour: pop down and tell them I won't be more than a minute or so."

"You shouldn't be doing this," she said. "I could report you."

"Okay, Olive. I get the message."

D.I. Roxburgh walked out of the room, down the stairs, thanking her briefly, formally, at the door before making his way outside to the waiting car.

The first thing Waters noticed on being re-acquainted with the inside of Redfearn's mid-terrace was that the place looked cleaner and tidier than he remembered. "Not got a woman, have you?"

"Why do you say that?"

"Steady, Marcus, only asking."

The host lit the gas-fire with a match before taking off his coat. "After a while you get sick of living in a pig sty. Coffee, wasn't it?"

"Beer would be better."

"Not a drop in the house."

"You ought to be ashamed. You've brought me here under false pretences."

"You insisted."

"Don't be like that. Is there a problem?" Waters looked at his watch. "Okay, coffee it is, and then I thought maybe we could, you know, take a walk. It is Friday, long week and all that – for some of us, anyway."

"I think I'll give it a miss," said Redfearn, walking through to the kitchen to fill up the kettle. "I'm off the beer at the moment."

"Anti-biotics?"

Redfearn didn't reply. Returning to the room, he found Waters staring intently at the pages of manuscript left open at the piano. If he'd remembered he would have removed them, and hidden them; but their presence had taken on the invisibility of air, becoming the air that gave the room, the house, life.

Waters was taking the music down from the piano. In unison the two men swallowed hard. "It is sugar in coffee?" said Redfearn. "Actually, I may still have some whisky left from ..."

But his guest wasn't listening. He was busy turning over the pages of manuscript. *The fourth part*. The fourth part that had dropped through his letter-box that morning, and which he had only stopped playing long enough to go back over the preceding parts. It was music that grew every time it was played. And it was here, sitting on Redfearn's piano.

"You ought to hear that," said Redfearn, his voice at last penetrating his guest's distraction. This fourth part had arrived on his desk, unannounced, marked for his attention.

"Hear it?" said Waters. "Two hours ago I was playing it!"

Redfearn frowned. Hadn't Penny learned her lesson?

"You look surprised?" said Waters.

"To tell you the truth, Phil, she's a student of mine. She wanted me to give it the once over." Waters started to laugh, and at the sound of it Redfearn winced. "What's funny?" he asked, stiffly.

"It's some coincidence," said Waters, "when you stop to think about it."

"I don't follow."

"It's not necessary to play the innocent with me, Marcus."

"What are you talking about?"

"This is your doing, mate. You put her in touch with me, and for that I thank you. My top student, and she came by recommendation of one Marcus Redfearn, agent to the stars."

"I …"

But the thing had already spiralled beyond his control. Let Waters think whatever he wants to think and let him be gone from here.

"May I?" asked Waters, sitting down at the piano. "Because I think that together, my friend, we have discovered something rather special." Waters started to play from the beginning. Redfearn felt the passion swell as he listened again to those opening bars.

But it was passion cut with pain.

CHAPTER SEVENTEEN

On the unit the talk was: Oh, what a shame what happened to Evelyn's cousin, poor Norman Sidcup, poor, inoffensive Mr. Sidcup, who had given them all the creeps when he was alive, and who was practically a saint now. All he was doing was visiting sweet Evelyn, and who was there to visit her now that he was gone? Whatever anybody says, you still don't deserve to get chopped into tiny pieces for visiting your poor little cousin.

Bullshit! What did the fools know about any of it?

It was getting late. Friday evening was coming down on Penny like a fat storm cloud full of comic-book lightning. She'd come straight from college, spent the longest time with Susan in a dozen visits. Sometimes she wondered how Susan could stand being among these idiots. The sooner she was out of there the better.

She was chirpier again, though, even if the staff were too busy banging on about things they couldn't fathom to see it. Susan's brightness had nothing to do with their feeble ministrations, though. The things that mattered were things that they could never grasp, not in a thousand years.

Penny had hummed the completed parts of *Sextet* for her sister, and had seen the instant animation on her face. Susan was coming alive again. It was starting to happen. All the fear, the hurt, the pain – it was all receding. Susan was coming back from the dead. The promised resurrection was at hand. There were no limits to what the music, the magic, could achieve.

Forgiveness, Susan.

Another tune was emerging, though as yet nameless and faceless. It contained none of the chaos that had gone before it. Stillness was the order of the day this time, the heart of the mystic; no Norman Sidcup at the core of this one; deep fires burning.

Almost ... *a love song*.

No, that was too perverse. There had to be contrast though if the work was to truly come alive, breathing the fire back into the fractured heart of her twin.

The six had been six, not one. They had acted as one when they did what they did to her; but in retribution they were six and not one. One could not be made to symbolise more than one. One devil, six representative demons; and all to be cast into the same cleansing flames or else what in damnation had been the point of it all.

But where to look for this one: this five of six, this penultimate setting up of the shattering finale? Under which stone did this one fester? How would he reveal himself – how would he become known to her?

Perhaps he had already entered the frame.

Yes.

She glanced across her shoulder. Two cleaners - and guess who they were talking about? A little bit of poor, poor Evelyn; a little bit of poor Norman Sidcup, and more than a little of good-looking-do-you-reckon-he's-attached Detective Inspector Roxburgh.

But what kind of a name was that? He sounded like a loser, a pension sucking plod. Or did he? Perhaps the coin would show its real face; perhaps Roxburgh himself was one of the six, waiting for her in the dark on the pretext that he needed help with his enquiries. Time would tell. It would happen the way that it was destined to happen, and there was no point trying to force it with pale logic or murder-mystery intuition.

They were bringing Susan back to her room. It was time to think about saying some goodbyes. Time to leave this place of wretched light and wait in the shadows for the man who fitted the tune.

Penny walked down the road to the pub, and she found it full of human debris. The customers looked at her in the usual fashion, and as she took a swift Britvic at the bar there was any number of vermin she wouldn't have minded taking for a walk in the woods. None of them, though, made the melody come alive. It would be killing for the sake of killing, and that would make her no better than them.

There was nothing here. It was time to lift a different stone.

She stood outside, watching the traffic go by, finding no willing stranger, no poor Norman Sidcup to pull over and reveal himself to the night. Her bus came; she let it go, though she didn't know why. Instead she boarded a second bus, getting off half a dozen stops early, stepping onto the well-lit pavement close to the college.

But she still didn't know why.

She stood for a few minutes, looking at the dark hulk of the college buildings, remembering her earlier conversation with Mr. Redfearn. Wishing that she knew where he lived, because perhaps tonight was not the night for bloodshed; perhaps tonight was for sitting down with one of the few good men left in the world, and finding an hour of refuge from the insanity that was fermenting all around her and boiling within.

Blinking into the light she realised that the tune that had taken such a fierce hold on her earlier had now subsided. She watched a couple head into the park and wondered what it would take for people to heed the warnings.

Maybe it was time to go home. Walk up into Little Valemore High Street and get a taxi. Tonight was all wrong, out of kilter. The wrong patterns and the wrong shapes. *Sleep, rest, and wait, Penny.* Can't force the magic, can't disregard the fates.

Tonight she was nothing more than a young girl in ripped jeans and a torn leather jacket, standing alone outside the gates of a darkened public park with not a creature of prey crawling out to her from any direction. *Leave it, Penny. Go home, go home now.*

The wind was picking up and she felt it cut through her; blowing through like she wasn't there, invisible and unreal. She might have been dreaming, except that dreams were never so empty.

It was getting late. Her parents would be worried. Her parents were terminally worried. It would not be them if they were not sitting at home, biting their nails, trying not to stare at the clock. That was the life they lived, unable to take their eyes off time and unable to take their minds off tragedy past, present and waiting.

What would Mr. Redfearn be doing tonight? Drinking somewhere? He might be in the Feathers at this very moment, not even thinking about her or her music. And why should he? He had a life outside college, and he was entitled to that. He worked hard; he was a good teacher and a good man. The world needed more Mr. Redfearns to keep it from falling apart completely.

He said that he wanted to see her on Monday, to put some idea to her. He was excited, she could tell that. He liked her music, and it excited her to think what he might say to her.

What if he was in the Feathers now?

The thought kept returning. It was ludicrous. Even if he was in there, it was *his* time, and she had no right to intrude. If she were to walk in on his time he might look at her with contempt, even lose interest in her music altogether, and who could blame him? What good would that do?

Wait, Penny. Don't force it. Don't break it.

Did he realise the sheer weight of responsibility bearing down upon him? He was the only person in the world who could alter, or suggest altering, what was already written.

How could he possibly know?

Yet ...

What if?

The thought made her catch her breath. What if he was sitting in the pub all alone, wishing that he could talk to her about her music? What if he was frustrated because he didn't want to wait until Monday; wanted to say it all *now*? Make the changes that would nail it.

The excitement faded as quickly as it had come, like a gust of wind, all power and bluster, and then gone without leaving a single mark on anything. *He might not be alone.* He might be with a friend, even a lover. And why would he be sitting thinking about her, Penny Henderson, and a few hopeful pages of piano music? It was time to go home.

She looked towards the college. The Feathers was less than five minutes away, possibly less than three. *It was time to go home.* She started walking towards the college, back onto the main road that curved around to the east side of the campus. The Feathers pub stood waiting.

She was outside the door.

No, Penny. Better to turn around, go home.

Taking a deep breath, she stepped out of the cold and into the noise, the light, the warmth. He was not in there. She turned to leave, stopped, turned back. *He might be in the toilets*. Conversations were underway in every corner of the bar, and though people glanced her way she could be just another girl waiting for her boyfriend to park the car and then to come in and buy the drinks. Men were still capable of acting like gentlemen if there was something to be gained. She had a good minute or more before she would arouse anything beyond casual curiosity. Nobody was going to ogle too hard in here, not until they'd at least weighed up the boyfriend.

She looked at her watch. That simple gesture, she realised too late, effectively shutting down the possibility of an attendant boyfriend busy parking the BMW. Now she was a pretty girl who might have been stood up.

Fair game? Would someone – or something – emerge from the shadows?

More eyes were coming her way; had she already crept into conversations? Been undressed a dozen times and kicked back out through the door?

Still no Mr. Redfearn. *This is a bad idea, Penny.*

She felt the tug to leave, stronger this time. There was no business to be done in here. The tune was gone and good riddance ... if it had no more resilience than that. There was no immortality in empty melody. *Come on, Penny. Time to go.* She looked in the other room, the one with the jukebox playing hits from the sixties. No, he would never use that room, not Mr. Redfearn. It was time to leave – no, it was later than that. She was drawing too much attention. People were laughing.

She opened the door and stepped quickly out into the night. There was nothing left but to get home and get home fast. She didn't need to wind her parents up any more than she had done already; didn't need them watching her any closer. The wrong day, the day gone all wrong, that's all; start again tomorrow. *Just get home, Penny. Home.*

A taxi was coming over the brow of the hill and she waved it down. She could see the way the driver was looking at her. Bald and turning to fat, but he wasn't past fancying his chances.

Was that the tune again, starting to worm its way back, thinking it could seduce her into a second chance? She opened the door and climbed into the back seat, feeling at the thing that was inside the pocket of her leather jacket.

"Where can I take you, darling?"

She gave the name of the road, watched him watching her in the rear-view mirror. Then the car lurched forward and the contempt that she felt for this man and his kind became an undigested lump in her heart. Suddenly she longed, almost ached, to bury the knife into the back of his fat, ugly neck.

No music here, only false alarm; a harmless creep out making a living, storing up fantasies for the quiet hours. He kept staring at her in the mirror. If nothing else it was giving her the arse ache. At least he wasn't saying anything. At least she didn't have to put up with what came out of his mouth.

They were not a hundred yards down the road, passing the park gates, and already she was changing her mind. Maybe it would be better if he did talk, and break this filthy silence. And if he didn't glance at the road occasionally they were going to both wind up dead anyway.

The urge to call up the tune rose savagely. It was almost enough to imagine that it was there.

Who was she fooling? How could that serve anybody, least of all Susan? Gratuitous violence sickened her. The tune was nowhere. It had deserted her. What if the whole damned shooting match was over?

The gloom, dark as treacle, was spreading and sticking. Susan wasn't coming home this Christmas or any other Christmas. It had all been delusion, a way of dealing with the darkness, postponing the craziness, the real craziness still awaiting her and her family. It hadn't all come down yet. They hadn't even reached the bottom yet. My God, it was going to crush them when it came, like an Old Testament deluge.

He was still looking at her.

And he belonged in hell.

Past the park gates now, coming to the crossroads – there! Mr. Redfearn! Like an angel burning out of the darkness. Not alone, but with a friend. A *male* friend. Penny looked back through the rear window. The two men had come from around the side of the park. They were walking quickly. She knew where they were going. "Stop! I said *stop* - here."

"What the ..."

The bald fat man jerked the car to a halt, and Penny leapt out. He shouted after her, and silently she cursed him. What if his obscenities caused the men to turn around? But already they were too far up the road, and too engrossed. She took flight towards them.

Putting the yards between herself and the blaspheming driver, she began to slow down. She could hardly overtake them. But the driver didn't appear to understand the plan, already reversing his car back up the main road, past her, squealing into the entrance adjacent to the park gates.

Now the two men stopped and turned around as the taxi driver got out of his car, lighting up the scene with language flares bright enough to burn down a church. Penny saw Mr. Redfearn start back towards her, squinting with dim recognition. The man with him was falling behind, the couple or so paces that were always enough to display the colours of the bona fide coward. Mr. Redfearn was shouting something, though it was lost beneath the sustained vitriol of the fat taxi driver, the frustrations of an entire, miserable lifetime choosing that moment to explode out of his ugly fat mouth.

She was backing towards the park gates and he was still coming towards her. Mr. Redfearn was closing in behind him, trying to make himself heard. From the shadows a voice sounded behind her. "Is everything alright here?"

Two uniformed policemen emerging from the park.

The taxi driver had stopped in his tracks, and looked about ready to remember that his unlocked cab was a few yards back up the road. Mr. Redfearn was right behind him and his friend the standard number of yards further back. The policemen didn't like the look of at least one of the gathering, and one of the officers was already radioing for assistance.

Dangerous times had come to Valemore.

How did these things work themselves out? What psychopathic gods of fate laughed behind these human games of chess?

Sitting in the Feathers, around a corner table, Marcus Redfearn on one side of the triangle drinking lager-shandy with a dash of lime, and on the other, as unreal as a lottery-winning dream on a rain-soaked December 25th, Phil Waters, the name flashing at once like a blade in Penny Henderson's mind.

The policemen had seemed most interested in the taxi-driver, and so had the policemen's chums when they arrived. After taking a few details from the others at the scene, they had offered the driver the hospitality of the local police station, and set the rest free to go about their business on this cold and unfriendly night.

Penny had seen the twinkle in the policeman's eye - the first policeman, the one who had turned the thankless and friendless task of patrolling dark parkland into a night of high adventure, calling the cavalry. Things had added up in the mind of that young and excitable constable. Facts and theories unknown in the public domain were causing a nuclear reaction in the ambitious heart of that young officer of the law.

Penny's story:

Visiting her poor abused sister, feeling lonely, coming back on the bus, calling in at the pub near to the college, classmates sometimes called in and they might be in tonight, the need for company, that's how it gets you on the worst days, but nobody there, only strangers, waited a few minutes, just in case, giving it up and getting a cab, worried about her parents, wanting to get home so that they wouldn't be worried about their little girl, and then the taxi-driver starts coming out with all this obscene stuff and the little girl is frightened, panics, asks him to pull over and he pulls over but she thinks he's going to, you know, try something, so she jumps out of the car and runs for it, and he comes after her, drives the car backwards, tires screeching and everything and he's out of his car, cursing and yes, officer, you know the rest, and the police offer her a lift home, but no, she doesn't want to be brought home in a police car - what would her parents imagine when they saw her getting out of a police car? - and then Mr. Redfearn, who tells the police about being a teacher - Penny's teacher - asks if she wants to come to the Feathers where she can ring her parents, tell them that she's okay, and then he'll organise a cab and take her home himself - and then this Phil Waters, his eyes lighting up when he realises who she is, though she hasn't heard his name yet and so doesn't realise why he's so interested all of a sudden – this Phil Waters, going one better than Mr. Redfearn, hands her a mobile phone and says to ring them straight away as they're bound to be fretting, yes, that's the word he used like he was talking about a dog or something: *fretting.*

And she plays the whole thing down on the phone, because the police have already gone now, taking Mr. Fat and Ugly with them, and the two Sir Galahads are courteously out of earshot and yes, yes, it wouldn't be Mum and Dad if they didn't go absolutely apeshit.

But they're old school types; short of a doctor, a teacher is your most trusted member of an uncivilised community. Can't trust the police any more, not all of them, but curiously the medics and the teachers still get the Henderson Seniors Seal of Approval.

So if Mr. Redfearn is good enough to take you for a stiff brandy to calm you down, and if he is good enough, so close to Christmas and on such a cold and frosty night, to see that you get home safely – then, our child, our precious, precious child, of course you have our blessing. And we'll be up waiting for you. And we will reimburse all concerned, of course, and blah and blah. And the best way to cut short this call? Remind them that this is somebody's mobile phone. Mr. Redfearn's, actually – well, what's a little white lie on a night like this? And suddenly the phone call's over. Cannot waste the phone bill of a teacher kind enough to blah, yes, I won't be late coming back, but I'm in safe hands now, blah, and I could use that drink, blah, and I don't think it will turn me into a raving alcoholic.

Easy, in the ascendancy, and rolling off the tongue deliciously. The conversation leaving behind the duty-bound investigations and speculations, and moving into the mutual land. Talking about music, and all the time something curious happening. Mr. Redfearn sipping at his shandy and lime, Mr. Waters throwing back three pints of bitter in less than half an hour, and Penny nursing first a brandy and then a Diet Pepsi. Getting to the music like it's the taboo subject of the night. Like it was sex or something wicked like that.

What were they so frightened of? And the curious thing starting up like it did, out of the blue. Mr. Redfearn acting like he hardly dared look at her. Waters making bad jokes and messing with his glass. The two of them exchanging glances that were meant no doubt to be discreet. Hard to interpret. Friends but not friends. Conspirators? *Rivals?*

All strange enough, but on top of that: *the curious thing*. The tune starting up again; every time she looked at them, whatever they were saying or not saying. Everything was bringing it on. And some tune it was, now that it was free to cut loose. More powerful than anything that had lived on the inside of her head before, startling in its intensity.

But why should it come to her now, like this? Waters was a jerk and his postal course was what you would expect from a jerk. But he was nothing worse than that. He wasn't worth this inspiration. He drank too fast, made facile jokes, spoke without first considering and held her look a bit longer than was necessary. So what? It made him a jerk. He was trying to fleece the gullible – he needed a smack in the eye.

So what was it?

And what was it about Mr. Redfearn?

And when Mr. Redfearn suggested that it was time they sorted out a cab, what was that look from Waters supposed to mean?

Mr. Redfearn sorted out a ride home and insisted on going along to see that she got home safely. It was the least he could do. Then Waters insisted too, and they'd exchanged looks again.

On the ride home she ended up with Waters sitting next to her, though he wasn't saying much by that time. Mr. Redfearn was in the front seat and saying even less. The taxi driver probably thought he was taking home the leftovers of a funeral party.

By the time Penny was getting out of the taxi and saying her thank yous again, the tune inside her head was splitting her skull down the middle. Her parents were already at the front door, and they waved the taxi off in a gesture of gratitude for bringing their daughter back safely.

She stayed up long enough to condemn Mr. Fat and Ugly to an eternity of brimstone, wringing a few tears from her mother's eyes, soaking up a handful of warnings and a tide of kisses, both maternal and paternal, and offering her sincere promise to be more careful in future.

Penny fell asleep long after she had heard out the last of her parents' sad and pitiful bedtime sounds. Fell asleep with a raging melody in her head and the face of two men, Waters and Redfearn, pasted onto the inside of her eyelids.

CHAPTER EIGHTEEN

Detective Inspector Nigel Roxburgh woke up on Sunday morning feeling heartily sick and more than a little tired. The pressures from above and below were starting to squeeze him like a Christmas walnut on Boxing Day afternoon.

But that was only half of it. The other half was Olive.

The case he had played by the book, more or less; the hours he had put in documented meticulously. All that was missing was that elusive piece of luck.

The unofficial idiot's guide stated: Play it straight; keep hounding at any, even the most desperate, lines of enquiry; be on the case twenty-four hours a day, or at least give that impression; bring people in from time to time, keep asking questions, questions, questions and under no circumstances allow the public or the politically motivated a clear shot at making a case for ineptitude or lack of commitment.

Yes, he had done that. All boxes ticked. Yes, he was still doing that. All by the book, even the tab on Waters. Yes, even the tab on Olive. Luck - it would come. You just had to keep the faith.

He reached across the empty double-bed and squeezed at a pillow. What did she see in that loser Waters? He thought back over the events of Friday. Olive giving him time; Olive letting him look around the house. Wasn't there a sign there? But she had only gone so far, not allowing him to look a little closer, a little deeper, to turn over a few rocks. That letter on Waters' desk, for instance. Would Olive have taken a peek later? No doubt about it. Could be there was nothing to see, but then again.

Olive had given him more than he had expected. Why? What did it mean? Did she have her own suspicions about Waters, suspicions that she wasn't ready to voice? Or was she letting personal feelings affect her judgement? What, finally, did Olive value most: the interests of justice, or her personal life?

No, Olive was a woman of integrity, despite her falling into the arms of a twat like Waters. But Olive was also a woman of needs, the most basic needs, and Waters – no, he didn't need to go there.

Or did he?

What would motivate a man like Waters to go around mutilating and murdering innocent men? What secret life was he inhabiting that might be the key? Waters was a man of secrets; of things hidden away. Nothing was ever hidden away without good reason. That was the detective's job, to find what was hidden and why.

Instinct suggested that Waters was not the one. Due a fall, most certainly; a walking hard-on with his greasy paws all over Olive - guilty as charged. But murder? That would be a miracle sent from heaven. Nail Waters and release Olive. Instincts could be wrong. Yes, they could be wrong.

He lay across the pillow, thinking over the details of Waters' reported movements on Friday night: walking down to the college; meeting up with Redfearn, the teacher from Valemore College, already interviewed, and the man who Waters had apparently been trying to find on the evening of the fourth murder. The two men proceeding to Redfearn's house, emerging later, walking back towards the college. Then the incident with the taxi-driver and the student: Miss Penny Henderson. The taxi-driver knowing nothing about the two men, but very pissed off about the fare-dodging young lady.

Then it turns out that Redfearn teaches Miss Henderson at Valemore College. The three of them go to the Feathers for a drink. *Cozy.* A taxi takes the three of them, drops the girl off - all very innocent and civilised. How thoughtful, noble, even. A young girl has an unpleasant experience at the hands of a taxi driver you definitely wouldn't trust your daughter with, if you had one, and it so happens that her music teacher is passing. *Convenient coincidence?* And what a stroke of luck that Redfearn and Waters are not the kind of men to take advantage of an attractive and vulnerable young girl's misfortunes. Almost too good to be true. The taxi drops Redfearn off.

Now: something interesting - possibly. Redfearn gets out of the cab and offers to pay. Waters gets out too but Redfearn tells him to get back in, it's late, he's going to bed. Waters, clearly inebriated, isn't ready for bed and starts sounding off. Redfearn walks away and opens his front door. Waters is still sounding off, not making much sense. Half-baked accusations centring on a girl.

Miss Henderson?

The plain-clothes officers in the unmarked car are as close as discretion allows, but can't catch all the words. Waters is clearly incensed about something – almost certainly to do with the girl. Redfearn gives up trying to pacify Waters; goes into his house, and the front door closes. Waters gets back in the cab and goes home. He doesn't come out again that night or even on Saturday.

The detective sat up.

Olive goes to town on Saturday morning, calls at a couple of High Street stores and then – whoa! Would you believe what a small world it can be? She bumps into her estranged detective husband and they end up going for a coffee. Good old Roxy plays it cool, avoids asking any obvious questions, but still manages to pick up that Olive is less than happy with lover-boy this morning. Seems he came home a bit drunk and a touch moody on Friday night, but no more is said about that. Looks like lover-boy's heading for that fall, could be soon, and what a tragedy that would be for all concerned.

And then, right off, she says it. After Roxy had left the house yesterday, Olive, bless her, had gone back into

Waters' work room. Reckoned she needed a stamp; must have thought he keeps his stamps under his letters in progress, but, what the hell - we'll forgive you this time, seeing as Mr. Secrets is the nearest thing in all of this to an injured party.

Something in the letter catches her eye. She doesn't like the tone of the letter he's writing to one of his postal students, the one whose music he keeps playing day and night. This was getting interesting enough for a second round of coffees, and that's what happened. And cool as a cucumber, Roxy asks who the student is, asks it matter-of-fact.

But Olive is still far too cute to fall for that one, suggesting that she's said too much already, though it was bugging her and oh, what the hell, what was she doing having this conversation with the man she used to love and who happens to have more important things on his mind right at the moment, like catching -

"Used to love?"

"Don't, Nigel."

"Don't what?"

"Don't play games with me. This is hard enough."

"Let's suppose ..?"

He started the sentence, but couldn't pluck up the heart to finish it.

"Let's suppose what, Nigel?"

"Nothing."

Then, after a long pause, all the while aware that she was studying him, dissecting him, he said, "I think it's good that we're starting to talk again."

"You do?"

"Yes," he said, lightly stroking the back of her hand. "As a matter of fact I do."

She didn't move her hand away, but held his gaze. "You were a bastard," she said.

"I know. It took me a long time to realise it, but I know it now."

Roxy got up and dressed. It was early Sunday morning, and still dark outside. He washed, shaved, drank two cups of black coffee and finished off the two slices of cold pizza that his stomach had bucked against the night before.

It occurred to him that if Waters and Redfearn both had the hots for the student - both of whom they were teaching, one way or another - then something was going to break and soon. It was the kind of out-of-the-blue turn-up that he and Olive needed. Open her eyes to the real nature of what she was shacked up with. She was getting the idea already, no doubt about that, but a touch of up-front scandal could save a lot of time and trouble.

It was right that he should take the lion's share of the blame for what had happened between them, no doubt about that either. He was more than prepared to take the lot and done with. There was nothing to be gained by pride, and everything still to be lost if he got into that point-scoring rubbish again. He would happily trade that grand, empty bed and throw in the whole ridiculous five bed-roomed façade and live in a tent, if it meant that he could reach over in the night and ... his foolishness, his unreasonableness over the years had driven her into the arms of Phil Waters, and this was the turn-around stroke of luck that he could have got down on his bended knees and prayed for.

Fastening his tie, he smiled into the mirror. "There's hope for you yet, Roxy, old son."

He glanced at his watch and turned his thoughts to the other business of the day. The team briefing, the press-conference, and the hour he would have to spend in the Chief's office, spinning out nothing and making it sound impressive. Fooling nobody, but that was hardly the issue, was it? Going through the motions expected of a man in his position - that was the point. Pity, he thought, that the gods of good fortune who were smiling once again on the holy institution of the Roxburghs could not extend their generosity. Could they not find it in their hearts to spare a little nod in the direction of catching one measly psycho with a penchant for cutting off dicks? Round off the year in style?

It was asking too much, asking for everything, really; yet if the gods of good fortune wanted to go all the way this Christmas and tie up the bundle to perfection, making none other than Phil-the-twat-Waters that measly psycho, then his gratitude would know no bounds.

"Hey, you up there!" he said, looking directly above. "Do it, make my day." He put his face up close against the mirror. "There's not a dick in town's gonna rest easy in its underpants until that sonofabitch is nailed. Now let's do it, Punk. Let's kick that ass all the way to the Human Zoo."

With a wink he left the house, full of bounce, full of belief that today was going to be a good day and that this good day was going to be the first of many good days and that the good days were about to turn into good weeks and that he stood on the threshold of a good rest of his life.

CHAPTER NINETEEN

It was Sunday afternoon when the call came. Penny was alone in the house. Mum and Dad were paying their Christmas visit to their parents' graves, something they always chose to do prematurely, as far as Penny was concerned; tying it to the date that her Mum's mother had died - a good three weeks before Christmas.

Penny and Susan had gone with them on previous years, though in truth they had long found the whole business morbid and more than a little dull. Penny asked if she could stay at home and finish some college work. Given the circumstances her parents didn't play up about it, driving off in silence down the street. She was playing over the four completed sections of *Sextet* on the piano when the house phone rang. Later, this coincidence would strike her as too remarkable to be dismissed as mere chance. It was a sign, a confirmation.

Earlier in the day she had spent time trying to work up ideas for the troublesome fifth part. But the melody that had swooped down on her in the company of Mr. Redfearn and that Waters guy, seemed reluctant to go anywhere in the bland light of home. There was nothing particularly wrong with it, at least nothing she could point a finger at. It was quite a strong melody, in fact; full of shape and flavour. It had character, *but whose?*

It was proving to be nothing more than a beautiful widow, a stranded orphan, sad and alone, incapable of hooking into what lay around it; tightly closed, unwilling to unfold, reluctant to develop. Sad and lonely widows and stranded, abandoned orphans could form the basis for magnificent music, but they were simply not the order of the day.

The image of the taxi-cab driver flashed into Penny's mind, and she imagined herself carving out the notes on his fat and hideous flesh. The thought amused her, but brought with it no great design; no interesting route out of the cul-de-sac down which her latest tune had taken her. Cutting off the dick of a creep like that might do the human race a favour, but gestures of that kind would not further her sister's cause. To become sidetracked now would be to abandon Susan. She had to remain focused or it was all in vain. To hell with art for art's sake, everything needed purpose, a direction, a goal as far as the magic was concerned. The music brought with it the magic and the magic brought with it the music, the perfect circle. And they had made that discovery together, the two of them. Little children, six years old; learning to play the recorder; starting to mess about on the piano; quickly discovering the possibilities, the applications.

There had been no first time, no great moment of revelation; at least, not one that Penny could recall. There were so many early examples, and they all blended in, forming a divine mush in the mind, providing no certain and concrete starting point. One of them had been hurt; one of them crying. It didn't seem important which one. Penny this week, Susan the next, tit for tat. The music soothed. In those first days it probably wasn't magic at all. A promise of what might be, a glimpse - if the path was followed.

To begin with it was comfort and little else. The healing came later, developing out of the knowledge that the other sister's musical balm had been created out of love and blessings. For a considerable period of time that was magic enough to make a difference.

But with age came experience, and the fall of innocence. No child can believe in Father Christmas forever. Or at least, not a *child's* Father Christmas. The fairy stories are held up to the light and a choice has to be made, and the girls together made their choice.

And together they kissed goodbye to the mundane visions of the adult world and opened their hearts to the angels and demons who sang in their dreams. And once the magic really kicked in, the possibilities appeared limitless. And in seeming to be limitless, became so. For all limits are set by minds. They knew that; they had discovered that. So long as they believed, so long as they kept the faith and locked the secret in their hearts and nowhere else, it could never fail them.

It didn't fail them. Not once, not ever. Physical hurt, sorrow, the harsh words and actions of those playground monsters who knew that there were secrets around them but couldn't find the way in to share them - to all the pains and sufferings of two young girls growing up in an unspectacular outside world, the magic had no limits.

The girls had grown up, their musical abilities had blossomed and the complexities of their healing rituals had surged forwards at an impossible rate. Talented as they were, they entered the terrifying gates of the teenage-kingdom and wept with joy and fear.

The power of their imaginations soon left behind their precocious talents at the keyboard and, in Susan's case, if only for a short while, the violin. (Penny still remembered fondly the day Susan declared that the violin was not her instrument. It was only after some digging on her part that she discovered the deeper reason: that the music teacher at school had chosen another girl to be first violinist in the school orchestra for the Christmas concert that year. It explained why Susan had made a doll that looked a lot like the teacher, and why she was sticking Mum's sewing needles into its eyes when she thought that Penny wasn't watching.)

To become mere virtuosos seemed wasteful of both time and energy. Vulgar displays were for the attention of others, and drew the attention of others. In bed at night in the darkness they preferred to talk glibly of curing the most wretched of human conditions through the power of their compositions. Imagining entire symphonies constructed to cure a range of cancers and schizophrenic delusions.

They had the keys to their own kingdoms, untouchable by the forces and the curses of the humdrum world. Yet even this fantastic dreaming had its own condition: for though there would be nothing in heaven and hell that they could not achieve with their secret gifts, they would gladly, in the fashion of highest and most melancholy romance, sacrifice their lives each to the other. Die a slave's death if need be.

They had been fine and inspiring times, those early teenage years. Innocence allowing everything to remain possible, experience turning them away from the world and back to the precious hearts of each other. And nobody, they swore, could ever break into their circle. Parents, teachers, classroom contemporaries, all were rigorously denied the knowledge of what the sisters could achieve together in their secret life.

They didn't boast; they knew the dangers of pride. What they had discovered and developed was too precious to be spilt on playground shows of strength; too fantastic for the mind of an infantile adult world that had chosen to live in false light.

The pacts had been drawn up. There would never be the crossing, never be the shedding of experience. Even at an age too young to understand the full implications of what they were promising to each other, they knew the gravity of the oaths they were taking. They were dazzling times and it was sufficient to be frequently astonished.

As the years passed the magic grew as surely as their limbs and their inquisitive, restless minds. Their progress was relentless.

Then Penny's fever struck one day. Her temperature wouldn't come down. Almost a week passed, the doctor calling twice a day, talk of hospitals, Susan sitting at the side of the bed holding her sister's scalding hand, singing her songs through the night, singing so softly that Mum and Dad never knew what fantastic medicine was being taken in the room next to them. Penny begging: *not hospital*; and Susan promising: *no, never.*

Over the years it evened out, more or less, though Susan would always hold the whip hand when it came to healing, as Penny held it when it came to suffering. And then the night of nights came, changing everything.

The night when they should have stayed together, instead of allowing others to come between them, forcing them apart. An examination of their allegiance, and they had failed. How could they have allowed it to happen, and so easily?

The phone was ringing through the empty house.

Penny stopped playing, her hands suspended above the keyboard. By the time she reached the phone it had stopped. She stood staring at it, waiting for it to start up again. A long minute passed; she almost gave it up. Then it started again, the voice at the other end professionally calm but recognisably excited. She could hear the thrill inside it, hiding underneath. Asking if Mr or Mrs Henderson were available, Penny telling the caller that they were not available, but that she could pass on a message; confirming that she was Susan's sister. Tension but not fear: bad news didn't come from a phone voice that was concealing excitement, unless they were employing psychos in the NHS these days.

The thought briefly amused Penny. *A career option, perhaps?*

"She's spoken," said the voice.

"What was that?"

"Susan. She's spoken. We thought that you ought to know right away."

"Yes, yes, thank you. But what did she say?"

"You will want to come over and see her?"

Yes, yes, yes, yes - but what did she say, what, what?

Penny put on her jacket and scribbled a note for her parents. Then she called a cab, hoping that Mr. Fat and Ugly was still helping the Roxburgh Blues with their enquiries.

CHAPTER TWENTY

Phil Waters looked at his watch. There was still no sign of Olive. He gummed down the flap on the A4 envelope and sat back in his chair. *Damn her if she wants to play games.* She'd got the grumps because he came in pissed on Friday night and hadn't wanted a shag. One night off; shore-leave - every man's entitlement, for God's sake! Why did women have to take these things so personally? Okay, so it wasn't like him, especially not after a couple over the eight, but what the hell, take a break once in a while, it's nothing to get wound-up about. Women: different system of logic altogether. Mars and Venus? *Apples and fucking pears!*

She'd given him the quiet treatment, like he'd been caught with another woman. Chance would have been a fine thing, with Marcus Redfearn as unofficial chaperone for the evening. And to ram the lesson home, she'd made a point of being out most of the weekend.

It wouldn't surprise him if she was seeing old Roxy-face again. After all, that's what all that picking him up and whisking him down to the nick had been about. Roxy being Roxy and letting him know that she was still his woman and all that crap. Big Mr. Murder, and Olive falling for the glamour. Some social worker ethos she had, wanting him back now that he's playing in the big-league.

Waters picked up the A4 envelope and allowed himself a cold smile. The letter had been half-written days ago, but he'd been uncertain how to finish it. He wanted to hear more of this remarkable music, for sure; but he didn't want anybody thinking they could take the piss and get his services cheap just by showing a bit of talent.

Meeting her like that: it was like falling out of a Christmas tree and landing on top of Snow White. She was a belter, and ripe for it, too. And Redfearn - helping her with her music was he? Some dark horse he had turned out to be. But he kept in a fine malt whisky, even if he'd started drinking orange squash for a living.

They'd got into that stupid argument about some of the girl's music being familiar, and where had they heard it before. Next thing they're ploughing through Redfearn's music collection and still nothing even comes close. But the whisky's good and there's worse ways of spending Friday evening. As it turns out, it's no big mystery anyway; so one of her themes sounds like a playground version of some old movie tune. So what?

Then back to playing her music at the piano, and the two of them acting like a pair of old boxers padding around, sizing each other up. How they didn't get to putting on the gloves and sorting it out that way, he still wasn't sure. The next thing Redfearn's getting pissed off big-time, not his usual self at all, and can't put it down to the booze because Phil Waters is still the only one drinking. Then they're out through the door, Mr. Orange Squash suddenly on a mission, saying it's time for an overdue pint at the Feathers, like he's trying to prove something. And then they run bang into the girl and the heart goes out of Redfearn, who compromises with a shandy.

Waters kissed the envelope. There was a post-box at the end of the street; it would catch first post Monday morning. Now the Redfearn business seemed about as important as the Olive business and the Roxburgh business. What mattered was what was inside that envelope.

He licked his mouth at the prospect of the girl opening it. In his mind's eye he watched her reading it, watched her reaction. It was time they stopped messing about with bits of paper flying around the postal system and got down to some real business. She must come around, bring anything that she's working on. He was excited at the prospect of working with her and what a great opportunity it would be for both of them.

He kept it reasonably restrained for the most part, but couldn't help letting some of his enthusiasm leak through into the last few paragraphs of the longest letter he had written in his entire life. They could come to some arrangement for payment for his services, but she was not to worry about that. There was always a way around these things. He'd also suggested that they could speed up their correspondence by using email. After all, if the technology was there, why not use it?

Waters was going out through the door as Olive was about to come in. There was a moment of stalemate before she let him pass, looking all the time at the envelope in his hand.

"Something for your new girlfriend?"

"Speaking again, are we, Ol?"

She went inside and Waters followed her. She was taking off her coat. He watched her take it off. Underneath was one of his favourites, a clingy white cotton dress that always made her arse look so inviting that he wanted to get down and take a bite out of it. He felt a hardening inside his trousers. She knows what she's doing, he thought. Keeping that thing pointed at me. She was taking off her shoes. He waited, forgetting why he had been so angry with her. His eyes were still fixed squarely on her behind when the question fizzed up onto his tongue. He asked it more politely than he might have, under different circumstances.

"Have you been to see the policeman?"

"So what if I have - what do you care?"

She turned around. The show was over. "Aren't you going to post your precious letter?"

"Have you been going through my things, Ol?"

"Oh, come on."

"I'm serious. Have you been reading my letters?"

"It was on your desk."

"So that makes it okay? Why did you go to see him?"

"Is that any of your business?"

A thick edge darkened the tone his voice. "You never read the final draft," he said, holding up the envelope and disappearing out the door.

Mr and Mrs Henderson arrived on the unit, having returned home from visiting the cemetery to find Penny's note. Scrambling over to Eaglesfield only a few minutes behind their daughter, the staff nurse told them how it had happened.

Susan had been sitting in the main lounge when the detective came in, wanting to speak to one of the staff. He had been to the home on a few occasions because of what had happened to Evelyn's cousin, the late Norman Sidcup. One of the care staff had said to Susan that the big dishy policeman was back again, and Susan had started crying. The care worker asked if she wanted to return to her room, and Susan indicated that she did. And once inside her room, she spoke.

She had been looking at the care worker in a way that had been described as "strange and intense" and the carer had asked if she was okay. Susan was opening and closing her mouth as though trying to form a word, her facial movements becoming more animated. The carer heard a breathy sound, as though something was struggling to come out. (She had made a song and dance about it, likening the whole process to childbirth.) She'd placed an ear to Susan's mouth and then heard it, the word finally delivered.

"Penny."

The family went in to visit Susan, but it seemed she had shut up shop once again. Penny insisted on a few moments in private with her sister before they all made their way home.

Sextet

In the privacy of Susan's room the sisters held hands. "The magic's working," said Penny. "It never went away. We just stopped believing. Four of them dead, Susan: you'll be home for Christmas." A tear bubbled onto Susan's lower eyelid, and trickled down her pale cheek. Penny kissed her. "I'm going now. I'm going to find Mister Five. It's all for you, Susan."

As the three of them made their way along the corridor, they passed the detective coming in. He nodded at them collectively, but seemed to single Penny out for a smile.

Inside her head the thoughts exploded like so many devices placed along a gunpowder trail. She thought of the cab-driver, Waters, Redfearn, Mr. Humanities.

Which would you care to investigate next, Mr. Detective?

As though he had heard her thoughts, he turned back. Penny heard his voice like an endless echo that she could not outrun.

"Mr and Mrs Henderson?"

They turned around.

"Penny Henderson?"

She heard him introducing himself, heard it as though his voice was trapped inside a thick fog. Then the word *Susan* struck and the fog instantly cleared, like a wand had been waved through it. He was offering his sorrows for what had happened to Susan, making out in that official way that he knew how hard it must be for them. Then, casually, like it was of little importance, he asked if any of them had met Evelyn's visitor. He recalled the exact evening for them, reminding them of the poor unfortunate man's description, all precise in detail yet remarkably matter-of-fact in delivery.

A seasoned practitioner. A man not to be trusted.

Evelyn's visitor? No, they hadn't seen him. Penny had been visiting that night, but no, she hadn't noticed him. Was she sure? Yes, of course she was sure.

Was she imagining it, or did he carry on looking at her?

Detective Roxburgh apologised for detaining them, after listening respectfully to Mrs. Henderson's brief soliloquy on what a good job the police were doing against all the odds stacked against them. As the family walked away, Penny looked back over her shoulder, and caught a momentary glimpse of how deeply one human eye could look into another.

He was on to her.

Or was he like all the rest - merely a man with a man's eye?

The music was back inside her again. And she knew precisely how the days of the future were numbered.

When Phil Waters returned from the post-box, Olive was already soaking in the bath-tub. He would have left her to her privacy if she hadn't called out to him.

He took his place on the adjacent toilet seat and tried to keep his eyes off her breasts. She asked him if he loved her and he told her that of course he did. He asked her if she was thinking of going back to her husband and she said that she wasn't sure what she was doing, she was too mixed up. She asked him if he really was having an affair with the woman he had written to, and he answered her truthfully that he was not.

The thing inside his trousers was asking its eternal question again. Being nothing more than its mouthpiece and its advocate, he asked her if she wanted to make love. Within an hour they had made love twice, and Olive had smoked precisely the same number of cigarettes.

And no one was more surprised by anything in the mortal world than Phil Waters, waking a couple of hours later, discovering Olive's half of the bed empty, going downstairs to find her, large glass of brandy in her hand, crying her little heart out.

CHAPTER TWENTY-ONE

Monday morning Penny could not take her eyes off Mr. Redfearn. The very air around him seemed alive with possibilities. She watched him and listened to him. It was a pleasure. Mr. Redfearn had unexpectedly grown quite beautiful. Beauty, she knew, could be many things. Sacrificial lambs were nothing if not beautiful.

At break there were no signals from Mr. Redfearn. Lunch came and still no signs. She was back early for the afternoon, but nothing. Afternoon break - was that the first hint? That single raising of the eyebrows? And then - not when she was alone with him in the classroom, early once again, the first one back; but rather when the class was dribbling drowsily back in - he said, almost as though it were some long-distance after-thought and quite probably the least important thought in a long and drab day filled with them, "Could I see you afterwards, Penny?"

She watched him fumble through the remainder of the afternoon, and when the bell brought it all to an end, she thought how he looked scared enough to leave his skin behind and orbit the planets for a while. That's how it looked from the back of the classroom, through the eyes that never left him.

Penny waited until the class had left and the room had fallen silent. She walked out to the front and took a chair next to his desk, and let the moment grow. The door was still open, of course. Mr. Redfearn had been teaching teenage girls long enough to know the rules. She watched, without breathing, as he took it from his desk drawer. The first four parts of a student's humble offering to the pain gods and the rain kings that watched over this sad world.

Her masterpiece. *Susan's medicine*. What would he say? What *could* he say? "Penny," he said. "I'm afraid I have a confession to make." She let him make it. "I have not been able to find a single thing to fault here." That wasn't it; there was more to come. "To tell you the truth, I have not been able to stop playing your music, or to get it out of my mind, for that matter. The other night ... that ... unfortunate incident ..."

He was playing with his tie. He didn't need to explain anything. *Relax, Mr. Redfearn.* Dispense with this rambling and *tell it.* He coughed, begged her pardon; tried the sentence again. "I didn't realise he was familiar with your music. Well, what I mean to say - not until earlier that evening. I must apologise."

She yawned, right in his face. It was a cruel thing to do, but she had to stop him somehow. And the end justified the means. It shut him down. The apologies, the fidgeting - all done with. *So where do we go from here, Mr. Redfearn?* He was taking a breath. In the second before he spoke, she felt the room electrifying around them.

"I think, Penny, that you have a remarkable talent. More than that, I think that there could be a market, of sorts, for your work." He was hesitating, unsure how to deliver his conclusions. This was costing him, and there were beads of sweat breaking out, bathing his face. "I wish I knew how best to advise you from here, but I think that you should without doubt seek some route of publication. I mean it." He *did* mean it. *But all that effort to say so little?* There had to be more. He was starting to shuffle the papers around his desk.

"I would like to hear you play my music, Mr. Redfearn."

He glanced at his watch, though he knew as she did that he had nowhere else to be but there with her now.

"I really would love to hear you play it for me, Mr. Redfearn."

"Here?" he asked, stupidly.

"Where else?" asked Penny.

"It's just that, I mean, I didn't wish to embarrass -"

He was looking at his watch again, holding the look as though he couldn't work out how to read the dial.

"You're right," she said. "It isn't very private, is it?"

He was starting up on his old hobby horse, how the college really should improve practice facilities for students. This was safe ground. He could talk this talk until spring came, but there still wouldn't be the facility.

"Do you have a piano at your house, Mr. Redfearn?"

The question appeared to stun him. Could a man fall dead to the floor because he was too afraid to say yes and at the same time terrified of saying no? She could not leave him to suffer like this. "I mean, it's just that it would be more private, that's all. I really would love to hear you play my music. I haven't heard anybody else play it and I think it would be very helpful."

Of course, he would have to make the correct objections. But the decision had been made. It was already a blush stretching from his collar to his hairline. Whatever arrangements he might seek to impose, whatever discretions, there was no question that before this day was over she would be entering the private place where Mr. Redfearn dreamed his most intimate dreams. And from Mr. Redfearn's palace of dreams it would be a mere stone's throw to completion.

And for Susan: resurrection.

Penny, in the eternity it took Mr. Redfearn to lower the flag on the remains of this monumental day, remembered the time when Dad thought he'd got cancer. Finding a lump somewhere delicate. Of course, she and Susan weren't supposed to know anything about it. They were still at school and had to be protected from the fears and truths of the grown-up world. Dad was being Dad and doing his best to appear cheerful and unconcerned.

Though they weren't supposed to know anything, the day he changed back was as obvious to them as the change in light when the clocks move forward at Easter. They could have told him exactly what the feared illness was, along with the dates of its imagined onset and the lifting of its curse.

And during those tense - yet with hindsight, almost laughable - days, the two sisters had tried extending their magic; tried its application outside of the usual parameters.

They had composed a piece of music, beginning all soulful and forlorn but leading to an uplifting, rousing finale. They had completed the piece two days before the lifting of the curtain surrounding Dad, and so inevitably believed again in their own supernatural ministrations. This belief had metamorphosed into something even richer. The girls, treating their own minor ailments in this fashion, had always been able to stand as close witnesses to the process. They had seen and felt, from inside and out, how quickly and thoroughly their efforts had been repaid. With Dad this had been different: he didn't know the powers that were working for him and therefore could not possibly have enlisted the rewards of applied sympathy.

There was another way of looking at it: he had not been ill in the first place. It had been nothing but a false alarm - nothing to cure and so nothing proven or disproven. But there were always two ways of looking at anything. You either had faith in what you were doing, in your own gifts, or else you languished in cynicism and scepticism like almost every other member of the human race.

The dawning of these ideas had at first been too painful for Susan and Penny, and they had resisted them. It seemed to lessen the gift, at least in terms of its wider potential and implications. In time though it taught them a special secret, and became the most profound lesson of their childhoods: that all people lived in separate worlds and that rarely did two worlds collide. What they had might well be unique, it was certainly rare enough. Most importantly, it must never be compromised or risked for the sake of experimentation, or for the sake of trying to widen a closed circle. Dad's phantom illness had been a warning, and once they had recognised the extent of the warning, they had written from it an absolute law.

Penny had never seen anybody look at a watch as often as Mr. Redfearn on that late afternoon. It was the first thing he did when they entered his house, when he asked if she wanted a drink, when he offered to take her jacket. Perhaps he timed everything and made copious notes that filled volumes.

While he switched on the kettle and started organising the drinks, she looked through the library of sheet music that filled the shelves on either side of his piano. It was an interesting collection, she thought, eclectic yet comprehensive; a man with a passion for music; a man of some considerable taste.

She smiled to herself: All that huffing and puffing back in the classroom - like he was Napoleon working out a strategy that would bring him the world. And all it had amounted to was her ringing her parents to say that she was staying at college to finish off some course work, and then a discreet walk through the deserted campus and down through the few streets that led like a fated arrow to Mr Redfearn's comfortable little home.

"Sugar?" he shouted through from the kitchen. She wanted to shout back, *Yes, Honey?* He would have died on the spot! "No sugar, thanks. And white, please, Mr. Redfearn."

He'd asked if she had any ideas for parts five and six. Some, she told him. Nothing worked out. *Having difficulties with Part Five.*

More out of chivalry than anything else, she suspected, he offered to assist - if that was appropriate, of course.

He came back out of the kitchen carrying two hot mugs of tea, one bearing Rupert the Bear, the other Wagner. He gave her Rupert and then he was back to looking at his watch, or glancing over at the piano. Mr. Redfearn was clearly not practised in the art of entertaining young ladies.

At last he made his move. Taking her by surprise in his sudden decisiveness, he went over to the piano and took out of the stool a copy of her music. The room closed in around them as he started to play.

Penny eased back in her chair. This was unreal: Mr. Redfearn playing *her* music.

The first movement was ending already. He was halfway through the second part. Over before it had started, she could see that now. The third became the fourth and already he was sitting motionless at the piano. The concert was finished.

How long had it taken? Now *she* was thinking about time.

She was not writing pop songs. She was going the distance, journeying to the other side, to another world. One could not travel that road in the blinking of an eye.

He was looking at her thoughtfully. She said, "How long were you playing?"

"I didn't realise we were timing?"

You've timed everything else. "You play well."

Whatever Mr. Redfearn was seeking, it was not praise, and he gave her an embarrassed, almost shameful smile.

"Sorry," she said. "I didn't mean to patronise you. I think I can see where I've rushed the ideas. Where I can slow it down and develop some of the themes."

"I think that what you've written so far is perfect."

"No, you don't have to -"

"It's beautifully balanced. I wouldn't change a note of it."

"It still has two parts to come."

"I realise that," he said.

"How can you say it's perfectly balanced when you don't know what comes next?"

"Everything leads the listener forward. If it ended there it would be unbalanced. But it doesn't end there, and frankly I can't wait to hear what follows."

"That's the problem," she said. "Nothing does."

He had a look of expectation, as though she was going to finish it there and then. Penny stood up, walked over toward him. "May I?" she asked.

He got up, leaving her to the keyboard.

"This is all I have," she said. "I don't know where it's going."

She began to play, filling out tunes in her head, extemporising around them. She played for a couple of minutes and then stopped. "I don't know where to go with it, honestly."

Mr. Redfearn was frowning. "That's really all you have?"

"Why do you say it like that?"

"Because I don't believe it. Would you like another drink?"

He sighed heavily and turned away, taking the look of disappointment with him.

Penny got up from the piano and stared at the back of him. Was this it? Was he framing it out of gross inexperience, or was this an act by a consummate artist? He might turn around and reveal himself the fumbling amateur, or he may have about him the gleam of a man who is turning in the performance of a lifetime. The difference mattered - as life and death. The music itself would turn on the answer to that mystery.

She could feel the blade in her jacket.

He was turning now, and the breath was catching in her throat. He was facing her, but it was not the face, not any of the faces, that she had expected. He sat at the table, the weight of the Earth crushing down on him. "Would you say that you tend to work from inspiration?" He gestured for her to join him at the table, and she did so.

"Yes," she said. "I think I do."

He eyed her for a moment. "I never used to believe in the idea of inspiration," he said. "I used to subscribe to the old adage about creativity owing more to *perspiration*. But then what do I know? I've never created anything."

He had stopped looking at his watch. He was trying to say something, and the effort appeared to be taking up all of his available head space. "I used to imagine, as a child, that the great masters simply wrote it down in a white-heat of inspiration. The Mozart model, you might say. But then I grew out of that way of thinking and went totally the other way."

"I thought that was how Mozart *did* write."

Redfearn shrugged. "How can anybody know what goes on inside another head? I think that all art is a series of experiments in the mind. Some work it out on paper, others, perhaps blessed merely with a greater memory work it out on the inside. Mozart might well have improvised inside his head." He paused. "Are you sure you wouldn't like another drink?"

"I don't know what point you're making," said Penny, again ignoring his offer. He was looking at his watch again. The certainty struck her: he knew exactly what he wanted to say. His mental battle was over. It was a matter of choosing the words, framing the sentences.

"An idea," he said. "Everything has to start somewhere."

She let his awkward pauses go untended. Maybe he had even rehearsed them, timing them to perfection. The whole thing orchestrated like a true Wagnerian.

"Even if the greatest artists played mind experiments," he said, "mental jam-sessions, there still had to be some spark, and there still does."

Was he getting to it, or was he moving away again? It was difficult to tell from his words alone. But his face, yes, his expression was contorting towards the punch-line.

"The key to you moving on with this, Penny, is to get back into the mind-set that brought you this far. Go back to the beginning and remind yourself *why*."

Mr. Redfearn had never sounded so esoteric. His practicalities had always been his founding-stone and his anchor. That was part of his appeal. But this junk - what was he doing?

With his next question he unclothed her.

"Penny, who were you thinking about?"

Her mind was reeling. It was as if she had missed a line. How had he got from that to this? She said, "I don't know what you mean."

He brought off an awkward smile. "A young girl," he said. "You must have some, oh, I don't know - some romantic ideas. *Ideals,* even."

The blade, cold and hard, was burning through the thin material of her shirt.

"I can hear some of the yearning in your music, Penny. I think that you have somebody very special in mind. I believe that is what gives this music such a solid structure. Substance. If you can remind yourself of your purpose, then you have a chance of finishing this thing."

He put his face into his hands and shook his head. "The old cliché was never more apt: those who do, do, while those who can't ... teach. That's me in a line, Penny. That's me in a nutshell. Sad but true. I wish I could *do*, but the *do* part is missing. So I try to be profound, and it sounds like an old fool trying to say something clever."

Was this a line? Was she supposed to put an arm around him and comfort him all the way upstairs to his waiting spider's web?

"I think I will have that drink, Mr. Redfearn."

She watched him go into the kitchen. Music was erupting inside her, chaotic and confused. She tried to focus on Susan but couldn't even see her sister's face.

Standing up she opened her jacket, and began unbuttoning her shirt.

Mr. Redfearn's voice rang from the kitchen. "Tea again - or coffee this time?"

Penny hesitated. Her shirt was open and her hands moved to unfasten the belt on her jeans. "Don't mind," she shouted back. "Surprise me." The music was ebbing away, deserting her. Susan - drifting, already miles from the shore line. She re-buttoned her shirt, fastened her jacket. In a moment she was sitting back at the table, barely holding herself together as Mr. Redfearn came back from the kitchen. She felt the collapse beginning as he set the drinks down. Dimly she heard him trying to comfort her, though she couldn't distinguish his words for the thundering of blood inside her ears.

He was taking her home in a taxi, and if it was Mr. Fat and Ugly driving then he must have kept his fat and ugly comments to himself. The ride was a silent affair. She had told her tale to Mr. Redfearn. He had listened and then he had taken her home, and everything from there was dreamy; him saying something as he helped her to the door, something that she didn't catch, maybe nothing at all, her parents thanking him profusely from the doorstep like they wanted to fall down before him and kiss his feet. And then she was lying in bed, the kisses from her parents washing over her, and she was falling away from them as the darkness beckoned.

CHAPTER TWENTY-TWO

Penny's sleep was as brief as it was haunted. She was back in time, trying to get Susan to understand that they had to get the music finished. Susan saying it would wait, Penny insisting it wouldn't. Telling Susan that he was just a pimply-faced dork wanting a feel of her tits, and Susan smiling back provocatively - and it hurt, it hurt like hell.

Penny feeling the lump in her throat and trying to talk around the lump. Trying to tell Susan that it might destroy the magic forever letting a stranger into the circle. Susan looking at her like she was stepping through the portal, out of childhood and into the badlands of an adult world.

But the lump wouldn't let the words out right, and she could feel Susan moving away from her into a new orbit that she couldn't quite comprehend, not yet. Breaking the magic, that was why it happened in the first place. Susan brought it down on herself. She would not listen.

The boy, the pimple on legs, had nothing to do with it, not directly. Susan never got to the date. He had been the poor excuse for temptation, and it had proven enough. The devil, his eye on the target, can make good use of the most pathetic tools.

In the dream, if it was a dream and not some exposed tunnel that led straight to hell, Penny was pinned to the dark sky above the abandoned theatre, fixed there for eternity to look down and relive. The policeman was there this time; his back turned as they raped Susan and tore the heart out of the poor girl. All the time his back was turned and he was scratching his head trying to work it out like it was Chinese algebra, when all the time it was as easy as pissing with the wind.

She punctured the dream with a single cry, and the next thing Dad was talking gently on one side of her and Mum was sobbing on the other.

Whatever time it was, with Mum full of pills and sleeping, and Dad still full of fight and story, she listened as he told her the tale about when they were fourteen.

They had a tortoise-shell cat called Bubbles, and they thought he was dying. The two girls were playing the piano, and didn't know that Dad was eavesdropping outside the door. They had stopped playing and were chattering about saving Bubbles.

"You were saying to Susan about making up a tune so that Bubbles would live." Mr. Henderson laughed, squeezing his daughter's hand as he did so. "And he did live. Another year until that fool down the street backed over him." Mr. Henderson shook his head. "There was something very wonderful about your naivety over that cat. You were both so convinced that you saved Bubbles' life."

Penny looked at her dad, amazed.

"That tune you made up - the one that *saved* poor old Bubbles - it was a good one. It had both of you in it though I think it was yours to begin with." He laughed again, softly. "It drove me mad when I heard you playing it again last week."

Penny felt herself sliding up into a sitting position. "Last week?"

"I knew I'd heard it before. I'd assumed it was off the radio. Never thought it might be something my daughters once made up for a cat that needed worming."

Marcus Redfearn lay staring at the ceiling. His mind was full of music and story. All of that pain inside the poor girl; it made him want to weep. Better to help than to empathise. Quite how was another matter. Two sisters using music to keep the evil of the world at bay; using it to heal the sickness around them – it was incredible. And now this terrible thing had happened to one of them: it was like Penny had been cut adrift. If he could help her it would be the best thing he had ever done in a largely fatuous existence.

But what ... and how?

At some point he found a brief port of sleep, and in it he dreamed about Penny completing her precious *Sextet.*

He saw her sitting at his piano, playing it, writing it down; holding up the finished thing. Saw but didn't hear it, as though someone had turned off the sound so that he could only imagine the beauty of the music. The most incredible part of the dream was right at the end, when the music was played for the first time through loudspeakers. Susan lying in front of the speakers in an empty classroom at college; Penny and he joined in prayer as the music filled the room. Susan standing up filled with light, the music finding its climax.

Susan walking towards them, *restored.*

He got out of bed long before his alarm clock signalled the start of the last day of term. The images from the dream were so clear and sequenced in his head that it was less like the remnants from a crazy dream and more like scenes from a remembered film. Making himself a strong coffee, he thought of what she had said about Phil Waters' competition; about her wish to immortalise the music for her sister.

He went over to his collection of CDs and picked one at random, taking the disk out of its box, turning it about in his fingers. He imagined it bearing the name: *Penny Henderson,* and the dedication: *For Susan Henderson.* Everything that he had ever thought about faith, religion, and superstition – all the conscious or subliminal fragments that had passed through his head over the years - bombarded him, and he knew, absolutely, that Penny had to accomplish all that she had set out to do. Even if the completion of this thing made not a jot of difference to Susan's ruined life, it could make the difference between sanity and insanity for her tortured sister.

He would see to it that she finished her *sextet*. And he would see that the finished work was recorded - at his own expense if necessary. There was nobody else to buy for this Christmas, except his mother in Chester who would herself be richer in the CD department this year with the unwrapping of a requested Richard Clayderman collection. A rod for his own back, as she would doubtless play it through Christmas lunch, through New Year, and every time that he went back to visit for the next twelve months.

He looked at the CD in his hand: Beethoven's Ninth, Karajan conducting. He hadn't played this old favourite in years. Carefully erasing the prints he had scattered over the disk, he selected the final movement: *Ode to Joy.*

A revolution had occurred. A tale had done it, changing him forever. He listened to the music, glad to be alive.

CHAPTER TWENTY-THREE

It was two against one. Mr and Mrs Henderson, bleary and dazed, did not think their daughter fit to make the journey to Valemore on this ice-crisp December morning, be it the last day of term or the end of civilisation.

"I'll ring the college," said Mrs. Henderson. "Mr. Redfearn will understand ... given the circumstances." The last part of the sentence was uttered sotto voce, and it had the paradoxical effect of making it sound like it was spoken over a PA system to a crowd of thousands.

Penny had no argument, though she knew that she had to be somewhere. It was written on the inside; part of the inevitable march to a sacred climax that would rescue Susan. But how to put *that* into words?

It turned out that she didn't have to. Fate had decided to change the cards. The signal came with Mrs. Henderson's words about Mr. Redfearn understanding still hanging in the air.

The tell-tale sound at the front door: Penny shot through the hallway and liberated the letter from the jaws of the letter-box. Taking it upstairs to her room, she tore open the envelope to find a three-page letter paper-clipped to what appeared at first to be a single sheet of blank music manuscript paper. The manuscript page was not blank, though; not quite. There was no musical notation on the page, but a number had been handwritten at the top.

'5'

The letter was from Waters. He was banging on about how great it had been bumping into her like that. Then there was some meant-to-be-funny stuff about the fat taxi-driver. The tone wasn't genuine, though it was trying hard to be.

She couldn't pin down exactly the phrase that it conjured in her mind, but "too familiar" was close enough.

And all that crap about a sextet traditionally implying the number six, and that five usually came before it, then a string of sloppy conceits and skin-crawling homilies - the man was practically jerking-off on the page. *Easier face to face; come to some arrangements about payment.* The creep wasn't even subtle.

Penny could hear footsteps on the stairs, her mother's light tread, and then her father's voice, short and sharp, the footsteps halting, a brief exchange, barely above a whisper, footsteps descending. She looked again at the horn-driven missive in her hands, and the light inside her head switched on.

Five.

He was right. It was the only way forward. My God, it was perfect.

She looked at the address in the top-right corner of the letter's first and least obscene page. She had walked that street, even looked at the house. The significance had been there from the beginning; it had needed a little nudge to bring it to life. Her deeper mind, where the magic soared, had been ahead of the game all along.

She placed the letter and the manuscript page back inside the envelope, and went downstairs.

Mum and Dad were standing in the living room looking uneasy. Mum was by the phone, staring at the handset like a guilty child seeking confession. "I rang the college," she said, tilting her weak chin as though finally confronting a dark fear. "There's no problem, Penny." Mrs. Henderson glanced nervously towards her husband. "Is there, dear?"

Mr. Henderson edged forward, looking at his daughter with an appeasing smile that was clearly not of his own making. Penny spared him. He was about to do the honourable thing and come to his wife's rescue. Penny didn't need to see that. "I'm sorry," she said. "You're right, and I'm not going in." Her head was bursting with the music. "I'm going back to bed," she said. "I need to rest."

Mr and Mrs. Henderson exchanged the briefest of smiles. "Good girl," said Mrs. Henderson. "My good, good girl."

Olive did something that morning that her colleagues at the office would be profoundly proud of. She had left the bed of one man for the bed of another. Less than two hours separated two mighty orgasms, two very different pricks involved. And to paraphrase a recent, drunken sermon courtesy of the *Right Reverend* Phil Waters - *Emily Pankhurst practically whooping out a jig for the soil-blessed worms to dance along to*.

Phil had been back on form, no doubt about that. But she had been riding somebody else's horse. He had been the stallion of old, but in his eyes there was some other undressed mare, and Olive was too long in the tooth not to realise that she was no longer seeing some other facet of her own reflection in those deceiving eyes. Still, she took the ride and it was good, though it didn't stop him being an arse-wipe of the first order. And it didn't stop her making her decision, there and then, in the heat of it. A suitably fine swansong, but then the finale *ought* to be something to remember, she thought. Still, her bread was buttered more wholesomely in another, older place, and she was going back.

Olive had rung work from her car, though not to tell the girls in the office that she was halfway through a historic double. That would wait until she could tell it in person. For now it was enough to say that she was ill; that something hadn't agreed with her.

Then she'd called Roxy - and he was grateful for the call. This case he was working on was going nowhere and the pressures were building. The man needed some good loving, and he would never be able to resist his one true baby.

Olive drove across town like a bat out of heaven. She was going to see D.I. Nigel Roxburgh with vital information, and who would stand in her way? Who, in this excuse for a town, on this day of days would halt her with that kind of promise hanging from her lips? So what that the information had less to do with murder and everything to do with calling off the legal machine and saving a marriage.

Roxy was waiting. He had nowhere to go except through the motions, giving the public a professional illusion, the appearance of decisive action when there was nothing to act on. He was waiting for her, and she was coming to him like a guided missile ticking down to zero.

She was barely through the door, her own front door, and already they were kissing, the urgency of it killing the need for awkward preludes and cautious reunion speeches. Fireworks! All cylinders firing in a blaze of glory! Fire and smoke! She could still remember, in the post-coital glow, what she had seen in Phil Waters. But all of that was here with old Roxy too - all of that and more, a sight more. Absence had put the lead back in his pencil, and absence had opened his eyes to what he had taken for granted for too long. She had looked into Waters' eyes not two hours earlier and seen somebody else reflected; looking into Roxy's eyes now was like being deified on an altar, or at least a silver screen. It didn't get better than that, though it might.

Roxy made some phone calls and then they went out for lunch, eating lightly and talking heavily. They rushed home again with fire in their hearts, leaping the stairs, tearing each others' clothes off, acting like teenagers again.

Olive was getting her breath back, putting the colossal rush of thoughts into dazzling perspective, when he reached across the feather-stuffed pillows and took her hand. The look in his eye was as bright as a star and her reflection even clearer inside it this time. And she was moving again, back towards him, her breathing picking up once more. If there had been any doubt, on either side that the light had gone out, then that doubt was being nailed to the cross in D.I. Roxburgh's bed.

Marcus Redfearn moved through the last day of term like a ghost. The day had been over before it had started. A note from administration: three students would not be attending. The absence of two of them didn't surprise him.

He almost made it through the day before the axe fell in the final session. A chance remark; one student choosing that moment to bad-mouth another – absent - student; some end of term extemporisation. A meagre-talented girl coming close to making a fool of herself at the piano; attempting to improvise around the theme of *Silent Night.* A kind remark from Mr. Redfearn misinterpreted, and then a sarcastic riposte as the girl returned from the piano to her desk, lighting the fuse, completing the circuit. A moment ago he was surviving; now he needed the bell to ring, loud and long.

Falling to pieces in front of them, he had to be out of there.

When the bell did ring, and the classroom was finally emptied for the last time that year, Redfearn sat still behind his desk, unable to move. There was nothing to be done and nowhere to go. They had gone and closed the door behind them.

A weight was pressing down on him so heavily that he thought it would bury him. He sat at his desk, staring at the closed door. After a while he rested his head onto his folded arms and wept.

CHAPTER TWENTY-FOUR

Penny felt as though she was about to burst through the walls. There was enough energy, enough fury stoked up inside her to take the Henderson house to the moon. Number Five was out there. He had a face, a name, even. The key to the success of *Sextet* lay here. It would point inevitably to the climax. Climaxes were easy; they wrote themselves on what preceded them. It was finding the pathway to it that took the craft.

All of that was academic, with Penny holed up in her bedroom like the pampered prisoner that she had become. Mum and Dad appearing at regular intervals with hot drinks and sympathy; a small child with a high fever.

They wouldn't leave the house. Christmas almost on them and they couldn't find a reason to join the crowds of sheep forming disorderly queues in every worn-out crevice of this arsehole town.

She'd considered it all. The drainpipe, the bolt downstairs and out through the door; a hundred lies and none of them convincing. The morning was all but gone already. Waters' face; Waters' words; filling her brain; calling to her.

Dad was standing in the doorway. "I know what's on your mind," he said. He walked into the room, and stood at the window looking down into the untended garden below. "I know what you have to do," he said.

Penny waited for him to turn around. She said, "Do you think Susan could still be home for ..?"

She paused, heard his sigh.

"We could make it a quick call, I suppose," he said. Penny frowned, though she knew well enough what he was saying. Still, she let him spell it out. "Your mum's popping over to town after lunch. I think we can safely assume that two hours will not prove fatal."

Susan hadn't spoken since her one-word outburst a few days earlier; but when Mr. Henderson gave the two sisters a few moments privacy, she spoke Penny's name again before turning her head to one side, as if to indicate that she was ready to hear what her sister had to say.

"It's happening," said Penny. "It's coming together." She took Susan's hand, and felt the power of her grip.

When Mr. Henderson returned to the room, the sisters had softened their fierce handshake, exchanging unequal kisses, accepting one-sided goodbyes. And then father and daughter were holding hands, walking through the corridors, out of the building and towards the car park.

It had arrived. The moment.

Penny stopped walking, smacked her head.

"What is it?" asked Mr. Henderson.

Divine innocence, thought Penny. Or else *playing* the innocent. Were all men so full of deceit? What did it matter? "I forgot to tell Susan something."

Mr. Henderson waved a finger and pretended to look paternal. "You girls," he said. "What am I to do with you?"

"I could get the bus, Dad."

She should have walked away then, not waited. The hesitation returned the initiative, the cue to saying something to ease the awkwardness. "What do you get up to, Penny?"

She pushed out her bottom lip and shrugged.

"You're not writing the music again?"

"You know I am, Dad."

"I don't mean that. I know you write for college. What I mean is …"

He stopped talking. Penny saw the thought falling into place behind his eyes, and the tearful mistiness rolling in across his face. He took her in his arms and it felt like he was going to pull her through his flesh and right the way into his heart. "Penny," he said. "How do we stand it?" She felt his weight shifting, the pressure easing. "You do it," he said. "You write it, Penny. Make her well again." He took a note from his wallet. "Taxi, okay?"

"Okay."

"I can cover for you until four. After that you're on your own."

She watched him drive away. Into the rapidly descending gloom she whispered, "Goodbye, Dad."

In the back of the taxi Penny felt the burden of her thoughts leaving the demon-riddled landscape of Phil Waters and head to a better place. *Mr. Redfearn.* He wanted to help. Everything about him proclaimed it. And he had pointed her in the right direction without having the faintest notion of where she was heading.

He could have made a worthy Number Five, but deserved better. His place, as clear as the North Star on a freezing-clear night, could never have been as mere penultimate. He was the love waiting for her when she spilled out of Waters' wicked door; the warm-hearted giver whose reward would never comfortably fit inside the kingdom of misery where the damned alone thrive.

Penny sat back as the taxi passed Valemore College. There was only one setting for her song of songs.

Mr. Redfearn's image began to dissolve, and in its place returned one less deserving of pity.

CHAPTER TWENTY-FIVE

Detective Inspector Nigel Roxburgh's mobile phone was in the pocket of the jacket he had left over the back of the rocking-chair when its plain, shrill tone cut like a blade through the blissful reunion. He jumped out of bed and padded over to retrieve it. "Yes," he said, with quiet authority.

Olive lay gazing happily at her husband's naked body. In spite of herself, she couldn't help making comparisons with the body she had left behind. Okay, in purely physical terms it was a Waters victory. But on points; not a straight KO. Old Roxy had shed a few pounds along the way and the loss hadn't done any harm at all. And in every other department, Roxy took back the points. Even his arrogance seemed tempered these days.

Yet Olive knew that absence could do strange things to a man, and usually on a temporary basis. The signs did look good though, and from her cheerful position as she watched his impressively firm behind shimmer deliciously, she decided that she was more than willing to take the chance.

Ending the call, he put the phone back into his jacket pocket and slid his exposed jewels into a pair of sleek boxers. "Sorry," he said. "You know how it is."

"How could I forget? Are you going to be long?" She waved her hands. "I know, don't ask."

He laughed. "Actually," he said, thoughtfully, "I'm hoping I won't be too long. I know a great restaurant. We could check it out later. Why don't you stick around? Re-acquaint yourself with home sweet home."

After he had kissed her goodbye, Olive rested her head back on the pillows. The queen of all she surveyed. Waves of contentment washed over her, quickly consuming her.

A fairy tale princess again, her eyes suddenly heavy, sinking deeply into enchanted sleep.

Penny asked the taxi-driver to pull over a couple of streets down from Waters' address. She settled the fare and walked up towards the intersection, arcing back around to her fated destination. She watched the driver go past, watched him checking his mirror the way that men seemed compelled to when driving past a female.

It was getting late in the afternoon. Mr. Redfearn would have let the class go home by now, making his way to his lonely little house, perhaps via a pre-Christmas pint.

She was entering the street already. The first house on the even side was Number 88. Less than a minute would do it. Even walking slowly the numbers seemed to zip by. As she came to the green door of Number 40, she noticed a car opposite with two men inside. They were pretending not to notice her. *So they were staking out Waters' house.* A faint stirring of panic kept her walking, and she soon spotted another unmarked police car outside Number 14. Plain-clothed amateurs keeping each other company or else ringing around their respective families as part of the run up to the big day.

Penny crossed over the road and walked back towards Waters' house. What was going on? Unless the force was employing psychics, how could they have an inkling of what was about to take place here? They were messing with the natural order of things. How could a girl get her work done and heal her sister when every other car was full of policemen playing nosy neighbour?

She crossed the road again, back to the even side. Glancing back, she heard a car start up, and turning back along the street, she tried to give an impression of having forgotten something. The driver was still chattering away to his companion as the car passed her. They saw her and made it obvious. Did men never get sick of the need to stare, to ogle? Did the itch never leave them? And did their behaviour mean that they really weren't police officers at all, or were they simply obeying the laws of verisimilitude?

The other unmarked vehicle moved, settling for Number 66. Why did they need two? Were there others that she hadn't noticed? Was Waters more than some perv trying his luck?

She was back outside Number 40. There were more important matters to consider than the possibilities of a psychic police force. Yet what if Waters was more than she could handle? Penny smiled to herself. *Then it might be as well to have half the local police force hanging around outside.*

She walked into the short drive-way, making her way up towards the dimly-lit front window of the semi-detached property, noticing that one of the surveillance personnel, the one in the passenger seat of the vehicle now parked outside Number 66 had a handset pressed to his face.

Roxy, from the privacy of his car, returned the call to the officer stationed outside 66. There were things that bore repeating.

Like the fact that a young, attractive woman was approaching the home of Phillip Waters after walking up and down the street looking like a cross between a nervous burglar and a trainee hooker. And that was interesting enough. After all, if the murder investigation was dying in the water for Christmas, at least he could use all the resources available to him to nail that bastard's balls to the tree, and show Olive what she had been dealing with.

At the back of his mind was the twitching of a favoured thought that he could only put down to wish-fulfilment: nailing two birds with one stone, or one bird with two stones. Showing Olive the real Waters, that was a given. But what if the case was breaking?

In technical terms Waters was still under surveillance. A suspect for one murder. But what if there was a way to nail him for all four?

Instinct was still rebelling against it, and most of the facts, too. But there had to be a fit. A little Christmas fantasy unfolded in the D.I.'s head: nailing Waters for the murders, Olive back for good, mince pies and loving with the promise of promotion in the New Year. *Thanks, Santa.* And now Waters had a visitor. A young woman, Penny Henderson, involved in a recent altercation involving a local taxi-driver, an incident also involving Waters and the woman's teacher at Valemore College, Marcus Redfearn. *Waters and Redfearn.* And the woman, this Penny Henderson, with a sister in the same psychiatric unit that Victim Number Four had been visiting the night he ended up in the mortuary fridge.

Susan Henderson.

Attacked by six men outside the old Regent building.

All very interesting.

Roxy got out of his car with a troublesome itch for company: alibis or no alibis, Waters was close enough to the heart of the matter. Close enough and yet not quite. Something needing to fall into place. The itch was strong and getting stronger, though for the moment it was playing second-fiddle to catching Waters red-handed with a nubile student. He had Olive's number on speed dial. In this game it paid to be prepared.

Roxy checked with the officers outside Number 66. The woman, not much more than a girl, really, had been inside the house for a few minutes already. Her entry into the property had followed a protracted conversation with Waters on the doorstep. After inviting the woman inside, Waters had been observed looking both ways up and down the street in the time-honoured fashion of the dishonourable rogue.

Roxy took Olive's key to the property out of his pocket. He could square this later; easy as candy from a child, because a woman saw what she wanted to see, and when she had reason to be on your side she could look at the horns growing out of your head and still believe that you were born of sainted stock.

A light was on in the upstairs room, Waters' music room. Roxy smiled, kissed the key and walked around to the rear of the house. They wouldn't hear the back door open, not from up there. Not if there was a cosy little lesson going on around the piano.

Opening the back door, he heard it; music drifting down the stairs. He took the phone from his pocket.

Penny had rang the doorbell, and rang it again. She hadn't been able to resist looking up and down the street, despite knowing that she was being watched. Finally, the shadow had appeared in the doorway, the door opening to reveal a lecherous grin that the creep didn't even have the good grace to try and conceal, along with the cheesy comment about how he would have answered the door sooner if he'd known that he had such a special visitor waiting. Still, he kept her freezing on the doorstep, going on about his precious letter and how he hoped she would *see the advantages.*

The knife had never stopped beating against her heart as Waters completed his doorstep routine before finally inviting her inside.

"You thought we could do a little business, then?" he said, showing her into the living room, where a television was on with the sound muted. It was some late-afternoon cookery show, its tone of domestic drudgery further antagonising her as she stood trying to take everything in.

"Can I take your jacket?" He was practically rubbing his hands together. She took a step backwards and instinctively her arms went up in the air. She could not spend a moment alone with this creep without the re-assuring feel of the steel blade next to her heart. This one, more than any of them, was the real thing. This one, this *man,* was the bone, the flesh, the mental aberration in physical form that had done what had been done to Susan. He was the rabbit's foot carved into a cloven heel, and when he was added to the pot it would cause the bubble and froth to erupt into magical lava and open the door to the final healing.

Only not today. Not with half a police force lined up outside in the street.

What have you been up to, Mr. Waters, you odious little toad?

She let him bumble on about the promise in her work. How everybody needed someone who could recognise the spark and then help fan it into living flame. Oh, yes, he was full up to the eyes with it, and she let him pour it out.

"My piano is upstairs," he said at last. He led her to the foot of the staircase, and then insisted she lead the way. *The perfect gentleman.* She felt his eyes burning after her as she climbed to the top, ushering her into the room to the left of the wooden banister rail. "Are you sure I can't take your jacket? I want you to feel comfortable."

"I'm okay," said Penny, pulling her jacket in closer, watching him smile at the gesture, licking his lips at her childishness. "Your piano?" she said, nodding towards it.

"No," he said. "That's my flying saucer. It is, actually; it transports me to places you wouldn't believe. Or maybe you would."

The stupid laugh: *Nervous?* She hadn't considered that possibility; that someone like him could actually be nervous. Was it conceivable that this self-satisfied prick hadn't done as much *entertaining* as he would like people to believe? Or was the truth more sinister than that? Did Waters have an agenda every bit as dark as her own? Was he the personification of what made her parents panic every time she went out the door and didn't return before dark?

The thought brought with it a swell of fear, though the feeling quickly subsided, to be replaced by a determined reaction stirring in her gut. She visualised Susan walking out of the unit, Mum to her left and Dad to her right. They were all four of them humming the music together. She could hear it clearly now, the theme she had been looking for. It was forming in her mind like a foetus in the womb.

"Okay," he said, sitting at the keyboard. "Here's something to help you chill out and make you feel right at home."

He began to play the first part of *Sextet*. He played from memory. His playing was stiff to begin with, but he was starting to ease into it. As he started to relax, she felt her own tension change in shape and intensity. Closing her eyes, she placed a hand over the blade, and listened, visualising it all.

It was coming. Not today but soon. *Soon.*

Roxy edged to the foot of the stairs. He listened to the music, eyeing his phone as he did so. Then the music stopped. He moved deeper into the shadows at the side of the stairwell, noting the cupboard under the stairs, a possible bolt-hole in case of an emergency. He almost laughed at the idea. He was catching the gist of what was happening up there. Waters was quite an artist, it seemed, when it came to complimenting young females on their musical prowess. Roxy's fingers hovered over the front panel of his phone, but for the moment he didn't press the button that would summon his beloved.

Phil Waters was laughing. It sounded perverse and urgent from where Roxy was standing. Waters wouldn't want to drag things out unnecessarily. Not his style. That laughter said wham bam and not even a thank you.

The girl wasn't saying much of anything. And now she was laughing with him; a regular party going on up there. Roxy pictured the girl from that time at Eaglesfield. A good looking girl, not quite his type, not as seasoned, not as voluptuous as the divine Olive - but then who was? What a fool he'd been, and how lucky to be on the threshold of winning her back. Waters didn't know what he was about to lose.

Roxy thought again of the brief meeting with the Henderson family at Eaglesfield. Did her parents realise the company she was keeping? Something about her was tickling at the back of his mind. How he hated that. It was a sleep killer every time. He'd meant to fish out Taylor's old files on the rape case. Taylor was retired now and playing more golf than Tiger Woods in his prime, by all accounts. When Roxy had taken his job from him, Taylor had put all the still-open-but-going-nowhere-slowly files in good order, and the two men had briefly gone over them together. Good practice did sometimes get results, though the passage of time was rarely the policeman's friend.

He recalled Taylor commenting about it not being politically correct to close the case, though he hadn't at the time chosen to elaborate. The case had seemed straightforward and unlikely to be progressed, and Roxy hadn't wasted valuable time digging into it, or into Taylor's cryptic remark. After all, Taylor could be a bit of an old chauvinist, according to legend. Whether he meant to imply that the victim in the attack had brought it upon herself, or that she was not raped at all but wholly compliant in having six men screwing her half to death out on waste ground - only Taylor knew the answer to that.

Seeing Penny Henderson, the victim's sister, had reminded him to look up Taylor and maybe get in nine holes before lunch one day. Taylor would understand:

talking about some dead-end case as an excuse for being spotted on the golf course whilst making zilch progress on the dick-chopper murders.

Why hadn't he done it already? He knew well enough the answer to that: *Olive*. The ultimate distraction in every sense of the word, God bless her. When she was around there were a lot of things that went by the wayside.

He resolved to ring Taylor just as soon as he had shown Olive what Waters got up to when she was out earning a living. Maybe Taylor would have some thoughts on the case. It would be strange if he didn't. Taylor had thoughts on everything, though not always helpful ones. He would be following it on the news and in the papers, no doubt. Formulating theories and likely expounding them to anyone who would listen.

The music was kicking in again. A different tune this time, though even Roxy could tell that it was not entirely unconnected to what had gone before. "Some time for a concert," he muttered to himself, looking at his watch. "What is it with kids today? They don't have any understanding of priorities."

He allowed himself a quiet chuckle, and then looked again at the phone in his hand. His thumb twitched over the send button.

If he summoned Olive and this turned out to be some bona fide music lesson, then some mighty explaining would be required. He had to consider the progress that he and his estranged wife had made already, and hold it against the urge to nail this sack of shit. Showing her that Waters could be honourable around attractive young girls was not an impressive game plan, and neither was breaking into her boyfriend's house in a desperate bid to reveal him in an unwholesome light.

His thumb slid from the send button. This needed some more thinking about.

He held his fire. He didn't hold it long. The second piece of music was ending. Roxy heard the girl say, "That was beautiful." Then Waters: "It's not the only thing in this room that is."

The phone trembled in Roxy's hand. "Go for it, Mr. Waters. Make my day."

The girl was telling Waters that he probably used his charm on all the young girls. "*Charm?*" muttered Roxy.

Waters was telling her how amazing she was and it was starting to sound like a particularly bad night at the amateur dramatics, when the girl said, "Play some more first." The music started up again.

"Fuck's sake!" said Roxy. "How much is there?"

He'd heard enough to play the percentage game. This wasn't heading down the road that any respectable music lesson ought to be heading, and it didn't take a detective to work that out. And even if it didn't end up with Olive walking in to find the two of them bouncing around the keyboard in the buff, there was going to be plenty of embarrassment on the faces up there when she arrived. Enough to justify all that needed justifying.

Roxy pressed send.

It took Olive no more than half a dozen rings to wake up from the sweetest dream, and no more than three minutes to get dressed, out of the house and into her car.

Roxy listened to the music, and played out an imaginary conversation with Olive. She wanted to know what he was doing in the house, what this had to do with police business, and why it was considered important enough to merit the ringing of the bat phone when half the male population were having their dicks chopped off and nobody seemed any wiser as to who was doing the chopping.

Sextet

There was no doubt about it: Olive could be a more severe interrogator than any number of chiefs of police. He would have to be clear - clear, yet at the same time nicely vague. There was an art to doing that, and most people, even the more astute ones, couldn't see it when it was done well enough.

It would run like this: He had wanted to talk to Waters again anyway, but then a young and attractive student, acting suspiciously, turns up on his doorstep, so naturally he's curious, particularly noting Waters' own apparently edgy manner. Of course, it would be professional suicide to divulge exactly what he had wanted with Waters, but something about the girl, *that girl,* turning up at the house ...

Roxy halted in the telling of his imaginary tale. Fact and fiction were merging a little too closely. Things were in danger of becoming *too* confusing. *What about the girl turning up?* What about that girl, Penny Henderson, sister of Susan Henderson? *Eaglesfield. Norman Sidcup.*

The music was ending. Roxy strained to listen. He caught Waters' voice.

"I want you, Penny."

Roxy grinned. "You know you do."

Then the girl: "No, wait. Play the fourth part first."

Waters' again: "I can't wait."

Roxy checked his watch. "You're only flesh and blood, after all," he said. "And personally, I reckon we've waited long enough."

The girl: "You won't have to wait long now."

"Let's hope not," muttered Roxy.

Then something about a sextet. Roxy blinked. *Six,* he thought. *Six parts.* Musical Neanderthal he might be, but he could work out that much.

All was quiet again up there. If this *concert* was going on for much longer, he might have to keep an eye on the road outside and intercept Olive.

What was that? The girl was saying something. *Sextet.* That word again. She wanted to write the fifth part here, now. Finish it *now*. Waters asking about her inspiration, and the girl answering - something to do with her sister; then asking Waters one more time to play the fourth part.

Roxy clenched his teeth, the veins in his forehead squeezing at some elusive eureka.

The music started up again. It was more melancholic this time. There was a quality to it that drew you in. An undeniable charm, and under different circumstances he could have stood more of it. Except that these were not different circumstances. He wanted the music to end so the real business could start: Olive arriving and the whole thing done with and tied up as neatly as an anniversary bow.

On the other hand, he didn't want it to end. It wasn't that it made him want to tap his feet, exactly, or even to hum along. It chilled him, if anything. It wasn't unlike the stuff you heard in the better-class horror movies: not all gothic and Vincent Price, but right under the skin, elusive, escaping the fingers that tried to button it down.

A little like the nagging idea that wouldn't quite make the great leap forward from the back of his mind: Penny Henderson, and her sister on the unit at Eaglesfield: *Susan Henderson*.

What was Taylor saying? He had to ring him, get the file out. Six animals hammering the life out of one innocent teenage girl; lucky she wasn't dead - or was it? How did a family come to terms with that? Had Taylor sold them short, making his mind up that the girl had it coming? *Made it up*?

The music was building, and it took Roxy's concentration with it as he stood, not breathing, at the foot of the stairs. Approaching its zenith, he waited, felt it peak, coming back down, cooling, spiralling. *Sextet*, he thought. *Six*.

But what was behind the thought? What was the hidden significance? He promised himself a good long chat with Taylor once Ms. Henderson's liaison with Waters had run its inevitable course. In the meantime, he killed time, calling off the surveillance. *I think I can handle things from here*, he told himself in a smug and victorious whisper. Let the boys be getting on with some paper work instead of idling away the hours. There was too much time wasted by the police these days, and the public didn't know the half of it.

The music was ending. It kept dying, and then starting up again. Broken, fragmenting; stabs of sound like a dying man trying to get off the floor, only to sink a little further into death with each desperate attempt.

He didn't like the feelings it brought with it, but there was something in there; something that he couldn't get a handle on but needed to. He'd heard the arty types come out with that kind of bullshit. Music was music, at the end of the day; it either did it for you or else it didn't.

Without warning the music ended. But it was like it hadn't really ended at all. Like it was to be continued: *Four down, two to go*, he thought, straining into the almost perfect silence.

The silence held. And then it broke.

Olive was scarcely a mile from Waters' house, but the traffic was conspiring against her. Temporary lights were everywhere. *Hey, says the Council, seeing as it's Christmas week, everybody's busy, everybody's needing to get around - so let's dig up the road again!*

Roxy had sounded excited on the phone, in that quiet way of his. Cool bugger, she thought. She'd known him long enough to recognise that bloodhound nose twitching at the other end of the line. Phil Waters was onto some college slag, and it was going to cost his scrawny bollocks one good kicking.

*

As Waters played on, Penny had taken the knife from her jacket, visualising how perfect it would have been inviting this odious specimen to become the fifth part of the healing. Slicing into his miserable, lustful, greed-riddled flesh; leaving him to spend his last agony-filled moments choking on his own dick.

Penny cleaned the knife, handle and blade, before placing it carefully beneath the clutter on the desk. Then she waited for Waters to stop playing. At the end of his performance, as he turned around, Penny unfastened her leather jacket and started to unbutton the cotton shirt beneath it. She watched his hungry eyes feasting on her, running his tongue along the rim of his dry lips. She could have thrown up there and then.

"I've tunes in my head, Phil," she told him.

"You mean," said Waters, easing himself up from the piano stool, "you need me to help you *get them down*, so to speak."

She winced at his schoolboy vulgarity. "You run a course in composition, don't you?"

"I'd forgotten," he said. "Lack of money does things to the memory."

"Oh, I see," she said, pulling her shirt together in a gesture that quickly raised his hand. "No," he said. "I was only joking, I didn't mean ..."

His words petered out as she opened her shirt again. "I have a confession," she said. "I always write naked." His jaw dropped so fast that by rights it ought to have cracked. "Have I shocked you?" she said. "*Offended* you?"

He shook his head, seemingly incapable of further conversation.

"I expect my collaborators to have the decency to work on my level. Do you have a problem with that?" Waters shook his head again, still unable to speak. "You do understand what I'm saying, don't you, Phil?"

The name, *his* name, stuck in her throat, though he didn't seem to notice. She watched as he took off his sweater and tee-shirt, placing them carefully on the piano stool. He looked at her and smirked.

"What's funny?" she asked.

"I was wondering," he said, regaining his powers of speech, "whether the great masters ever applied this technique."

"It's not mentioned in the history books. Anyway, you're still looking over-dressed."

"I'm an old-fashioned kind of guy," he said. "I insist on ladies first in all things."

She turned her back on him and unfastened her jeans, slipping out of them. Feeling his hands on her, she stifled the scream, moving away from him, turning back around. "Your turn," she said.

In a moment he was standing naked before her. Good and ripe.

"To work?" he asked.

"Just a moment, please." She slipped her jeans back on and buttoned up her shirt.

"What are you doing?"

She moved close to him and took his hands, placing them on the collar of her shirt, either side of her throat. "I like it rough, Phil."

"I see."

"Do you, though?" She pulled down hard on both of his arms, in turn tearing the top buttons from her shirt. "Is that all you've got?" she asked him. "Harder, Phil."

This time he needed no assistance, tearing down on her shirt until all the buttons had popped, exposing her. "I can feel a tune coming on," he said, licking again at his lips.

Penny moved to the sash window, lifted it and leaned out. And then she screamed. "Help me! Please, help me. Rape! *Rape!*"

The surveillance vehicles were barely out of the street, though already out of earshot. But Roxy was on the stairs, charging up them two at a time.

The door burst open and D.I. Roxburgh stood face to face with the erect and naked Waters, reading him his rights while radioing for back up, the surveillance vehicles u-turning for all they were worth, Waters speechless, Roxy looking like the cat who had finally got the cream, more footsteps coming up the stairs, more plain-clothed police entering the room, Waters being led away in a blanket, a policewoman entering the scene, taking over the niceties while police cars with flashing lights brought the neighbours out onto the street.

A woman was leaping from a blue VW Beetle, rushing towards Waters as they ushered him inside one of the flashing cars. The woman was shouting, demanding to know what was going on. Roxy went over to her as she stood transfixed, staring with disbelief at the still blanketed Waters.

"Got the bastard," he said.

From the rear seat of the squad car, as they drove him away, a stunned Phil Waters looked back at Olive.

"Will somebody tell me just what the hell is going on," she said.

Roxy, adopting a look of utter professionalism - a senior detective carrying out his duties without time or inclination for feelings of personal satisfaction - said, "It's a bad business, Olive. But it's over now."

CHAPTER TWENTY-SIX

Mr and Mrs. Henderson sat together on the sofa in shocked silence as D.I. Roxburgh told them of their daughter's ordeal. Penny was trying to downplay it, saying that she was okay and that it was all really nothing.

It didn't sound like nothing, not according to Mrs. Henderson. "I'm beginning to wonder if this world's safe to bring children into," she said. "First Susan ..." Mrs. Henderson broke down, and Mr. Henderson comforted her as best he could; sobbing himself as he held his wife close.

Roxy gave them a few moments. "Your other daughter: Susan. She's still on the unit at Eaglesfield I understand?"

Mr. Henderson started to speak, but emotion quickly got the better of him. "That's right," said Penny. "Susan's still there. She's starting to make progress, though. We are hoping she will come home soon."

Roxy was itching to ask more. But with both parents unable to speak for crying, he decided this wasn't the time. Better to get the formalities completed and call it a night. He made another mental note to contact Taylor and discuss the Susan Henderson case with him. But that too could wait. There had been enough good work done for one day. Waters was back in custody. The world was beginning to make sense again. His mind drifted over the contours of Olive, and it took a mighty effort to wrestle it back.

When Penny had made her statement, Roxy stood up to leave. "If you want my opinion," he said, "this wants taking the distance. It's the only way to keep maniacs like that off our streets."

"I agree," said Mrs. Henderson, feeling a little better. "We must prosecute." She turned to her daughter. "Mustn't we, sweetheart?"

"Scum like that deserve all they get," said Penny, still regretting that she had not been able to turn Waters into the fifth part of her work. She was wondering whether the police had got around to finding the knife that had killed four men, buried beneath the papers on Waters' desk.

Before D.I. Roxburgh left the Henderson house, he again urged Penny to take the case all the way. It struck her as strange. It was almost as though this detective had a mission to nail Waters. *A personal vendetta?* It might turn out that he was nothing more than a policeman trying to do his job, but she didn't think so. She sensed that the fates were moving again in the right direction: a knife in the work room of Phil Waters, and a detective who wanted to see the low-life go down.

That evening, Penny asked to go over to Eaglesfield, and her parents took her. There was no way they were letting her through the door on her own, "what with one thing or another" as Mrs. Henderson put it. There was a psychopath out there and rapists on every corner. What was the world coming to, that's what Mrs. Henderson wanted to know. Waters was in custody, but as far as Mrs. Henderson was concerned, Waters was merely the tip of the iceberg. There was a killer on the loose out there.

Maybe Waters was the killer, suggested Penny. Mrs. Henderson doubted it. She didn't have any evidence to back up her theory that Waters was not the killer, though; it was all a matter of feeling, instinct. She still thought that Waters ought to swing by his testicles for what he had done to Penny.

Before the Henderson family left the unit that evening, Penny had her usual few minutes alone with her sister. Susan hadn't been any more communicative than usual in front of her parents, and staff on duty hadn't suggested any further developments. But as soon as Mr and Mrs. Henderson had left the room, everything changed.

Penny had taken hold of her sister's hand. "Susan, listen. I had it all worked out ... it's just that things didn't go to plan. That's how the best stuff goes sometimes, you know that."

"Christmas," said Susan.

Penny felt a bolt of excitement. "Yes, *Christmas*. It won't be long now."

"Christmas," said Susan, tightening her grip on Penny's hand. Her strength was building. This was the best sign yet. It was all working, the magic was working.

"You will be home for Christmas, Susan. You have my word on it."

"Christmas," said Susan. "*Christmas*."

Penny was quiet on the way home, and her parents put it down to the day she'd had. "It was too much, coming out this evening," said Mrs. Henderson.

"That's Penny all over," said Mr. Henderson, glancing back proudly at his daughter sitting forlorn in the back seat of the car. "No thought for herself, that one. A good girl and a good sister."

"They're both good girls," said Mrs. Henderson. "Why do bad things always happen to the best people?"

Mr. Henderson shook his head, as baffled by it all as his wife was.

Penny went straight up to bed, and Mrs. Henderson switched on the television while her husband made hot drinks. The local news was still jammed with speculations over the killings, but there seemed little in the way of progress. Reading between the lines, the police appeared clueless, though a local man who had been arrested for an apparently unrelated offence was helping them with their enquiries.

Mrs. Henderson shuddered at the very mention of the beast. Her husband brought in the drinks and she told him what she'd heard: that the man who had attacked Penny was helping the police over the killings. "Maybe Penny's right," she said, then folded forward, her face in her hands. "What if he was planning to kill our daughter?"

Mr. Henderson put the drinks down. "We don't know that, do we? We have to be patient. Let the police do their work."

"But what if it is him? What if Penny was that close to being killed by that animal?"

He hugged his wife, allowing the rest of her tears to fall, before handing her the drink that he had prepared for her. "Get that down you," he said. "That's what you need."

"No," she said. "I don't believe it. The killer's still out there. It's not safe out there. It's not safe anywhere."

The news the next day revealed that a weapon had been found at the home of the man helping police with their enquiries, the man who had attacked a local female student. Was there a suggestion that the weapon was used in the killings? Was the killer extending his range, no longer content to murder and mutilate men, now going after vulnerable young women too?

Penny watched the news with her parents. She thought about the detective, more convinced than ever that D.I. Roxburgh was determined to take Waters down for the whole shooting match.

That evening Mr and Mrs. Henderson remained adamant that Penny was not leaving the house alone, whether the psychopath was behind bars or not. She agreed to a lift. "Want to show Susan what you've written?" said Mr. Henderson, eyeing the folder that his daughter was carrying.

"Be nice to play it for her, one day," said Mrs. Henderson.

Sextet

The mood seemed a little lighter as they drove out to Eaglesfield. And when Penny asked, as usual, for a little time alone with her sister, her parents went to the canteen for a sandwich. As soon as they had gone, she took out the pages of manuscript and showed them to Susan, watching as her sister looked over them. She studied her sister's expression carefully, though it was hard to read. Difficult to tell how focused Susan was, or what effect, if any, the notation was having on her.

She turned each page, giving her sister time to take in the music. At last she asked what Susan thought, but Susan didn't say anything. "Tell you what," said Penny, "I'll give you a rendition." She hummed the melody from the fourth part, holding Susan's hand as she did so. But seeing Susan looking away, disengaging, she stopped. "What is it?" asked Penny.

Susan looked at her. *"When am I coming home?"*

At the impromptu meeting with the consultant, following an hour of what Mr. Henderson later referred to as "bureaucratic dyslexia," it was Mrs. Henderson who finally put into words the question that was on everybody's mind. "Can Susan come home for Christmas, yes or no?"

In the end it was pointless arguing. The consultant was adamant. He needed to see more signs of progress, consistent progress. It was no good setting Susan up to fail. The meeting ended and another one was scheduled for the New Year. When Penny went in to say goodbye, she hadn't the heart to tell her sister the truth. Instead she told her, "I've got numbers five and six lined up, Susan."

"When am I coming home?"

"Tomorrow I'm going to buy myself the tools to see the job through."

"When am I coming home?"

*

Roxy felt like celebrating. Waters behind bars, Olive back in his bed. There could be a promotion in this, though that would require Waters fitting the bill for four murders, not merely for trying to get inside the knickers of a college student who he had seduced through some shitty correspondence course.

Was Waters the man? The knife said he could be, though Waters was saying that he'd never seen it before, and that he had no idea how it got there. There were no prints on it, which seemed odd. Why dust off a murder weapon and then leave it on your work desk?

Had he been planning to kill Penny Henderson? Why kill four men, sexually mutilate them, and then go after a teenage girl? Waters fitted the bill for the girl; he was the type to do that. But was he the type to go around chopping off dicks and stuffing them down throats?

Still, if he *could* nail Waters for the murders, there would be no going back as far as Olive was concerned. Not that she would go back to Waters now, surely; not after she had seen what he got up to when she was out of the house, albeit in the arms of her estranged husband. Maybe Olive had a theory. She had a theory on most things.

When Roxy got back home that evening, Olive was waiting. He was all for pouring them both a large one, maybe calling for a takeaway or even a late supper out. Get her thoughts on Waters as local serial killer.

Olive, it turned out, wasn't in that kind of mood. Olive was in the mood for asking questions of her own. According to Olive it didn't add up. What was he doing taking her key, going into her house to spy on Waters, regardless of whether a young woman was visiting him or not? Was this a set up? She knew how badly Roxy wanted to nail him. Had he put the young woman up to it?

"Olive, that's a terrible thing to say."

"It would be a terrible thing to do, too."

"You think I could stoop to that?"

She eyed him carefully. "I hope not."

They looked at each other. "Tell me," she said, "that the knife wasn't planted."

"Okay," said Roxy. "The knife wasn't planted. Look, I'd like nothing better than to see Waters go down, we both know that. But do you think that I would risk my career - risk sending myself down - to see that happen?"

With the inquisition at an end, or at least temporarily suspended, Olive agreed to supper. They drove out to a little French bistro that served late. After eating, as Roxy was gathering back some of the warm glow of victory, Olive said, "Why would Phil murder and mutilate four men? Why would he do that, it makes absolutely no sense. A young woman being lured into his web, okay, I can see that - but the rest ... no way."

She had a point, and she had voiced *his* thoughts. Still, the bottom line was this: Waters not having a clear motive was something he could live with so long as it didn't stop him fitting the frame.

CHAPTER TWENTY-SEVEN

Marcus Redfearn watched the news in disbelief. *Phil Waters arrested for the attempted rape of a seventeen year old student.* They weren't naming the young victim, but Redfearn had an uneasy feeling in his stomach.

What the hell was going on? He knew nothing good would come of that competition, though he hadn't expected anything like this. What had come to Valemore? Wasn't it enough that there had been four horrific killings, without Waters adding to the horror, attacking young women, grooming them through his correspondence course.

He had to get away again, but where to? He hadn't long returned from visiting his mother, and she would be suspicious if he turned up again so soon. On the other hand, it would earn him a few more Brownie points, pose as his Christmas visit and keep her off his back until spring. The change of scene would do him good. He would ring her up and give her the news. It would make her Christmas, and possibly his too, the way things were going.

He sat at his piano, playing over some old jazz standards. It was as good a way to relax and take his mind off things as he knew. Beer used to have a similar effect, but his taste for the stuff had deserted him.

Playing some Gershwin his mind drifted: falling out with Waters; Waters attacking a young student, a student from Valemore College at that, almost certainly a student that they both knew. *Penny Henderson*? None of the other students had mentioned Waters' competition, and Waters hadn't mentioned any other students from college.

As he played on, his thoughts circled around Penny and her sister. How much grief did one family have to bear? How were the parents coping? Some people had no luck in this life, it wasn't fair. It was a damn shame. There was so much pain in the world. Why did people do such terrible things to each other? How could they? It was a messed up, screwed up world. And yet there were good things and good people too. People like Penny, people who cared.

He thought of how desperately she had wanted him to look at her compositions. The poor girl had all of that going on with her sister, and she was pouring out music that was nothing short of remarkable. Maybe the two things weren't unrelated; her way of dealing with it, getting all of that pain out. The emotion in the music was coming from a deep place, and you couldn't fake it, not to that extent. Was that what gave it such power, such purpose?

Yes, that was the word: *purpose*. Trying to express the inexpressible, as maybe all art does. She had a gift, clearly. The tragedy was that such talent should require immense suffering to bring it to fruition.

He stopped playing; he could have cried for the poor creature. It wasn't likely that he would see her until term started in the New Year. That seemed a long time. It *was* a long time, *too long*. He needed to know that she was okay.

But how could he make contact? He couldn't just turn up at her house, out of the blue, and tell her parents that he was doing a well-being check on their seventeen year old daughter. That wasn't in the rules, especially not now, after what had happened. Not in Valemore. People quickly got the wrong ideas when middle aged men, *professional men,* in positions of responsibility started taking that much interest in the welfare of young girls.

Switching from Gershwin, he began playing Penny's music. It was too painful, he thought. *Beautiful*? Perhaps beautiful wasn't quite the word. *Raw*? Yes, *raw*. Filled with darkness and suffering, yet it had beauty, too. He wondered how the rest of her 'sextet' was coming along. It was a strange project, writing a sextet for the piano. She knew well enough what a sextet was. It was peculiar to apply that term to what she was doing. But then she was hardly your average student, hardly your average teenage girl full stop. She seemed to come from a different place. She was unlike any other student that he had come across in all of his years as a teacher.

Maybe she had what it took to make a big noise out in the world one day. You couldn't get an angle on Penny, the same as you couldn't quite get an angle on her music. It was elusive. *She* was elusive. *Sextet*, he thought.

He opened a drawer of his desk and took out a pile of papers, quickly finding what he was looking for. Phil Waters' ad; the one Waters had been so proud of. There, that word: *Sextet*.

It was too much of a coincidence. She must have decided on the project after seeing that ad. Sometimes titles kick off ideas. He could see how the number six must haunt the poor girl, her sister being attacked by six men. *Six pieces of music representing six assaults on Susan.* Yes, it made a kind of sense, when you thought about it in the right way.

And Phil Waters had exploited all of that, cheapened it. Waters deserved everything he had coming to him.

Redfearn felt a swell of anger, and he tried to contain it. If only there was a legitimate way to get in touch with Penny, he thought. Make sure she was okay. She knew where he lived and she would always be welcome. But what if she didn't visit? And why should she? And if she did, how inappropriate was that? A vulnerable child - that's what she was, after all: a *child* - having been attacked by one pervert already, a pervert pretending to be interested in her music, when his mind had been on ...

A sense of loathing rose up inside him. *How dare Waters act like that?* The man was a monster, and he had once been something close to a friend.

Suddenly Marcus Redfearn felt dirty. As though the sins of Phil Waters had infected him, debasing his very essence from mere contact with such a loathsome example of how low a man can sink. No, Penny Henderson didn't need another middle aged man in her life. She'd had all the advice she needed. More than she needed, most probably. What could he, a college teacher, pass on to somebody who could write music like that? She had a gift that he knew nothing of. He knew a lot of technical stuff and an abundance of history, but when it came to actually composing music Penny Henderson had something he would never have. Something he could only dream of.

He went back to playing Gershwin. It felt like nothing but killing time. *Killing time until what, though?* Until he went to Chester to visit his mother? *Until it was time to go back to work and see Penny Henderson?*

Later, he switched on the television to catch the news. It was full of the local murders again. Waters' attack had intensified public fear and ratcheted up the pressure on the police to make the streets safe again.

The news confirmed what he'd suspected: the police investigation had stalled. They were tearing around the town like headless chickens, interviewing everyone in sight. But as sure as he was sitting eating a corned beef sandwich lathered in pickle, they were getting nowhere.

That night he lay in bed circling over the same ideas that had been haunting him all day. The facts as he understood them; the possibilities and the permutations. He fell asleep thinking over them and awoke soon after with his head full of Penny Henderson. At some point he dreamed of her playing her music to a packed audience at the Royal Albert Hall. At the end of the performance nobody was clapping, silence descending on the hall like a death cloud. The spotlight shifting from Penny, alone at the piano, staring like a frightened kitten into the darkness

- now illuminating the faces of the silent audience, none of them moving; every one of them dead. Blood soaked, mutilated, *dead.*

Christmas was tightening its grip on the nation. As Mr. Henderson drove the family over to Eaglesfield, Penny and her mother discussed arrangements. If Susan couldn't come home for Christmas, the family would spend the day on the unit. Whatever happened, it was still going to be the best Christmas ever.

They arrived at Eaglesfield to find that the Christmas decorations had already been put up. Artificial trees sprayed with artificial snow, and yards of tinsel everywhere. "They've turned this place into a winter wonderland," observed Mrs. Henderson, and Penny thought back to when Christmas Eve was the best day of the year, the anticipation making it even better than Christmas Day. Hanging up stockings for Santa to fill up, and pillowcases stuffed with goodies. The magic was back again. *No matter what the doctors said, Susan was coming home for Christmas.*

Susan seemed more detached than ever, staring at some invisible scene, while Mrs. Henderson stroked her hair and Mr. Henderson wittered merrily about the weather, the economy, and everything else that failed to concern him. And all the while Susan remained silent, sitting as wooden as a toy doll, betraying not the slightest flicker of emotion.

When Mr and Mrs. Henderson had left the room to speak to the staff on duty, Penny took her sister's hand.

Susan glared at her.

"What is it?" asked Penny, startled by the intensity of her sister's expression. "Look, I've brought something to show you." She took a knife from her jacket pocket. "What do you think of that, then?"

The knife was almost identical to the one that the police had found in Waters' room; the one that was going to earn him a good long stretch, at least if D.I. Roxburgh had anything to do with it. "I got it off the market. Cash. I said it was a Christmas present for my brother who's into fishing. The guy on the stall didn't even blink. He was too busy looking at my tits and fancying his chances."

Susan looked at the knife; *smiled*.

The staff had little to tell Mr and Mrs. Henderson. Susan had been fine; quiet, possibly, but nothing that had given any cause for concern. They rejoined their girls, and the visit didn't go on much longer after that. Susan's frozen silence had resumed in the presence of the family, unnerving them all. Better to go home and try again another time, suggested Mr. Henderson. Likely it was just a bad day.

"We all have bad days," agreed Mrs. Henderson. "She'll be better tomorrow, you'll see." On the journey home Mrs. Henderson again broke the gloom. "Maybe Susan's heard about what happened. She may have heard something on the news."

"Penny's name's not been mentioned," said Mr. Henderson.

"I know that. But Susan's a bright girl. She is a very sensitive young lady. You'd be amazed how much she picks up. Doesn't miss a trick and never has done. Mark my words: our Susan understands a lot more than she lets on."

Penny sat quietly in the back seat. She was thinking about the way Susan had glared at her. Her smile at the sight of the knife had been re-assuring, but something was wrong. The rules of the game had changed again.

Marcus Redfearn awoke with a splitting headache. He'd planned to make the journey to Chester that day and then decided instead to delay his plans and travel on Christmas Eve. It would give him more time to sort himself out, and give his mother less grounds for suspicion. Your only son turns up on Christmas Eve, what's to explain?

As he lay in bed formulating his plans, he recalled the dreams that had infested his dismal night; still vivid and filled with weirdness and violence. *A natural subconscious outpouring?* It would hardly be surprising with all the murder and horror that had been going on lately. The reports on the media were enough to give anybody nightmares.

Penny playing to a dead audience? What was that about? There had been other dreams involving Penny, too, though he could only recall snatches of them, and nothing that made much sense. But then he rarely made sense of any remnants from a night's sleep.

He got up and made a hot drink and took some painkillers, switching on the radio as he did so. It didn't appear that the police had made any further progress. The news machine was treading water until something broke or a bigger story came along. It amazed him how people could spend half their lives listening to aimless speculation, and adding to it. He heard it in the staff room at college. It was like an addiction for some people.

He switched off the radio, and after scalding himself under the shower for as long as he could stand it, he got dressed and walked out in the direction of Valemore Central. If he was going to Chester, he'd better go armed.

Penny sat at the piano. The music seemed anything but magical now. The fire had gone out. It was rubbish and it had always been. *Cat healing shit*. Waters had lied, had other agendas. He probably told all his 'clients' that they had 'something' just to get their business. Money, it always came down to money in the end, money and sex. And that low-life was obsessed with both.

She'd expected more of Mr. Redfearn. Thought he was one who could be trusted. What a fool she was. How could he have heard anything of value in this crap? He was as cheap as all the rest, merely a better actor. She'd seen the way he looked at her when he thought nobody was watching. He was no different to Waters and all the others. It would only have been a matter of time before he made his move. Had she learned nothing of the ways of men, *all men, every last one of them*? Redfearn was the lowest of them all, his ability to deceive making him the most dangerous - and therefore the most deserving.

The door opened and Mr. Henderson walked in. "What was that you were playing?" he asked.

"Oh, just a thing I made up ... once upon a time," she said.

"It sounded familiar. It was like that thing you were playing the other day, only different."

"The same only different," said Penny. "Yes, that sums it up."

Mr. Henderson placed an arm around her. "We'll get through this."

"I know, Dad."

"I think," he said, "that we're all a bit shot at. I think we need to rest and take it easy. I have faith, Penny. I have faith that everything will work itself out." She saw the mist rolling into his eyes. "Maybe," he said, nodding at the piano, "you should play something Christmassy."

She played a mournful arrangement of *Good King Wenceslas*. When she'd finished playing, he clapped, sarcastically. "Well, that's got the party going," he said. Then he kissed her, and left the room, closing the door behind him. Penny returned to her own music, playing it in the style of a funeral march; *thinking about Mr. Redfearn.*

Marcus Redfearn walked around the town centre until his legs and back ached. He still hadn't bought anything for his mother, other than that Richard Clayderman collection. The shops, despite being packed-out, seemed empty, and he couldn't stop thinking about Penny. Wondering how things were working out. Hoping everything was alright. He was on his way home, passing the college, when the image of the young student playing to a dead and mutilated audience returned. *Where did dreams come from? Where did such bizarre and surreal images originate?* He'd read all the theories, dabbled with Freud, Jung and all the usual suspects. Weren't dreams supposed to represent hidden truths? Repressed material, realities too hideous to be allowed out into the light? What truths lay in such monstrous and strange images? A young, sweet, innocent girl grieving for her lost sister - and an audience of dead people, carved beyond recognition. *Is my subconscious telling me truths that I can't – won't – admit into my waking thoughts? Am I reading too much into a bad night's sleep?*

He was home, shattered; an evening of mindless television and then a hot milky drink that he took up to bed. He'd intended reading but ended up thinking instead, *thinking about Penny.* He couldn't get the girl out of his mind. It had to be pity and compassion. What else could he be feeling for a seventeen year old student?

He finished his drink and turned out the light, though he didn't feel the least bit sleepy. He thought about switching the light back on and selecting a book, but the energy to do so, or the inclination, had deserted him. Instead he lay there in the dark, the thoughts crowding in. At some point he realised that he was afraid to fall asleep. *Afraid of what, though*? That in his dreams he would find Penny Henderson naked? That his dreams might become erotic, and that he would find himself acting ... despicably?

Was that the fear? Discovering aspects of himself that he had kept hidden even from himself?

He was on the cusp of sleep and slowly it was dawning: to fall asleep and dream of loving Penny was not the thing that he feared at all. What he feared was something else entirely; an altogether different truth hidden beneath layers of deceit.

He was falling, falling at last, falling under sleep's consuming spell.

Not the dead. Not the dream about the dead.

CHAPTER TWENTY-EIGHT

Penny sat at her piano. *What now?* Her plan to kill Waters had turned to shit and left her a man short. Which meant moving Mr. Redfearn from Six to Five or else leaving him in place as the ultimate sacrifice and finding somebody else to take the vacant fifth spot. It seemed the better plan, she thought. There was something poignant in climaxing with the sacrifice and slaughter of a basically decent man.

The plan was flawed. Any further killings would take Waters out of the frame, unless there was a copycat killer doing the rounds. Stuff like that only happened in the second-rate thrillers that her mum used to watch on Saturday evenings before all of this came to pass. They might even start to think that she had planted that knife in Waters' room. She was a connection between Waters and Mr. Redfearn ... what if they bailed Waters for the attack on her, deciding he wasn't a murderer, *merely a rapist* ... in which case killing Mr. Redfearn would be back on the cards: *Waters killing Redfearn.* Would that be credible? Someone like Waters taking that kind of a risk - killing his friend over a college student straight after coming out of the nick? He might though. He was one screwed up prick. As long as nobody else got carved up while Waters was in custody, it could work. She could make it work, one way or another.

The clock was ticking. What to do? Susan wanted to be home for Christmas, and she had promised. With Waters still in custody further killings were not an option, not for the time being. She had to go and see Susan. Buy some time. Susan would understand.

At the end of the visit, Penny remained in her sister's room while her parents went to get drinks in the canteen. Susan had been unresponsive and Mrs. Henderson had become upset, struggling to contain her tears. As soon as her parents had left the room, Penny felt the tightness spreading through her chest and down into her stomach. How to tell Susan that she wouldn't be coming home for Christmas? No easy way.

The two sisters sat in silence, staring at each other. Sometimes Penny swore that her sister could look into your eyes and read your mind.

The moments were becoming minutes, and Penny felt the pressure building, like something was about to blow. She couldn't stand it. It would have to be the truth. She leaned forward and touched the back of Susan's hand. In a voice not much above a whisper, she said, "I have to tell you something. I went to see a man named Phil Waters. He was perfect for Number Five. I had it all worked out but in the end I couldn't do it. I didn't bottle it, nothing like that. The police had him under surveillance. They had him as a suspect, so if I'd done him they would have had me." She squeezed the back of Susan's hand. "They took him in though. I screamed rape. But we're going to have to lie low. If I kill another one they'll know it wasn't him. I planted the knife. If I do any more they'll come for me."

In her sister's eyes a silent anger appeared to be raging.

"I'm sorry, Susan. I wanted you to know. I want to be upfront. You're going to have to be patient a little longer."

Susan continued to stare. The intensity was savage.

"Please," said Penny. "Say something. Speak to me."

She cracked. Letting go of her sister's hand, Penny dissolved, her face buried into her jacket, heaving out the tears. And still her sister said nothing; looking down on her, not moving a muscle.

When Penny at last stopped crying and looked up into the silence ... the storm broke.

"Finished? Or would you like to cry some more?"

"Susan ..?"

"No, you've had your say. Now it's my turn."

The voice was shocking; seething with restrained venom. Susan Henderson, in the minutes that followed, folded back the weeks; talking as though a wand had been waved and her speech, her vocabulary, her ability to communicate had all been restored. "Do you think I'm stupid? Do you think that I don't know what's been going on?"

"Please, Susan -"

"I've told you once already: it's my turn to do the talking. And you're going to listen until I've finished."

Penny edged back in her chair, trying to gain distance from those blazing eyes.

"You thought that I stole your boyfriend. So you had a word with Daz. Arranged to have me gang raped - no, don't deny it. Six of them ... down by The Regent. You think I didn't know that you'd set a trap? You think I could have let that happen to me? I screwed six boys, Penny. I took them, one at a time, and I spat them back out. *Screwed six boys: not raped by six men.* See the difference? Oh, I was full of their juice alright, but my head was as clear then as it is now. This was all for you, Penny. *Payback.* I wanted to see your reaction when they brought me here. I wanted to see whether you were riddled with guilt or bursting with joy. I watched you trying to say the right things; hatch your stupid little-girl plans; wasting your time writing all that shit and believing that there was ever any magic in the first place. I watched you throwing your life away, sister, digging your own grave you *multiple murderer you.* What are they going to do with you when they find out - when they come to take you away? How long will you spend in a place that has none of the comforts of Eaglesfield?"

Susan raised a finger. "No, I haven't finished. I'm disappointed in you, Penny. It was bad enough watching you believing that such crap could heal anything or anyone. But you couldn't even finish what you started. All of those promises! I should call you Schubert; the one who left her 'masterpiece' *unfinished.*

"I'll tell you what happens next, shall I?"

Penny nodded, like a child waiting to find out its punishment.

"This unit is going to witness a miracle. Progress isn't the word - they'll have to invent a new one. Doctors are good at that sort of thing. So what I'm saying is: don't lay the table for three this Christmas." Susan's face widened into a consuming grin. "That's right, I'm coming home. Tell Santa I'm off the naughty list."

CHAPTER TWENTY-NINE

Redfearn had fallen asleep, begging to the gods that ruled his mind that he wouldn't dream again about Penny playing her music to an audience of butchered corpses. His begging fell on deaf ears.

The dream had grown darker. This time, as the music stopped and Penny Henderson looked out on the dead audience, groans of pain and terror emanated from the back rows. He watched her climb down from the stage, walking over the dead to get to the barely living. Watched her take an axe (or was it a sword, a machete?) and lift it high above her head. People were screaming but Penny was swinging the weapon down, again and again, silencing the screaming, victim by victim, until there was only one left.

Up in the balcony, above the bloodshed and terror, one man was crying. And Penny was climbing up into the balcony like a spider coming to consume the last desperate fly caught helplessly in the web. *It was him.* "She's coming to kill me. She's coming to kill me. She's coming - "

Redfearn sat up in his bed, sweat raining out of him. "No," he said. "Penny wouldn't hurt a fly."

He got out of bed and went down to the kitchen, drank a pint of water, refilling the glass. He didn't believe in the superstition of dreams. He didn't believe in omens that came in the shape of subconscious outpourings. He was a grown man, for God's sake, and a teacher at that.

Yet something was badly wrong. No – get a grip!

He would check that Penny was okay, not because of a dream, but because he was her teacher and he had a duty, and every right to be concerned about her welfare. He switched on the radio. The late night music was hardly to his taste, but there would be a news bulletin along any minute.

The police were appealing for information and continuing with door-to-door enquiries in the hope that some lead would emerge. It sounded desperate.

Were they still holding Waters?

Redfearn went back to bed, though the night, he knew, was in ruins. He tried reading though he was far too distracted. Thoughts were bombarding him. Thoughts about the evening he had sat in the Feathers with Penny Henderson and Phil Waters, Penny sending material to Waters, the competition giving her the idea of writing a 'sextet'.

One victim had been visiting a relative on the unit where Penny's sister was.

So what? What did that have to do with anything? Penny needed help, but not that kind of help. Dreams meant nothing - you couldn't read anything into dreams.

He couldn't stop the thoughts from circling. He couldn't get Penny Henderson out of his head. "I've got to get away." *Away from what? The dawning truth?* "Stop it!"

It wasn't running away, it was visiting his mother for Christmas. It was escaping this madness that had come to Valemore, this death and mutilation.

Who was he kidding? He was running scared. *Scared of what? Who?* He would visit Penny before going to Chester. *Why? What for?* To check that she was okay, that's what he would do. That was the right thing to do. Check she's okay. He started to relax, felt himself floating towards sleep. Then it started over. The same dreams, the same fears.

They let Phil Waters go. They had no choice. Roxy knew it: the man's alibis were too good and Olive wasn't budging. Not an inch. Could she have got some of the times wrong, Roxy asked her, more than once. Could she have been just a little *mistaken*?

"You want me to fit in around your theory, is that what you're saying? Why don't you tell me what times you're thinking of and I'll change the truth to suit you, how about that? In fact why don't you write out exactly what you want me to sign up to and done with?"

"You know that's not what I'm saying, Olive."

"Are you sure about that? You hate Phil and you need to get someone behind bars fast."

They were still simmering down from kicking up a rumpus, but the coldness that had seeped into the bedroom was far from congenial now. Olive shook her head. "You thought we could smooth things out under the sheets, didn't you? Thought a bit of rumpy-pumpy and I would give you the head of Phil Waters on a plate."

"Those are serious allegations, Olive."

"Too bloody right they are. Look, maybe I should just go." Olive hurriedly dressed as Roxy looked on helplessly. "Back to Waters now, is it? You can't wait, can you?"

"You're being ridiculous."

"Am I? At the very least the man's a danger to women. He tried to rape a student, or had you forgotten about that? You're supposed to be a social worker."

"What's that supposed to mean?"

"I thought you were a champion of women's rights and all that."

"Oh, for God's sake grow up, will you. You throw this in my face every time. It's always there, isn't it, an inch beneath the surface. And when you don't get your own way, out it comes. You and Phil - you're two of a kind!"

"Olive, listen -"

"I've heard enough. This was a mistake."

"Olive, wait."

"Happy Christmas, Detective Inspector."

CHAPTER THIRTY

Marcus Redfearn couldn't face the thought of travelling to Chester. He couldn't let his mother down either. She was always telling him that it might be her last Christmas. She'd been saying it for years, and making him feel guilty every time. He'd promised he would stay with her over the festive period and that was that. But he had to see Penny first.

Could he ring her? Speak to her parents? Would that be enough to put his mind at rest?

He took a long shower and thought it over. He could drop by the college - all the student details were kept on the data base; he could log in at the office and check Penny's contact details. He already knew her address; he could get her phone details and ring instead of visiting. *Better to visit, though*. He could photocopy her music; tell her he thought she might need it over Christmas. She'd have a copy of her own, of course, but how was he to know that? He could see for himself that she was okay.

He stepped out of the shower, and hesitated, tempted to step back in and take another. Cleanse out the remainder of his uncertainty. If he took the music to her, in person, would that be considered a reasonable thing to do? He could jot down a few extra comments, passing on feedback that she might find useful. He'd see her. Face to face. Then he could travel over to Chester and keep his mother happy.

What if Penny was out? Would he hang around until she returned? That might not look so good. What if her parents answered the door? Would he ask if he could go inside and wait for her?

What was he thinking of? He was acting like a lovesick teenager, not a middle-aged music teacher going to seed.

*

Susan was as good as her word, her progress little short of miraculous. Like something had clicked into place.

The staff on the unit were unanimous: Susan should be allowed home for Christmas. The consultant's blessing would be required, of course, and a meeting was set up for 23rd December. The bed would remain open, with 24 hour support available throughout the home-leave period.

Roxy was watching Olive disappearing out of his life for what seemed almost certainly the final time, when his phone rang. D. I. Taylor returning his call. Could he pop around for a coffee to catch up on the gossip?

Roxy was feeling less curious about the Henderson business. His mind was full of Olive and Waters, and he regretted digging out Taylor again. On the other hand, it might be interesting, finding out what the retired detective had been getting at with those cryptic remarks about the Susan Henderson case. What if there was a Waters angle? It was unlikely, but still.

"I have half an hour later," Roxy told Taylor, "if that's any good to you."

Taylor was looking well these days. All that golf had taken away the worst of the worry lines, along with a few pounds from around the man's gut. The two men shook hands, though neither seemed particularly keen to extend the pleasantries. Taylor got down to business. "There was something about that alleged attack that I never felt comfortable with," he said.

"I doubt Susan Henderson felt comfortable about it, either," said Roxy.

"That area is quiet at night, we know that," said Taylor. "There's no traffic, though pedestrians do use the shortcut to the bus station."

"So what's bugging you?" asked Roxy.

"A gang rape is usually quite a noisy affair. No screams were reported."

Roxy shrugged. "They could have gagged her."

"There was no evidence of that."

"They may have threatened her, then. A knife to the throat keeps most people quiet."

"That's true."

"What are you suggesting - that it wasn't a rape at all? That she was compliant in having six guys shagging the shit out of her?"

"There was clearly some compliance. The general lack of physical injury suggests that."

"People don't always put up a fight, if they're scared enough."

"Again, that's true."

"But? What is it?" Roxy asked.

"You rang me. You obviously have some thoughts about the case yourself. And we have this more recent incident with the sister, *Penny* Henderson. What exactly are you hoping to get from me?" asked Taylor. "You still think Waters is your man - I mean, for the killings?"

"It's a possibility."

"But you've had to let him go, despite him being in possession of what may turn out to be the murder weapon."

"We can't prove it's the murder weapon."

"And Waters is suggesting that he'd never seen the knife before - that it was planted?"

"That's about the long and short of it."

"Who would do that?" said Taylor. "Wasn't Penny Henderson the last person in that room with Waters? And why would a man going around mutilating and killing men suddenly attack a young woman - and a woman whose sister *just so happens* to have been attacked only a few months earlier? You know what I think?" Roxy knew exactly what Taylor was thinking. "I think something's going on with those two sisters."

On the Saturday before Christmas Penny got dressed and went downstairs. Her father was already in the kitchen. "Morning, Penny." He hadn't sounded this breezy for months. "Everything alright?" he asked her.

"A headache, that's all."

"Have you taken anything?"

"I need some fresh air."

"Probably all the excitement. You know, I don't believe that I've ever looked forward to Christmas as much as I'm looking forward to it this year. Right, then: time for your mum's weekend tea and toast in bed. Sure you won't have a slice?"

"I'm not hungry."

"You must look after yourself. I know, I know - I sound like your mother."

Penny left the house.

"Why would Penny Henderson, a seventeen year old college student, plant a knife in Waters' house? What's her motive?" Taylor shrugged, apparently baffled at his own questioning. "What's Waters' motive? And he has alibis, I believe."

Roxy thought for a moment. "Let me run something past you."

"Okay, fire away."

"What if Waters isn't working alone?"

"I would say unlikely. This type of killer usually works alone."

"There's a first time for anything," said Roxy.

"Of course, though I think you're clutching at straws. You have someone in mind?"

"I'm working on it."

After a moment Taylor said, "Look, Nigel, I'm not trying to tell you how to do your job. But don't you think it's a little strange that Susan Henderson, the girl whose alleged rape appears, should we say, highly ... *dubious*, has a sister accusing Waters of rape? And that a potential murder weapon was found in Waters' room immediately after Penny Henderson had been in that room - not to mention the fact that one of the murder victims happened to be visiting Eaglesfield on the night that he was killed. Ms. Henderson was on the unit that night, too - visiting her sister. How can you disregard -"

"Who's suggesting that I'm disregarding anything ... apart from you?"

The two men looked at each other in stony silence.

The meeting was over.

Walking out into the bitter daylight, Penny thought over her most recent visit to Eaglesfield. Susan had sat poker-faced, watching her run out of steam before turning the screw. "I'm going to make your life hell, Penny. But what's the best way to make you suffer?"

"It doesn't have to be like this."

"Doesn't it? Have you come to plead with me? Have you come to ask me not to go home? You'd rather consign me to this place until I rot than risk me opening my mouth around the table on Christmas Day. I could as easily spill the beans right here and now. The place, the time - doesn't really matter, does it? How can you stand the not knowing? How can you bear the uncertainty? When will it come, Penny, and where? I tell you ... *it's going to kill you.*"

As Penny walked on, she thought about Mr. Redfearn.

Phil Waters had been freed on bail for the alleged assault; the police obviously couldn't nail him for the murders. A pity, she thought, though it opened up opportunities. It might even prove to be a godsend. Waters and Redfearn were known to be friends. They had even been seen together by the police. There was a way to make this work.

Susan was going to wish she'd stayed on the unit.

CHAPTER THIRTY-ONE

Marcus Redfearn headed for the college with Penny's compositions tucked inside an envelope under his coat. The day was bright and cold and he had ventured into it with a cocktail of excitement and trepidation mixing nicely inside him, making his stomach ache like it was carrying a barrel-full of last year's ale.

The campus was deserted, as he expected it would be during the holidays. Everybody would be in Valemore Central, buzzing like flies in the department-store heat of the frenzied run-in to the big day. Using his security card, he entered the main office and logged into the computer.

Not a man comfortable around technology, it took him a few anxious minutes of messing with access codes and fumbling around the database to find what he was looking for. He thought about looking up Susan Henderson, while he was in the system, but decided against it. Not that there were likely to be any revelations. All the same he was curious. Penny had told him quite a bit about Susan, and he suspected that she had barely revealed the tip of the iceberg. There was a lot to those two, he thought.

He closed down the system and made a copy of Penny's music. Then the sheer stupidity of the situation struck him: accessing student records to get a phone number. Copying manuscripts so that he could carry two sets around, handing one back as though she wasn't sharp enough to have kept a copy. Not to mention calling at her home address during the holidays! What would her parents think? Wasn't everyone around Valemore suspicious and paranoid enough without a teacher acting weird? That was how reputations were made. *Or destroyed.*

He picked up a biro and began scribbling comments onto the photocopied manuscript. After a few minutes he stopped what he was doing. This was becoming farcical.

Give her the unadorned copy and be done with. Or go home.

Stepping outside, the temperature had taken a further plunge. As much to keep himself warm as to arrive at any particular destination, he set off at pace in the direction of Eaves End.

Penny Henderson was knocking on Mr. Redfearn's front door. The walk had done her good, the icy chill blasting away at her doubts and uncertainties, getting the blood flowing freely through her brain and nourishing the pathways of creative thought. It was clear as day to her now: if Mr. Redfearn was home, it could be done on Christmas Eve. If he was away, she would have to endure the season as best she could, and play out the moves on his return. Either way it would happen.

When Mr. Redfearn didn't answer, she waited for a few moments and then knocked again. "Just my luck," she muttered. So, it would have to wait. She would have to put up with Susan's cruelty a little longer.

Penny set off walking.

Marcus Redfearn's head was thumping so hard that he thought they would surely find him dead on the pavement. He had found the Henderson home too easily, as though fate had been blocking off all avenues of escape. There was the house; a gate to walk through, a knock on the door and it was done. What would he say when they answered?

He would say nothing. This was insane. His plan, if he remembered it right, was to hang around like a total pervert, attracting attention until somebody called the police and he spent Christmas in a cell. His mother would hear about it and she would never forgive him. The shame would finish her off and he'd have to live with the guilt for the rest of his life.

He waited out in the cold, looking for clues, signs of activity at the windows. Nothing. No clue as to whether anyone was in or not. He couldn't see a car. Maybe they didn't own one. There was a garage, but no way to tell if it was occupied with a vehicle or else filled with paint cans and junk. This was stupid. No, this was beyond stupid; standing outside the home of a student, playing silly little detective games. If they were in they would recognise him straight away. His stock was high with them; he'd brought their little girl home.

Or did that mark him down as over-familiar? When one of your daughters was at Eaglesfield - having being attacked in the most obscene way - you learnt to be suspicious. And with opportunists like Phil Waters around, trying to take advantage of your other daughter - my God, they were probably ringing the police already.

Redfearn hurried on, aborting his mission. He needed to get away, out of Valemore, and stay put until college started again. *The devil makes work for idle hands* - that was what his mother had told him, many times. She was full to the brim with stuff like that, and maybe some of it was worth keeping hold of.

They spotted each other at the same moment, and neither could quite believe it: Penny Henderson sitting on the wall, close to the bus stop; Marcus Redfearn moving down the hill like a runaway train. Penny Henderson thought that she was seeing things. Marcus Redfearn thought that he was seeing things: *Penny Henderson perched on the wall like she's waiting for me; Mr. Redfearn walking down past the college like he's coming to rescue me.*

He reached inside his coat, as though to take out the music manuscripts, and then hesitated: *Silly man. She'll ask*: *were you expecting to find me here? Why else would you be carrying those around?*

And then he'd have a choice of reply: I went to your house. I went to the college first thing this morning, accessed your records and took your telephone number, but then instead of calling you I walked to your house, though I was afraid to knock on your door; and so instead of calling to drop off these copies or even put them through your letter-box, I walked on until my feet were screaming and my heart with it.

Or else he could say: I was taking these copies to show to a friend. What friend? Phil Waters?

"What are you doing here?" he asked her. "Waiting for the college to open?"

She laughed at that, though she didn't find it funny. "I came to see you," she said. "I called at your house. I hope you don't mind. I need to ask a favour."

He opened his front door and went straight through to the kitchen to put the kettle on. "You'd better take a seat and tell me all about it," he said.

And over a cup of tea that's what she did.

"So," he said at last, trying to get it straight in his mind, "Susan's coming home for Christmas, which is great news; but you think ... this is the part I'm struggling with ... you think that - no, I'm still not grasping what exactly it is that you're trying to tell me, Penny. Are you saying that Susan wasn't as badly hurt in the attack as she led people to believe?"

"That's right, Mr. Redfearn. That's exactly what I'm saying."

"I see. And you think she may have faked some of her symptoms to make you feel guilty, because she blamed you for stealing her boyfriend?" He shook his head. "It's unbelievable."

"But it's true. Don't you believe me? Do you think I would make up something like this?"

"I, no, I mean - why are you telling me this?"

"I've got to tell someone. I don't know what to do. I'm desperate."

Redfearn scratched his head. "I don't have much experience regarding the love lives of teenage girls, I'm afraid." He coloured up. "What I mean is, how exactly can I help you?"

"I want you to come with me."

"Come with you?"

"To see Susan."

"Why do you want me to visit your sister?"

"I think you can help."

"I doubt that. Haven't you talked to your parents?"

Penny was busking it, and it was thrilling. Her plan was nothing more than a hazy sketch. It was the ending that was as clear as the blue frosty sky outside. But those in-between parts were open to suggestion, and it was like walking the high-wire to be sitting with Mr. Redfearn, filling them in as she went along. *Improvising*.

"My parents are so excited that Susan's coming home. It's all they ever wanted. But they don't know how disturbed Susan really is. They don't have a clue what she's capable of."

"You mean about exaggerating her symptoms?"

"It's more than that. Susan is planning something. Planning to ... do me harm."

"Oh, I'm sure that you're -"

"I'm not crazy. You probably think I am. Just a stupid little college girl -"

"No, Penny, I don't think that."

"Then come and meet her. See what you think. You could bring a get-well card and say you've heard all about her from her sister - your star-pupil." Penny laughed. "I'm joking, Mr. Redfearn. Don't say that, please!"

"But what will your parents think, me turning up at their house on Christmas Eve?"

"They'll be at church."

"Midnight Mass? Don't you think that's a bit late for me to be making house calls?"

"The Christingle service is at 5pm. They go every year. They used to take us when we were kids. They won't expect me and Susan to go, though they'll still make a fuss about *wouldn't it be nice.*" There was an edge to her voice that was unsettling.

"I don't know," he said. "I'm not sure that this is a good idea at all."

"Why isn't it?"

"Well, for one I'm supposed to be travelling to Chester."

"I'm scared, Mr. Redfearn."

"Now, now, Penny, what do you imagine is going to happen?"

She looked into her empty cup and mustered her best haunted look, raising her eyes, slowly, to meet his. "I don't know," she said. "Susan's changed. It's like I don't know her."

"Don't you think that you're being a little melodramatic? I mean to say ..." His words fizzled. Penny's eyes filled with darkness and fragility. He wanted to put his arms around her and protect her from the dangers of a savage world. "Okay," he said. "I tell you what: I will call, but I can't stay for more than a few minutes. And I'm not sure that it will achieve anything. But if it will put your mind at rest ..."

Before he could finish the sentence, she was on her feet and saving him the trouble of hugging her by hugging him instead. "Oh, Mr. Redfearn," she said. "I'll never forget this. You've saved my life."

CHAPTER THIRTY-TWO

It was the day before Christmas Eve. The Henderson family was up early. Today was the day. Susan was coming home. Mrs. Henderson was singing tunes from shows she had seen when she was young, while Mr. Henderson had a smile on his face that might have been chiselled for posterity. Their voices were light and bubbly, and they spoke excitedly about more toast, of jam and marmalade, making careless observations about the brightness of the day and the chances of snow.

It was all making Penny feel sick.

At Eaglesfield everything was ready. Susan's medication had been prepared in packs, enough to cover her leave with a few days to spare. All the contact numbers that could be needed in the event of any type of crisis barring a full-scale nuclear attack were provided, all conceivable eventualities covered.

Susan was quieter than she had been of late; the most subdued since the onset of her sudden, almost miraculous recovery. The staff on the unit suggested that this was to be expected. After all, Susan hadn't left the unit in months. It had become her home. Leaving the safety and security of Eaglesfield, even for the safety and security of her real home, was a major step, though a necessary one.

"What's the worst that can possibly happen?" asked Mrs. Henderson. "If Susan can't handle being home yet -"

The words caught in her throat, and Mr. Henderson comforted her. "Then she comes back to the unit and we try again in the New Year," he said. "But it's going to be fine. Everything's going to work out fine, isn't that right, Penny?"

*

In the car going home Mr. Henderson hummed merrily while Mrs. Henderson imitated a local travel guide, pointing out practically everything, regardless of its triviality; as though both of them were afraid of the silence stewing behind them. In the back seat the sisters sat side by side, staring blankly through the car windows.

As they finally pulled up outside the house, Mrs. Henderson turned to her daughters. "Home sweet home," she said. Neither of the girls responded. Both appeared on the edge of catastrophe.

"Cheer up," said Mrs. Henderson, despite her own forebodings. "It might never happen."

The day was spent walking on hot coals. Mr and Mrs. Henderson worked hard to maintain a facade of lightness and excitement, whilst feeling the weight of tension running through the house. They'd been warned that teething problems were highly likely, and they tried to hold on to the professional reassurance that all of this was to be expected. As the day wore on, the atmosphere continued to build. Since arriving home, the girls hadn't spoken a word to each other.

Mr. Henderson went into Penny's room and found her sitting on her bed, thumbing through a magazine. "Everything alright?" he asked, sitting on the edge of the bed. She continued looking at her magazine. "You seem a bit quiet," he said.

"I'll be okay."

"Is there anything you'd like to talk about?"

"I said I'm okay."

He left the room, but not before attempting yet another strained smile, and reminding his daughter that if she wanted to talk about anything, she knew where he was.

Susan spent time in her room, looking quietly through the window. Whenever her parents popped in she would tell them how good it was to be back home.

Everybody went to bed early. It had been a long day.

As Mr and Mrs. Henderson lay together in the darkness, they whispered about how wonderful it was to have both of their little girls back under their roof. Then Mrs. Henderson asked her husband if she thought Penny was okay.

"A bit quiet," he said. "I think it's going to take a day or so. I imagine there will be a period of re-adjustment for all of us. But she'll be okay."

They held hands and kissed goodnight.

Penny lay awake, trying to hear the thoughts of her sister in the next room. Long before it came light she climbed out of bed, walking the short strip of landing; standing outside Susan's door, listening. Hearing nothing, she turned the door handle and went inside; closing the door quietly behind her, she stood in the darkness.

"Come to finish the job?" said Susan.

Penny almost screamed.

The bedside light came on.

Susan stared at her blinded sister.

Penny, adjusting to the light, edged closer to the bed. "Can I sit down?" she asked.

"Be my guest."

She sat on the bed and tried to smile. "Hey, this could be like when we were kids. Like the Christmases we used to have. Do you remember the time -?"

Susan held out a pillow. "Cut the happy family crap and just do it quickly," she said.

"What are you talking about?"

"I'm offering you a way out: *suffocation.* I know what you are. So why not put an end to it, while you have the chance? No more playing games, what do you say?"

Penny held a look of astonishment.

Susan sneered. "We're two of a kind. I'm ashamed to say it, but there we are. Stop pretending, Penny. I'm sick of it."

"I don't know what you're talking about."

"Don't you? Then I'll tell you. I've fooled those idiots at Eaglesfield. I've fooled our dipshit parents and most of all I've fooled you. I could have told them months ago that you set me up; buying a favour off Daz for *stealing your boyfriend*. But I never did steal him. Oh, I thought about telling them everything - but what would that have achieved? They wouldn't have believed me. Better to pretend that I was too traumatised to speak. Make a slow recovery. *Then* tell them what happened. What you did to me."

"What do you want, Susan?"

Susan shook her head. "Not yet. You see, I knew that you would punish yourself if nobody else tried to punish you. That's the way you were made. That's the way you fell from the womb. Somebody tries to hurt you and you want to kill them. Somebody tries to forgive you and you can't stand it. I've been punishing you with silence for months and loving it."

"Then you're sicker than I realised," said Penny.

"Sick?" said Susan. "I've never felt better. I wanted to see what you would do, if you would turn back to the game. And you did, even humming that shit at me that you were writing. I don't know how I kept a straight face. Do you think even six of them could have taken that much from me?"

Penny asked again: "What do you want, Susan?"

"You still haven't worked it out? I want us to be sisters again; the best of friends. I want to enjoy Christmas with my family, and never have to spend another night on that unit with all of those losers who can't tell a lunatic from a genius."

"When are you going to the police?"

"You don't get it, do you? I want you to suffer, day in and day out. Every day you'll have to wonder if this will be the one when your world comes tumbling down. You'll hate the sight of me, if you don't already - but I'll love the sight of you, watching you squirm, watching you sweat, watching the hope dying in you. You'll plot to kill me, but you'd never pull it off, so it's never going to happen. They'd be onto you this time, Penny. They'd get you and you know it." Susan yawned. "So that's it. I'm feeling tired now, so if you'll excuse me, I need to rest. Goodnight."

Penny stood up, turning to leave when Susan said, "Hey - just like old times, eh?"

Christmas Eve, Mrs. Henderson was up early. There was so much to do. It wouldn't be easy, not after all Susan had been through, and now this attack on Penny. She wondered, and not for the first time, whether it was worth bringing daughters into the world these days, what with all the evil out there. But they would get through it. They were a family and they were together again. They could face anything, even this, together.

She'd hardly slept, or that's how it felt, though she must have because she could still remember dreaming about relatives who had died years ago. Not the sort of dreams you wanted at Christmas. She took a cup of tea into Susan and was surprised to find her daughter awake, sitting up in bed and beaming at her. "Oh, morning, love," said Mrs. Henderson, placing the tea down on the little bedside table, before hugging her tightly.

"It's good to be back, Mum, but I still need to breathe once in a while."

Mrs. Henderson let go of her. "You look so well, Susan. It's almost like none of this ever happened."

"I think the nightmare's over, Mum."

Mrs. Henderson launched at her again, hugging her more tightly than ever. Mr. Henderson came into the room. There were tears in his eyes as he watched. "Welcome home," he said. "And you're right: it's finally over."

Later that morning Mr and Mrs. Henderson went out to the supermarket, while Susan spent some time playing the piano in her room. She was playing part of *Sextet,* reading from her sister's handwritten manuscript. Penny stood in the doorway until her sister had finished. Without turning around, Susan said, "It sounds to me like death and destruction. You don't know the first thing about healing."

"Where are Mum and Dad?"

Susan swung around. "Why, are you going to tell them I've been nasty to you about your music? They've popped to the supermarket, if you must know. So we're free to talk."

"What's to talk about?"

"Murder, perhaps?"

"Bor-ing."

"I wouldn't know," said Susan. "I've never tried it. Not yet."

"You knew what I was doing. I was doing it for you, you ungrateful bitch."

"So I get fucked by six freaks and you go on a killing spree, murdering innocent men - and somehow it's all my fault?"

"You enjoyed it. Was six enough for you?"

"I made the most out of a bad situation. I'm not ungrateful. Anybody else would have got hurt, and that was the intention, I have no doubt. But they met their match that night, and they'll never forget it."

Penny felt the anger swelling inside. Then she thought about Mr. Redfearn, his five o'clock appointment, and smiled.

"What?" asked Susan.

"Thinking, that's all."

"I've been thinking, too. Wondering what makes a killer."

"And did you come up with a theory?"

"You could say that."

"Let's hear it."

"Well," said Susan, "you can't really blame the parents. They never starved us. Never beat us. No cruelty at all that I can recall."

"Not towards you."

"I can't remember them tearing out your finger-nails. I can't remember them sending you to bed hungry."

"It was subtler than that," said Penny.

"It must have been."

"You were always the favourite."

"Not that again!"

"It's true."

"Give me one single example."

"I wouldn't know where to start."

"There is nowhere to start, Penny. You always had a chip on your shoulder; you always thought I got the better deal. If I had something, you wanted it; but if I changed my mind and wanted something else, then you wanted that instead. The piano, for example; you were the one who insisted on having your own way, and I had to fit in around you. It was never any different. *You* were never any different."

"Don't rewrite history, Susan."

"You thought I stole your boyfriend, so you planned to have me attacked and left for dead. Don't you think that's going a little too far? Or is that how the books balance in that twisted head of yours?"

Penny didn't answer. She kept looking at her sister, and thinking about Mr. Redfearn, allowing her thoughts to simmer nicely on a boiling ocean of anger. *Susan would like Mr. Redfearn. Mr. Redfearn would like Susan. She would try to take Mr. Redfearn away from her; poison his mind against her. It would start all over again. Mr. Redfearn was no better than any of them. Mr. Redfearn –*

Susan's voice snapped Penny out of her thoughts. "How many lives have you ruined so far? How many more do you have in mind? You need help, but you need to ask for it. I won't do it for you."

"What are you talking about?"

"I won't turn you in, Penny. I will watch you suffer, every single day, but I won't end the misery for you. You'll have to do that yourself. And you will. One day you will."

"Hand myself in? Why would I do that?"

"Because you won't be able to stand it."

"You think you know me. You think you're so much cleverer. You don't know the first thing about me."

"No?" Susan started to play.

Chopin's *Funeral March*.

Penny held her breath.

"That's still the code between us, sister of mine," said Susan. "Nothing's changed. Blood's thicker than water, isn't that what they say?"

Susan stopped playing.

"I don't understand," said Penny. "Are you saying ... that we're alright?"

"I'm saying that I wouldn't count on hearing that music again anytime soon."

A car pulled up outside, and a few moments later the front door opened.

"We're back," shouted Mr. Henderson.

Mrs. Henderson marched up the stairs. "I'll have to use the bathroom, I'm sorry." She saw her two girls and sighed happily. "You'll never know how good it is to have you two back together. Two peas in a pod, you two are. Now, you'll have to excuse me or I think I'll have an accident.

That *Marks and Spencer's* tea-for-two goes right through me."

When the bathroom door had closed behind Mrs. Henderson, Susan looked at Penny. "Two peas in a pod - how wrong can a parent be? There's only one psycho in this family."

"Really?" said Penny. "And who's that?"

"Hi, there," Mr. Henderson shouted as he walked up the stairs. "How's it going?"

"Everything's fine," said Susan.

"Never better," said Penny.

Mr. Henderson shook his head. "You know, I can't get over how well things are working out."

"It's like a miracle," said Penny.

Mrs. Henderson emerged from the bathroom. "Fancy letting me drink all that tea," she said. "What's that about a miracle - our Susan? She is a miracle - you're both our little miracles. Now: anyone for a cuppa?"

Mr. Henderson rolled his eyes.

"Listen," she said. "We're going to the Christingle later. It would be lovely if you both came with us."

"I'm alright," said Penny.

"Thanks for asking," said Susan.

"I suppose you've got plenty of catching up to do," said Mrs. Henderson. "Well, I'm going to make a drink and start baking." As she headed downstairs, Mr. Henderson said, "I can still remember you two believing in Santa Claus."

"What's not to believe?" said Penny.

"Have you still got your Santa suit?" asked Susan.

"I gave it to a chap at work who has a couple of young kids. I could ask for it back next year if you like." Suddenly overcome, he took hold of Susan and hugged her. "It's so good to have you back home," he said. When he finally let go of Susan, he looked at Penny, and he hugged her too, before heading down to the kitchen to join his wife, whistling as he went.

"See," said Penny. "I'm always the after-thought."

"Grow up," said Susan. "Or at least change the record."

Marcus Redfearn rang his mother to confirm arrangements. "There's a train leaving at 6.07. The rest is in the hands of the train company and your local taxi drivers. Yes, Mum, everything's fine. I have to see someone first. No, I haven't a girlfriend and you don't have to ask me every time I speak to you. No, there's nothing different about me. Look, I'll see you later. What's that? Murders? I only know what I've heard on the radio and the television, same as you. It is shocking. Yes, I will be careful. No, I don't have to move - it could happen anywhere, even Chester. No, I'm not trying to frighten you. Okay, bye, Mum. Yes, love you too."

After ending the call, he switched on the radio for the local news. Police were still asking anybody with information to please come forward, but there was no mention of any more arrests or of anybody helping with enquiries.

The darkness was falling. He would have to think about setting off for the Henderson house. If he arrived on the stroke of five he could spare half an hour tops. That would give him ample time to make it to the station.

He still wasn't sure what it would achieve, meeting Susan. But Penny had clearly been deeply traumatised by what happened to her sister, and if giving up a few minutes of his time was going to help in any way, it would hardly be in the spirit of the season to refuse.

With that thought in mind he gathered his things together, feeling a little easier about the arrangements.

Penny could feel it building up from the pit of her stomach. Her mum had asked again about the girls going with them to church, and then suggested that for once she and her husband could miss going, if that meant spending more time together.

"No, Mum, you must go."

"Why must we?"

"It's important to you."

Susan had been watching and listening intently.

"No, I think our place is here with you girls. It wouldn't be right."

"We're old enough to be left on our own, I think," said Penny, glancing at Susan, who appeared absorbed in her sister's efforts.

"You never were keen on church," said Mrs. Henderson, "neither of you. It's something I've always regretted - that I didn't do more to encourage you."

"Maybe one day," said Penny.

"Oh, I do hope so. Look, I'll speak to your dad and see about us giving it a miss this year."

"No!" said Penny.

"Dear, whatever's the matter?"

Again Penny glanced at Susan. "You enjoy it so much. It wouldn't be Christmas if you two didn't go to the Christingle. Do you want to ruin Christmas before it's even started?"

Mrs. Henderson laughed. "Okay, you've convinced me. We do enjoy it, and if you're sure -"

"I'm sure. We're both sure, aren't we, Susan?"

"Sounds like it," said Susan.

After Mr and Mrs. Henderson had left for the Christingle service, Penny went upstairs. Susan was playing another section from *Sextet*. Penny walked into the room and stood behind her.

"So, what have you got planned?" said Susan, still playing.

"What are you talking about?"

"You were determined to get them out of the house. You couldn't care less whether they went to their precious Christingle. I'm intrigued," said Susan, looking back over her shoulder at her sister.

Penny nodded towards the piano. "Growing on you, is it?"

Susan stopped playing. "I don't mean to sour the Christmas mood, but you couldn't cure a hamster's cold with this shit. There's no soul to it. You should stick to what you do best."

"Meaning?"

"Shouldn't you be out there roaming the streets, looking for fresh meat?"

"They let you watch too much TV on that unit, that's your problem."

"And what's your problem, Penny? That the world hates you?"

Marcus Redfearn was well practised in the art of travelling light, a small rucksack ample to see him through the festive period. As he left his home that Christmas Eve, the night already coming down fast, he didn't notice the unmarked police car parked up the road.

He had decided to walk over to the Henderson house, rather than get a taxi. As he turned the corner, the officer in the unmarked vehicle, D.I. Nigel Roxburgh, made a call before putting the car into gear.

While the sisters traded insults, Marcus Redfearn made perfect time, arriving outside the Henderson house with a couple of minutes to spare. He felt the trepidation kick in again. Was it right, a teacher coming to the house of a student like this, a female student at that - and on Christmas Eve? It wouldn't look right, not in this cynical age. It would look like he had a sinister agenda. Middle-aged teachers and teenage students didn't mix, not in the context of making house calls, particularly after dark.

If the parents were in it might seem like an outrageous invasion of privacy; and if they were out - blatant opportunism. He couldn't win. He should turn around now, head for Chester. Visit his mother and forget about Penny Henderson until next term. Penny and her sister had parents to take care of them, they didn't need a teacher overstepping the mark and getting himself a reputation for his troubles.

But if he didn't turn up, what would Penny think? He'd promised. A promise was a promise, and that had been another of his mother's standard issues down the years. Maybe he should never have made the promise, but that was all water under the bridge now. The promise had been made, for good or ill, and he was a man who kept his promises.

On the other hand, he could always conduct his business on the doorstep, telling the little white lie that he had a train to catch, and that he was running late. He could hang around from the safety of the doorstep for a few minutes, adding credibility to the lie.

It was still a lie though. He didn't like telling lies; he was no good at it. He always felt the need to look away, finding it impossible to maintain eye contact. Wasn't that a sure sign that someone was lying? Penny would be looking straight through him, knowing that he was telling lies, and hating him for it. His mother always taught him that nobody likes a liar. Nobody trusts people who tell lies, any kind of lies. His mother had taken him to task more than once as a young child for telling lies. She would always know.

It was such a small lie.

There's no such thing as a small lie, his mother had taught him. *Small lies lead to bigger lies, and once a liar, always a liar.*

He had made a promise and he had given a time. Being late had been another of his mother's pet hates. Being late was almost as bad as telling lies. People who were late were not to be trusted. People who were late shouldn't be given the opportunity to be late again. They should be taught a lesson.

He'd given Penny a time and he would be there on the stroke. He wouldn't stay, though. Not thirty minutes, nowhere near. A flying visit, say hello, meet Susan, say his goodbyes, wish them a Happy Christmas, and head for the station. He couldn't be late for his train. His mother was waiting and she would never forgive him.

Marcus Redfearn opened the gate. He was bang on time when he rang the bell.

CHAPTER THIRTY-THREE

"Hi, Mr. Redfearn. Come inside," said Penny. "Susan's upstairs."

Upstairs didn't sound like a good idea. What if their parents came home and found him upstairs with their daughters? "I haven't got long," he said, hesitating on the doorstep. "Is everything okay? I can catch up with you after the holidays."

"Everything's ... sort of okay," she said. "I think you should meet Susan and make your own mind up."

"Why don't you ask Susan to come downstairs," he said. "I can meet her down here and -"

"She's playing the piano, can't you hear?"

He could hear the sound of music drifting down the stairs. Accomplished playing, he thought. "That's your music she's playing? I - don't want to interrupt -"

"I want you to see her playing the piano, Mr. Redfearn." He looked at his watch. "She's been playing since she came home," said Penny.

"She likes it that much? Fantastic! She's obviously a young woman of considerable taste."

Penny glanced towards the stairs. "I'm worried about her. Please, just five minutes."

"I - okay," he said, hesitating even as he crossed the threshold. "But I really can't stay."

She closed the door behind him ... and led him up the stairs.

When Penny tapped on Susan's bedroom door, the music stopped. Penny opened the door. "I've brought someone to meet you." She went inside and gestured to the teacher to follow.

"Who is it?" asked Susan.

"It's Mr. Redfearn."

Susan watched the strange man enter her room. He looked nervous, she thought. *Scared to death.* He walked over towards her, and held out a hand. But Susan didn't take it.

"He's come to see you," said Penny. "Isn't that kind of him?"

"What for?" asked Susan, not taking her eyes off the teacher.

"Actually, I was passing and ..."

"And do you always make house calls on your students at Christmas?"

"Don't be so rude," said Penny. "Look, why don't you two chat while I make a drink?" She hurried along to her bedroom, opening her underwear drawer, taking out the blade, the shiny new one from the market. Tucking it inside the top of her jeans and covering the handle with her tee-shirt, she walked back along the landing.

Susan and Mr. Redfearn seemed to be apologising to each other, but there was really no need. There was no reason for anybody to be saying anything. Actions would speak louder than words now.

"Forget something?" asked Susan, as Penny entered the room. "You said you were making drinks, remember?"

"Why don't you play something for Mr. Redfearn?"

"That would be nice," he said. "You were playing Penny's composition, I believe. A remarkable talent, your sister, wouldn't you say?"

"Oh, she's remarkable, no doubt about that," said Susan. "A quite remarkable piece of work is Penny."

Redfearn looked from one to the other, trying to work out what exactly he had walked into. If World War Three was about to kick off, then it might be better to leave them to it. "To be honest," he said, looking again at his watch, "I really must -"

"Five minutes," said Penny. "You promised. Please, Susan, just a few bars. It's Christmas, come on, don't be a party poop."

"Actually," said Susan, "there's a tune - it used to be one of your favourites, Penny." She looked at Mr. Redfearn. "I used to make music to heal, but I'm a little out of practice. Penny was more into sacrifice."

"Susan!"

"No, Penny; Mr. Redfearn needs to know what he's getting himself into - wouldn't you agree, Mr. Redfearn?"

"I really ought to be going," he said, turning towards the door.

Penny stood blocking the doorway, her hand hovering over the handle of the knife that lay hidden beneath her shirt. "Just five minutes ... pretty please?"

Susan struck out the sombre chords, the opening bars of Chopin's *Funeral March*.

"You play very well," said Marcus Redfearn.

"Doesn't she just," said Penny, the tears streaming down her face. It was the most beautiful music in the world. There had never been healing like this. There never would be again. "*Susan ..?*" she said, looking at her sister. "But I thought ..."

She saw it unfolding in her mind's eye: The knife flicking out of her jeans and at her sister's throat before Redfearn even knew what was happening. Blood flowing out of the wound as Susan hit the floor, death closing in quickly. Then turning to her dumbfounded teacher: "Oh, how could you, Mr. Redfearn?" Her baffled teacher looking at Susan; the blood soaking the carpet around her. "How could you?" she screamed, slashing at her left arm three times, drawing blood each time before swapping the knife to her left arm and slashing at her right arm twice, tearing her shirt open, slashing her stomach twice, and her neck for good measure. Thrusting the knife into her teacher's hand, forcing his fingers to clamp around the handle. "What kind of sicko are you, Mr. Redfearn? Stalking me, waiting until my parents had gone to church, entering our home, killing my sister, trying to kill me, forcing me to defend myself, and on Christmas Eve, too?"

All this in the blinking of an eye; the work of an imagination on fire. The teacher backing away, still holding the knife. "You can't run away from this, Mr. Redfearn. I won't let you. The killing ends here, *tonight.*"

The music stopped. The movie inside Penny's head stopped with it.

Susan sat laughing. "She's brought you here to kill you, Mr. Redfearn. To kill us both, actually. I'm crazy, didn't you know? Fresh out of the asylum. But I'm still not as crazy as my sister."

"Debatable," said Penny. "But that's one for another day."

"Look, you've had your little joke," he said, "but I really do have to be going -"

"I want to thank you, Mr. Redfearn," said Susan. "You've saved a life here tonight. Sometimes the sickness is too advanced for healing, and all that's left is sacrifice. Penny's served her time. The apprenticeship is over. I can't keep blaming her forever, can I?"

"You mean it?" said Penny.

Susan nodded. "These things happen. It's part of growing up. Tonight something ends and something else begins. This is Penny's domain, but I'm here for her now." Susan started playing again; the same sombre funereal chords.

"You *do* mean it!" said Penny.

Mr. Redfearn saw the blade in Penny's hand.

She had already drawn a bull's eye over his heart, and with a scream she lunged at him, plunging the knife deep into his chest, nicely between the ribs, all the way to the hilt, before ripping it back out of him, surprised not to find his still-beating heart attached to the blade. Marcus

Redfearn put one hand, then both hands, to the wound. The blood pulsed through, his life leaking out of him as Penny placed the knife into his blood-soaked right hand and slashed it across her own stomach and chest, glancing blows. Her shirt was ruined, there was no doubt about that.

"Best to ring for the police now?" asked Penny. "Or wait another few minutes to be certain?" The two of them watched death enter the room and take Mr. Redfearn to a better place. "Susan, I asked if it's time?"

"You're not taking the two of us tonight, then?" asked Susan. "This could be your last chance."

"How could you even think such a thing?"

"Well, if you've finished for the evening ... I'd say it's time to make the call."

Penny smiled. "Old times, what do you say?"

"I'd say look at all this mess," said Susan, "teachers bleeding all over the carpet. Still: always a silver lining."

"What's that?"

"An early Christmas present for the boys in blue. The stuff of promotions, I shouldn't wonder."

A key sounded in the front door.

"Even better," said Penny.

"Hi there, we're home," Mrs. Henderson called up the stairs.

"After three," said Penny. "One, two ..."

The two girls screamed.

Mrs. Henderson froze in the doorway. Mr. Henderson, who had been locking his car, dropped the keys and ran towards the house.

D.I. Roxburgh, sitting out in the unmarked vehicle, radioed for urgent assistance, before scrambling out from behind the wheel and heading towards the sound of screaming.

CHAPTER THIRTY-FOUR

Mr. Henderson was the first to the top of the stairs. In the shock of the scene that greeted him, his first thought was that the man soaked in blood on Susan's bedroom floor looked familiar. Then he saw Penny stumbling towards him, likewise covered in blood. "He tried to kill me, Dad. Oh God, what have I done?"

Susan stepped into view, shaking her head but not saying anything.

Penny threw both arms around her father. "He's been following me, Dad. He's a friend of that other pervert, that Phil Waters. I answered the door and he was standing there. He had a knife. I tried to close the door, but he got his foot inside. I ran up the stairs and he came after me. He said he'd got me a Christmas present. Oh, Dad, it was horrible. I thought he was going to kill me and kill Susan. I got the knife off him and - Susan, tell Dad what happened."

She looked to Susan for corroboration. But Susan was still shaking her head, and pointing back at Penny. "*She* had the knife, Dad. She went for him. *She murdered him.*"

Mrs. Henderson was still in the doorway downstairs, struggling to breathe. Roxy was behind her, getting out his ID card, trying to introduce himself while Mrs. Henderson was bent over, blocking the entrance, trying to stay alive.

Penny moved towards her sister. "You're lying. Why don't you tell him the truth?"

"You're sick," said Susan.

Penny looked down at the knife on the carpet next to the bloody figure of Mr. Redfearn. "Tell him the truth, Susan."

"I'm calling the police," said Mr. Henderson.

Penny picked up the knife. "Tell him the truth, you bitch. Tell him the truth or I will kill you."

"Penny!" Mr. Henderson caught hold of his daughter as she lunged at Susan.

"Get off me," screamed Penny. "She's lying. I saved her life. Tell him!"

As Penny swung to free herself, the knife in her fist caught Mr. Henderson in the right cheek. He fell back, clutching his face. D.I. Roxburgh, hearing the fresh sounds of violence exploding from the upstairs room, finally managed to push past the suffocating Mrs. Henderson, and bounded up the stairs.

He found Penny, the knife raised in her right hand, screaming at her sister to *tell the truth you fucking bitch.*

"Police!" shouted Roxy. "Put the knife down. I said *put the knife down.*"

When Penny continued to scream, and the knife remained raised, Roxy moved on her, grabbing the raised arm, overbalancing as she quickly turned. In an instant he caught the flash of the blade descending, felt the piercing sharpness as it was thrust into the side of his throat, collapsing to the floor, drowning in blood, images of Olive, Waters, and his beautiful career flooding through his brain in the final moments before it all closed down.

He didn't hear the reinforcements racing up the stairs, or recognise the attempts to resuscitate him as they took Penny Henderson away.

EPILOGUE

Susan sat in her room. Her parents had already left the unit for the day. Dad's face still looked a mess. It was likely that he would forever bear the scars, and that Mum would always have to take the medications that were keeping her lungs from collapsing, and her mind with them.

At least they had more time now, time at church, time to get old together. And when they finally did get back to work, they had both agreed it was time to cut their hours and think about downsizing; a smaller property in another town, and no mortgage.

They'd been to visit Penny again, and it had clearly distressed them. Six counts of murder; that was pretty impressive. The truth of it beginning to sink in - what their daughter had done.

It didn't sound like Penny was getting much pleasure out of the fulfilment of her ambitions, though. And yet, credit where it was due, she had succeeded after all. You had to hand it to the girl: six sacrifices and her sister healed.

Well, almost. Another few weeks on the unit, and it would be time to turn off the relapse and turn on the progress again. Get home for good this time.

One day it would be right and proper to visit Penny. Thank her for everything that she had done. The sacrifice that she had made, getting herself shut away so that her sister could lead a happy and fulfilled life.

The nurse knocked on Susan's door. A visitor was here to see her. It was the detective, the same one she'd given a statement to after they'd arrested Penny and taken her away. She'd told them everything, of course. How Penny had set up the attack on her through the late Daz Johnson, and how, on Christmas Eve, her sister had made arrangements for Mr. Redfearn to visit.

Susan told them how crazy Penny really was, planning to kill six men in a bizarre attempt to atone for what she had done. She told them how Penny had explained it all with Mr. Redfearn standing there, like it was being said to wind him up. How she had intended climaxing her grotesque plan by killing Waters and Redfearn, but then Waters had been spared because there were police outside his house already. So she had cried rape instead and left her knife in Waters' house to make it look like he was the killer.

She'd told them how Penny planned to kill her and make it look like Redfearn had done it, before playing the hero of the hour, trying to 'save' her sister and killing the teacher.

So what more was there to tell? What more could they possibly need to know?

"Your sister has suggested," said the detective, "that *you* arranged for six men to attack you, and that you subsequently faked the effects of psychological trauma. That you were made aware of your sister's plans to kill six men but chose not to tell anybody about this. And that you conspired with your sister to kill Marcus Redfearn at your home on Christmas Eve."

Susan responded with a wide-eyed look and a long hard swallow. "And is anybody expected to believe her?"

"You deny the allegations?"

"Of course I do."

"Do you believe that your sister arranged the attack on you?"

Susan hesitated. For just long enough. "I don't know what to think," she said. "Really I don't."

The detective made a few notes. Then he looked at Susan.

"Is there a problem?" she asked.

"Just some loose ends, really. You were raped by six men?"

Susan nodded, looking suitably ashamed.

"Did you scream?"

"They held a knife to my throat and threatened to kill me. No, I didn't scream. Is that an offence? Look, I'm tired. If you have any more questions, maybe you should -"

"One more question, that's all, if you wouldn't mind."

"And if I do mind?"

"You don't have to answer. Like I say, I'm gathering up any remaining threads, nothing more than procedure, really."

"Okay," said Susan. "Can we just get it over with?"

"So, if your sister was intending to kill you, and then make it appear that Marcus Redfearn was responsible ..."

"Yes?"

"Then ... why kill him first?"

Susan shrugged. "I hadn't thought about it, but isn't it obvious? I mean, if she kills me, then she might expect Redfearn to intervene."

"I see. And when she killed Mr. Redfearn, you didn't try to intervene? You didn't attempt to summon assistance?"

Susan felt the sudden and absolute glow of victory. They really were clutching at straws. This was the home strait.

She took a moment before giving the detective all he needed to hear.

"I was in a state of shock. I was terrified. I'm sorry that Mr. Redfearn died, I'm sorry that anyone had to die. I'm sorry that my own sister hated me so much that she had me gang-raped, if that's what she did, and then tried to kill me. If my parents hadn't come home when they did ..."

The detective closed his notebook. "You've been very helpful," he said. "I won't need to bother you again. I'd like to take this opportunity to wish you all the best, Susan. I hope that you get home to your family soon."

They shook hands.

After the detective had gone, Susan sat for a while, thinking. *Tying up the loose ends?* Understandable. In a bad business like this there are always questions to be asked, threads that could unravel. Better to get them out of the way. Only doing his job, after all and if it wasn't him it would have been someone else, maybe someone a little sharper, smarter, more tenacious and ambitious. Over with now, though. Done and dusted; time to move on.

Alone in her room ... Susan smiled.

THE END

Mark L. Fowler

Printed in Poland
by Amazon Fulfillment
Poland Sp. z o.o., Wrocław